A Clutch of

VAMPIRES

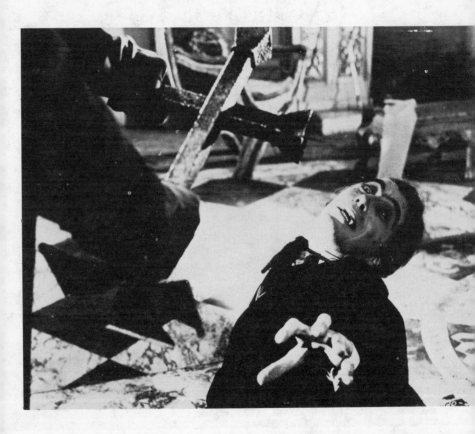

In the final scene of Hammer Films' *The Horror of Dracula* (1958), Dracula (Christopher Lee) disintegrates in the sunlight before a cross fashioned from two candelabra by Van Helsing (Peter Cushing). (Universal Pictures. Photo The Bettmann Archive)

A
Clutch of
VAMPIRES

These Being Among the Best
from History and Literature

by Raymond T. McNally

New York Graphic Society
Greenwich, Connecticut

Acknowledgments

"Vampire from Brooklyn, N.Y.": Copyright 1940, renewal 1968 Constance Seabrook.

"Vampire in Venice": From the book BALTHAZAR by Lawrence Durrell. Copyright © 1958 by Lawrence Durrell. Published by E. P. Dutton & Co., Inc. and used with their permission. Also reprinted by permission of Faber and Faber Ltd.

"The Living Dead" and "The Drifting Snow": Reprinted by permission of the author and the author's agents, Scott Meredith Literary Agency, Inc., 580 Fifth Avenue, New York, New York 10036.

"Drink My Red Blood": Copyright 1951 by Richard Matheson. Reprinted by permission of the Harold Matson Company Inc.

The author's special thanks go to Donald D. Ackland for suggesting a vampire anthology, to Pat Lambdin Moore, editor of this book, to Arch Getty and Bill Chase for their assistance with rights and permissions, and to Carolyn Thompson, who typed the manuscript.

To the memory of Augustin Calmet (1672–1757) and Montague Summers (1880–1948), holy fathers in the Christian faith and the spiritual fathers of all latter-day vampirologists

CONTENTS

Edvard Munch, *Vampire*, lithograph, 1895. In Munch's art
the kiss sometimes became an expression of the vampiric
woman whose demand for man's complete attention
drained him of his creative powers. (Werner Timm, *The
Graphic Art of Edvard Munch*, Greenwich, New York
Graphic Society, 1969)

Introduction

by Raymond T. McNally

In the vast genus of horrible beings, vampires belong to a distinct order. Unlike other monsters and demons, they exist alone—utterly alone in the twilight. region between life and death. Whereas the werewolf is a living human who has undergone change into a beast, and whereas the Frankenstein type of monster is alive—albeit not in the usual sense—the vampire is not alive at all. Nor is it dead, as are ghosts and poltergeists. It also differs from the zombi, a dead body that functions not through its own volition but through the will of a sorcerer. Indeed, among the many horror creatures, only the vampire fully merits the term "undead." According to the natural course of events, it really *should* be dead, but its body will not decay. Unable to return to dust, and driven to maintain its peculiar existence, the vampire wanders the earth, seeking sustenance in human blood.

Having studied the vampire in text, film, and folklore for many years, I am amazed at how little serious investigation has been done concerning the history of this creature. The only major researchers in this field have been two clerics: Augustin Calmet (1672–1757) and Montague Summers (1880–1948). Almost all contemporary works on vampirism crib from the writings of one or both of these men. I, too, am indebted to their works, although it has been my good fortune to supplement their findings with a few vampiric case histories that I came upon while studying in Transylvania.

This new selection of vampirana was put together so that in one volume the reader could find some of the best vampire tales and commentary from both history and literature, a few facts about the men who recorded or wrote them and the circumstances in which they did so, plus illustrations showing how artists working in various media have treated the vampire and related themes. Such a book seems timely. Today there is extraordinary interest in the occult and the unnatural—including the undead. A general anthology of vampire literature appeared in 1963; and articles about my research on the historical Dracula appeared in the *New York Times* as early as 1969, possibly helping to spark the veritable Dracula Renaissance that has marked the early 1970s. For whatever reason, in 1972, after years of neglect, Dracula was the subject of four new books. At the same time there appeared "a natural history of vampires." Also, both Lippincott and Addison-Wesley began publishing monster tales for children during the 1970s.

None of these books, however, was composed with the same intentions as mine. As far as I know this is the first anthology in English to present such a diversity of vampirana. It is my hope that it may help inspire a full-scale investigation into the lore and lure of the "walking dead."

Some minds, of course, may question whether serious study of the subject of vampires is worthwhile—whether it would in fact result in much ado about nothing more than a character from a nineteenth-century novel and the films that it has inspired. However, long before 1897, when Bram Stoker published his thrilling *Dracula*, other men were preoccupied with vampires. To be precise, the notion of the vampire reaches back into primeval history.

The term "vampire" itself is fairly new, having come into common usage during the eighteenth century, that so-called Age of Reason. Linguistic authorities differ over the origin of the word. For example, F. Miklosich, an eminent scholar of Slavic languages, claims that "vampire" derives from *uber*, the Turkish word for witch. But undoubtedly the source of "vampire" is the Hungarian word *vampir*.

Several authors have recently put forth the thesis that vampires are products of Christian civilization, overlooking the fact that in societies removed both in time and space from Christianity some concept of the vampire appeared; a single example is pre-Christian Mexico.

In its basic form, the vampire concept contains one or more of the following elements: association with night, a capacity for change into another physical shape, and a desire for human blood. Now for a brief look at the varied history of this creature called a "vampire"—a horror which evolved from primitive forms into the familiar Transylvanian count in a black cape, and which is still evolving.

According to an ancient Semitic myth, Lilitu, or Lilith, was the first woman on earth. In the Talmud, the book of Jewish civil and canonical law, Lilith was in fact Adam's first wife. Her ultimate role, however, was that of a night-roaming monster. In an

This popular medieval amulet was used during childbirth to protect mother and child against an attack by Lilith. (Joshua Trachtenberg, *Jewish Magic and Superstition*, Cleveland, World, 1939)

argument with Adam over who was the better, Lilith refused to concede Adam's superiority. Thus she disobeyed him and angrily left him, though three angels, Sanvi, Sansanvi, and Semangelaf, tried to convince her to stay. Because of her disobedience, Lilith's children were killed. Eve then came into the picture and bore Adam children. Extremely jealous, Lilith tried to kill Eve's children. Since all succeeding generations were considered to be Eve's children, humans had to defend themselves against further onslaughts by the night-roaming Lilith. Small children especially were in danger from her, and one means of protection was the wearing of amulets, preferably ones bearing the names of the three angels who had tried to persuade Lilith to stay with Adam.

Images of Lilith—or Lamia, Lamme, and Lamashto, as she was also called—were included in Babylonian carvings. In Assyria there were incantations to ward off her evil influence. It is also known that like the old god Proteus, Lilith could assume many animal forms.

When we encounter Lamia in Greek mythology, she has had children by Zeus. And now it is Hera, wife of Zeus, who succumbs to jealousy. She drives Lamia mad and kills her children as well. To avenge herself Lamia goes about endeavoring to kill as many children as she can. She also drinks their blood and eats their flesh. Once beautiful, she has become ugly.

In later mythology Lamia is said to devour handsome young men as well as children. In the post-classical period Lamia is mixed up with vampires, especially in the Balkans. Closely related to Lamia and vampires are the Greek *striges*—demonic nightbirds which steal children from their cradles, eat their flesh, and drink their blood.

Lilith was only one of many vampiric ancestors. Accounts of creatures who drank human blood are also traceable to the ancient Chaldeans, Assyrians, and Babylonians. And from ancient Armenia derive tales of the mountain spirit Dashnavar, which sapped the blood from the foot-soles of travelers until they died.

Later folklore, this time in Europe, not only includes references to vampires but also describes ways and means of coping with them. Centuries ago in Ireland the common people were so in dread of what they called "red-bloodsuckers" that they piled stones upon the graves of their dead in order to prevent vampires from coming out—just as other men have used gravestones to keep ghosts of corpses from rising up. Moreover, it is still said in Ireland that the newly buried dead can become active again at the New Year, rising out of their coffins, and causing their victims' blood to boil and flow.

In Serbia, Greece, and Normandy, among other places, was the belief that persons who were werewolves in life would become vampires after death. When the Norman French came upon a grave which seemed suspect, they would dig up the body, cut off its head, and throw the body into the sea or a river.

In Dalmatia, bodies suspected of becoming vampires were wounded so that they could not become "walking dead." In the Philippines, the feet of a dangerous corpse were slit for the same reason. In Burma, the corpse's toes were tied to the thumbs.

In Transylvania, the belief in vampires became so entrenched that precise details about their origin, attributes, and practices evolved. Heinrich von Wlislocki, writing in 1893 about the customs of the Transylvanian Saxons, stated: "The Nosferatu [undead; vampire] not only sucks blood of sleeping people, but also does mischief as an Incubus or Succubus. The Nosferatu is the still-born, illegitimate child of two people who are similarly illegitimate. It is hardly put under the earth before it awakes to life and leaves its grave never to return. It visits people by night in the form of a black cat, a black dog, a beetle, a butterfly, or even a simple straw. When its sex is male, it visits women; when female, men. With young people it indulges in sexual orgies until they get ill and die from exhaustion. In this case it also appears in the form of a pretty girl or a handsome youth, while the victim lies half awake and submits without resistance. It often happens

In this scene from Felix Murnau's film *Nosferatu* (1922),
Max Schreck portrays Count Orlock (Dracula) on board a
ship arriving in Bremen with a cargo of coffins. (The
Museum of Modern Art/Film Stills Archive)

that women are impregnated by this creature and bear children who can be recognized by their ugliness and by their having hair all over their bodies. They then become witches. . . . The Nosferatu appears to bridegrooms and brides and makes them impotent and sterile."

Among the horrors found in the folklore of the South Slavs is a creature named Mara, who, once she has tasted the blood of a living man, falls in love with him and must return night after night to torment him. In "nightmare," the element "mare" may be related to the vampire-like Mara.

As for the New World, a minor discovery was made there in the sixteenth century which would profoundly affect the visual image of the Old World vampire. While in Mexico, Cortes and his followers encountered blood-sucking bats, a species peculiar to Central and South America. Associating these animals with the blood-sucking horrors described in myth and folklore, Cortes called them "vampire bats." From this ultimately evolved the fiction-and-film image of the vampire: a figure wearing a great black cape (reminiscent of bat wings) who flies through the night.

The United States has contributed its share of historical vampirana. In Connecticut in 1854, the *Norwich Courier* told of an incident at Jewett, near Norwich, in which the townspeople exhumed the bodies of two brothers who were believed to be feeding on the living. Another account, tracing back to 1874, relates that in the village of Placedale, Rhode Island, a Mr. William Rose dug up the body of his daughter and burned her heart, believing that she was draining off the vitality of her immediate survivors. And in Chicago in 1876, Dr. Dyer, a noted physician, reported that the relatives of a woman who had died of consumption had dug up her corpse and burned her lungs since the deceased was thought to be drawing family and friends into the grave with her.

Various diseases may lie at the root of many historical cases of vampirism, including pernicious anemia, cancer, and tuberculosis. Especially the disease porphyria seems to lurk behind

In its artistic evolution, the vampire became inextricably linked with the bat. One of the few artists ever to have taken a kindly view of this nocturnal creature was—not surprisingly—the author of *The Adventures of Peter Rabbit*, Beatrix Potter. (Anne Carroll Moore and Leslie Linder, *The Art of Beatrix Potter*, London, Warne, 1972)

Pierre François Barrois, study of a bat for a natural history of quadrupeds. Barrois, born around 1770, was a copper engraver who specialized in vignettes and studies of animals.

vampire and werewolf stories from the past. This disorder usually causes deformation of the face, teeth, and nails. Another syndrome is extreme sensitivity to light. Thus porphyria victims in older times may have foraged for food at night, not because they were "nocturnal creatures" but because they could not physically endure the rays of the sun. Moreover since porphyria, being hereditary, is a "family" disease, its similarity to vampirism is all the more striking, for the vampire traditionally begins by attacking, thus infecting, members of its own family.

Dreams have been a major source for horror literature, to which vampire stories belong. The first Gothic novel, *The Castle of Otranto*, published in 1764, derived from a dream by Horace Walpole. *Frankenstein* was written after a vivid nightmare experienced by Mary Shelley. Edgar Allan Poe and the Brontë sisters wrote many stories based on their dreams. Robert Louis Stevenson while bedridden with an illness had a dream after which he spent three days writing *The Strange Case of Dr. Jekyll and Mr. Hyde*. And Bram Stoker's nightmare in the early summer of 1895 led to the greatest vampire story of all—*Dracula*.

During the nineteenth century the vampire became an increasingly powerful force in fiction as Romantic writers, fascinated by the mysterious, the ugly, the macabre, transformed what had been a fairly simple horror into a complex, sophisticated one. Among the earliest accounts from this time is John Stagg's ballad *The Vampyre*, written in 1810; it is prefaced by a learned discourse on vampires, and climaxed with the killing of a particular vampire in the traditional manner, i.e., with a stake through the heart. In the same place where Mary Shelley had her provocative nightmare, and at the same time—Geneva, 1819—John Polidori wrote the novel *Vampyre*. The vampiric character in it was based in part on Lord Byron, to whom Polidori was personal physician.

In Russia, Nikolai Gogol (1809–52) wrote "Viy," a tale in which there occurs not only a strange creature whose eyelids

An illustration from Thomas Prescott Prest's popular Gothic novel, *Varney the Vampire or The Feast of Blood*, first published in England in 1847. Although Sir Francis Varney victimizes the wealthy Bannesworth family, he is sympathetically portrayed as a basically good man who is driven to evil by circumstances. (Anthony Masters, *The Natural History of the Vampire*, New York, Putnam's, 1972)

touch the earth but also a vampire who sucks the blood from a sleeping child, then murders the mother and sucks her blood as well. From the pen of Aleksei Tolstoi (1817–75) came two tales about Serbian vampires: "The Vampire" and "The Family of the Vurdulak."

French writers, too, took up the theme of the walking dead. Prosper Mérimée composed a vampire tale and published it in 1827 as part of *La Guzla* (which he passed off as a selection of Illyrian verse, and which many persons initially accepted as being authentic folk poetry). Théophile Gautier (1811–72) centered his masterful novel *The Loving Dead* around *une belle dame sans merci* named Clarimonde, who loves a priest. She is kept alive by the priest's blood, nevertheless at the end of the tale it is the priest's fellow monastics who prove to be the real vampires. Baudelaire composed several poems about vampires, and the writer known as Le Comte de Lautréamont created a terrible dark angel, Maldoror, who enjoyed drinking children's blood, especially while it was "still warm." In *Children's Crusade*, the Frenchman Marcel Schwob (1867–1905) portrayed a character condemned to perdition who looks upon the vampire cult as an angry perversion of the Last Supper.

Having been used so profusely and variously in the nineteenth century, the vampire theme might be expected to have withered away in the twentieth. Instead it proliferated in the usual literary forms and in new ones as well: monster magazines, weird cartoons, science fiction, movie scenarios, and TV scripts.

Early in the twentieth century F. Marion Crawford wrote "For the Blood Is the Life," in which a girl returns from the grave to visit her beloved, a man whom she did not dare approach in life. A less menacing, though blood-seeking, modern vampiress appears in "Mrs. Anworth" by E. F. Benson. William Tenn's short story "She Only Goes Out at Night" depicts a young vampiress as the victim of a family metabolic deficiency. In James Hart's "The Traitor," there is a male vampire who succeeds in throwing off his undead nature through human love; and in Evelyn E. Smith's "Softly While You're Sleeping," the vampire hero fails at love, his lady renouncing him for life in the "real world." Modern poets whom the muse led to write of vampires include Stefan George, Gertrud Kolmar, Ingeborg Bachmann, and Johannes Bobrowski.

For science-fiction writers, vampirism has provided situations of high adventure and, at times, settings for social commentary. For instance, Ray Bradbury in his short story "Homecoming" tells of a family—made up of vampires, warlocks, witches, and werewolves—which lives in a hostile alien world; and in "Pillar of Fire" he uses the vampire to represent man's creativity, the striving for the real beyond the real—the sur-real as against the strictly scientific which has banned mystery and imagination from the world. In the novel *Something Wicked This Way Comes*, Bradbury writes about psychic vampires who feed on human souls.

Another sci-fi author, Richard Matheson, holds the record for the number of vampires invented. In *I Am Legend*, a world-wide plague has left the earth inhabited by a race of vampires, and a single human. This man has indeed become a legend in his own time. Finally he is killed by the vampires, and they inherit the earth. This story was the basis for the film *The Omega Man*.

Another of the numerous writers of vampire stories in this century is Robert Bloch, a master at creating realistic horror. His tales of the undead include "The Bogey Man Will Get You," "The Cloak," and "Dig that Grave." Even in his famous novel *Psycho*, there are undertones of vampirism: the hero's dead mother is kept around as if she were alive, and she destroys her son's identity so completely that in the end he thinks that he *is* his dead mother.

As for the history of the vampire in films, only a few highlights can be given here. Vampire movies have been treated in a variety of ways—even comic—by both major and minor scriptwriters, and in countries all over the world. By now more than a

An early 19th-century handbill for a penny play, *The Vampire*. (Theatre Collection, The New York Public Library at Lincoln Center. Astor, Lenox and Tilden Foundations)

hundred of them have been produced, one of the most recent using an all-black cast; most of these are listed in the filmography published in McNally and Florescu, *In Search of Dracula* (New York Graphic Society, 1972). On television, *The Night Stalker*, a "powerful chiller about a vampire killer loose in Las Vegas," has been the most-watched film ever created for the TV screen.

The walking dead—ugly and utterly dangerous—why should a creature like this be so fascinating? An explanation for its grip on the minds of people living in primitive and pre-scientific societies is easy: for such persons the fantastic being—vampire, ghost, or whatever—has been the only way of explaining certain phenomena. But how do we account for the lure of the vampire in the age of computers?

There is, it seems, some part of us that wishes to believe that the impossible is possible. Daily life becomes so dull and routine at times that one desires to escape it, to delight in the unfamiliar, the unnatural, the unreal. So we actually *enjoy* being scared by frightening tales and films about the dead returning to life. At the same time, these vampire tales touch on something deeper—our ignorance and fear of death. We wish, for instance, that our beloved dead were still alive, yet the dreadful question that comes to us is, what would they be like if they did return from the realm of death? In the eighteenth century the Marquise du Deffand stated, "I do not believe in ghosts but I am afraid of them." Though we live in a scientific, rationalistic age which makes no allowance for such creatures as ghosts and vampires, we know exactly what she meant.

1

Philinnion

From Phlegon's "Concerning Wondrous Things" in *Fragmenta Historicorum Graecorum*, Paris, 1849; translation by Montague Summers in *The Vampire in Europe*, London, Routledge and Kegan Paul, 1928; reprint Hyde Park, N.Y., University Books, Inc., 1968, pp. 35–37.

Phlegon was a native of the town of Tralles in Lydia and a freedman during the reign of Hadrian (117–138). He is famous for the *Olympiads*, a work comprising sixteen books which chronicles events from the time of the first Olympiad (776 B.C.) down to the 229th (A.D. 137). In it he describes the eclipse and earthquake of the eighteenth year of Tiberius' reign, which, some scholars claim, coincided with the crucifixion of Jesus Christ. Phlegon also traced the predictions of the Sibylline oracles, but only a fragment of that work has survived.

The following tale from Phlegon's surviving chronicle of "wondrous things" has sometimes been entitled "The Bride from Amphipolis"; indirectly it inspired Goethe's famous poem "The Bride of Corinth."

Philinnion, the daughter of Demostratus and his wife Charito, has been dead and buried rather less than six months. There is staying in the house a young man named Machates, and one night Philinnion's old nurse, noticing a lamp burning brightly in the guestchamber, peeps through the door to make sure that all is secure and discovers Philinnion lying in bed with the youth. Beside herself with joy, beholding the girl to all appearances alive, the nurse at once runs to the parents and loudly calls upon them to come and welcome their child who is living and well and has been restored to them by some kindly god. Charito, trembling with fear and joy, swoons away, but upon recovering her senses, she bursts into bitter tears at the thought of her daughter, and crying out that the nurse must be mad, orders her out of the room. The old woman, however, remonstrates very briskly and is certain that she has not been deceived. At last the mother agrees to accompany her, she steals a glance into the room, and there she certainly discerns her daughter and somewhat vaguely recognizes the night-rail [woman's nightdress], but feeling that at that hour in the morning, when all is dark and still, long before dawn, she could not ascertain the truth without raising the whole house, which naturally in such circumstances she is very loath to do, she resolves to say nothing until the morning, when she will be able to see if her daughter is really in the house, or at any rate she can ask Machates for an explanation of the mystery.

At the break of day it appears that the girl has vanished, whereupon Charito in the greatest distress most earnestly implores Machates to tell her the whole truth and to keep nothing back. The young man, who does not seem to have been aware that his host had lost a daughter named Philinnion, is greatly distressed, and confesses that an amorous pigsnie [darling] has shared his couch, and that his leman [sweetheart] whispered her name was Philinnion. Moreover, she charged him to keep their caresses very private. To confirm this story, he produced a golden ring with which she had presented him, and also a ribbon from her bosom that had been left behind. No sooner had Charito seen these two objects than she uttered a piercing cry, rent her clothes in token of lamentation, tore her hair and fell fainting to the ground. It was only too true that she recognized both the ring and the ribbon as having belonged to her dead daughter and as having been buried in the tomb with her. Immediately the whole house was thrown into the utmost confusion and there were shrieks and tears on every side almost as if a second funeral were taking place. At last Machates succeeded in quieting them by promising to summon them during the night should the damsel again visit him.

That night, as may be supposed, nobody slept; and at the usual hour Philinnion appeared. The young man himself was confused and amazed, he did not know what to believe, he could not think these warm and wanton limbs which he embraced were the cold and rigid members of a corpse, nor was it possible for a dead woman to eat and pledge him with wine. Rather he surmised that the gravediggers must have stripped the body, and sold the ornaments in the town. However, to the word of his promise, no sooner had she come than he made a sign to his servant who quietly slipped away and brought the girl's parents to the room. When they entered Demostratus and Charito were struck dumb with amazement, but a few moments afterwards with loud cries they flung their arms around the figure of their daughter. But Philinnion said in sorrowing tones: "Oh my mother and father dear, cruel indeed have ye been in that ye grudge my visiting a guest in my own home for three days and doing no harm to anyone. But ye will grieve sorely on account of your meddlesome curiosity. For presently must I return again to the place that is appointed for me. Do ye also learn that assuredly it was not contrary to the will of God that I came hither." Scarcely had she finished these words than she fell back lifeless, and a corpse lay stretched upon the bed in the sight of all. Charito now uttered the most piercing screams, the unhappy father lamented aloud, and the whole household could not restrain their grief at the second death (as it were) of one who was so dear to them all. The story was at once bruited throughout the whole town and in an hour or two caused an immense sensation. It seems to have been officially reported to Phlegon, who must have held some high and important position in the city. Early in the morning the theatre was crowded with citizens and after the matter had been debated it was decided to open the tomb in order that it might be ascertained whether the body of Philinnion still reposed where it had been laid six months before, or whether her place was empty. Accordingly the family vault was unbarred, and having passed by the bleaching bones of those who had long been deceased, they found upon the bier of Philinnion a ring which Machates had given the lady who had sought his embraces as a love-pledge, as also a parcel-gilt cup with which he had presented her. In great amaze, the magistrates repaired to the house of Demostratus, and then they found the corpse of his daughter laid out where she had fallen on the previous night. At this there was much wonderment and much debate followed until a certain seer and diviner, Hyllus by name, who was held in highest honour and esteem, addressing the authorities, bade them by no means to suffer the body of Philinnion to be replaced in the vault but to see that it was forthwith burned to ashes in a remote spot outside the walls of the city. He further enjoined upon them to see that solemn sacrifices were offered Hermes Chthonius, the psychopomp, who conducts the souls of the dead to the underworld; as also expiatory sacrifices to the Eumenides. Calling Phlegon aside privately he recommended him to sacrifice for the good estate of Caesar and the empire to Hermes, to Zeus Xenios, protector of the rights of hospitality and to Ares, all of which ceremonies were duly performed. The whole town was further ritually cleansed with holy lustrations. Machates, however, for love of his dead beloved, killed himself in a kind of despair.

2

Mennipus and Apollonius

From Philostratus, *The Life of Apollonius of Tyana*, original
Greek with an English translation by F. C. Conybeare, 2 vols.,
London, Heinemann, 1912; Vol. I, pp. 403–9

Philostratus was born ca. 170 and died ca. 245. He traveled through the
known world as the "companion" of Julia Domna, second wife of the
emperor Septimius Severus, and it was she apparently who commissioned Philostratus' biography of Apollonius. This work is based on
untrustworthy, and possibly fictional, memoirs by Damis, one of Apollonius' disciples. It was probably written in Tyre, where Philostratus
settled after his travels.

   According to the biography, Apollonius was a Pythagorean
philosopher and ascetic of the first century A.D. who had miraculous
powers to summon spirits, perform feats of magic, and predict the
future. The death of Apollonius is mysterious—Damis' own memoirs
include the phrase "if he did die." It is known for certain, however,
that Apollonius was worshipped as a miracle-worker for four centuries by defenders of paganism. Philostratus' biography begins remarkably like the Gospel of St. Luke, and some scholars have wrongly regarded it as a kind of pagan answer to early Christianity.

   The following story from Philostratus is about a kind of horror
known as *empusa*. The word *empusa* is generally rendered into English
as "vampire," its nearest equivalent. An empusa is, strictly speaking, a
demon which takes over a body, whereas a real vampire is a walking
corpse. Keats was partially inspired by this tale to write his poem
"Lamia."

A ghoul feeding upon the heart of a young bride. (From *Monde fantastique illustré*, 1874. Private collection. Photo Editions Robert Laffont)

Menippus [was] a Lycian of twenty-five years of age, well endowed with good judgment, and of a physique so beautifully proportioned that in mien he resembled a fine and gentlemanly athlete. Now this Menippus was supposed by most people to be loved by a foreign woman, who was good-looking and extremely dainty, and said that she was rich; although she was really, as it turned out, none of these things, but was only so in semblance. For as he was walking all alone along the road towards Cenchreae, he met with an apparition, and it was a woman who clasped his hand and declared that she had been long in love with him, and that she was a Phoenician woman and lived in a suburb of Corinth, and she mentioned the name of the particular suburb, and said: "When you reach the place this evening, you will hear my voice as I sing to you, and you shall have wine such as you never before drank, and there will be no rival to disturb you; and we two beautiful beings will live together." The youth consented to this, for although he was in general a strenuous philosopher, he was nevertheless susceptible to the tender passion; and he visited her in the evening, and for the future constantly sought her company as his darling, for he did not yet realise that she was a mere apparition.

Then Apollonius looked over Menippus as a sculptor might do and he sketched an outline of the youth and examined him, and having observed his foibles, he said: "You are a fine youth and are hunted by fine women, but in this case you are cherishing a serpent, and a serpent cherishes you." And when Menippus expressed his surprise he added: "For this lady is of a kind you cannot marry. Why should you? Do you think that she loves you?" "Indeed I do," said the youth, "since she behaves to me as if she loves me." "And would you then marry her?" said Apollonius. "Why, yes, for it would be delightful to marry a woman who loves you." Thereupon Apollonius asked when the wedding was to be. "Perhaps tomorrow," said the other, "for it brooks no delay." Apollonius therefore waited for the occasion of the wedding breakfast, and then, presenting himself before the guests who had just arrived, he said: "Where is the dainty lady at whose instance ye are come?" "Here she is," replied Menippus, and at the same moment he rose slightly from his seat, blushing. "And to which of you belong the silver and gold and all the rest of the decorations of the banqueting hall?" "To the lady," replied the youth, "for this is all I have of my own," pointing to the philosopher's cloak which he wore.

And Apollonius said: "Have you heard of the gardens of Tantalus, how they exist and yet do not exist?" "Yes," they answered, "in the poems of Homer, for we certainly never went down to Hades." "As such," replied Apollonius, "you must regard this adornment, for it is not reality but the semblance of reality. And that you may realise the truth of what I say, this fine bride is one of the vampires, that is to say of those beings whom the many regard as lamias and hobgoblins. These beings fall in love, and they are devoted to the delights of Aphrodite, but especially to the flesh of human beings, and they decoy with such delights those whom they mean to devour in their feasts." And the lady said: "Cease your ill-omened talk and be gone"; and she pretended to be disgusted at what she heard, and no doubt she was inclined to rail at philosophers and say that they always talked nonsense. When, however, the goblets of gold and the show of silver were proved as light as air and all fluttered away out of their sight, while the wine-bearers and the cooks and all the retinue of servants vanished before the rebukes of Apollonius, the phantom pretended to weep, and prayed him not to torture her nor to compel her to confess what she really was. But Apollonius insisted and would not let her off, and then she admitted she was a vampire, and was fattening up Menippus with pleasures before devouring his body, for it was her habit to feed upon young and beautiful bodies, because their blood is pure and strong. I have related at length, because it was necessary to do so, this the best-known story of Apollonius; for many people are aware of it and know that the incident occurred in the centre of Hellas; but they have only heard in a general and vague manner that he once caught and overcame a lamia in Corinth but they have never learned what she was about, nor that he did it to save Menippus, but I owe my own account to Damis and to the work which he wrote.

This winged cat-like creature, reminiscent of Western images of vampires, appeared in a 17th-century book about China. (Tony Faivre, *Les vampires*, Paris, 1962)

3

A Chinese Vampire

From Jan Jacob Maria de Groot, *The Religious System of China*, 6 vols., Leyden, E.J. Brill, 1892–1910; Vol. V, pp. 747ff. De Groot (1854–1921) lived and traveled extensively in the Far East.

From various sources we learn that among the Chinese there has been belief in a demon who takes over a dead body, preserves it from corruption, and preys upon the living. Another Chinese superstition has held that each man has two souls: one for good, one for evil. Should the moon or sun shine upon an unburied body, the evil soul will gain strength and come forth to seek human blood. In 600 B.C., Tsze-Chan wrote in the *Tsachiven* about a dead corpse which became a demon when the soul refused to leave the body.

In contrast to the European vampire, which infects his victims with vampiric instincts, the Chinese vampire apparently does not do so.

In Japan, as well as China, there has been a belief in vampires; aerial ones were called *Tengu;* the inferior Tengu had a bird's beak and wings.

Liu N. N., a literary graduate of the lowest degree in Wukiang (in Kiangsu), was in charge of some pupils belonging to the Tsaing family in the Yuen-hwo district. In the season of Pure Brightness he returned home, some holidays being granted him to sweep his ancestral tombs. This duty performed, he returned to his post, and said to his wife: "To-morrow I must go; cook some food for me at an early hour." The woman said she would do so, and rose for the purpose at cockcrow. Their village lay on the hill behind their dwelling, facing a brook. The wife washed some rice at the brook, picked some vegetables in the garden, and had everything ready, but when it was light her husband did not rise. She went into his room to wake him up, but however often she called he gave no answer. She then drew the curtains and found him lying across the bed, headless, though not a trace of blood could be seen.

Terror-stricken, she called the neighbours. All of them suspected her of adultery with a lover, and murder, and they warned the magistrate. This grandee came and held a preliminary inquest; he ordered the corpse to be coffined, had the woman put in fetters, and examined her; so he put her in jail, and many months passed away without sentence being pronounced. Then a neighbour, coming uphill for some fuel, saw a neglected grave with a coffin lid bare; it was quite a sound coffin, strong and solid, and yet the lid was raised a little; so he naturally suspected that it had been opened by thieves. He summoned the people; they lifted the lid off and saw a corpse with features like a living person and a body covered with white hair. Between its arms it held the head of a man, which they recognised as that of Liu, the graduate. They reported the case to the magistrate; the coroners ordered the head to be taken away, but it was so firmly grasped in the arms of the corpse that the combined efforts of a number of men proved insufficient to draw it out. So the magistrate told them to chop off the arms of the *kiangshi* (corpse-spectre). Fresh blood gushed out of the wounds, but in Liu's head there was not a drop left, it having been sucked dry by the monster. By magisterial order the corpse was burned, and the case ended with the release of the woman from jail.

4

Vampire in a Knight's Household

From Gualteri Mapes [Walter Map], *De nugis curialium, distinctiones quinque*, edited from the unique manuscript in the Bodleian Library at Oxford by Thomas Wright, and printed for the Camden Society, 1850; pp. 82–83. My translation.

Walter Map was born in Heresford, England, ca. 1140, to Welsh parents. He studied in Paris and elsewhere in Europe, and became a clerk to Henry II in 1162. He rose quickly in Henry's service and in 1179 was his delegate to the Third Lateran Council. In 1197 he was made Archbishop of Oxford, where he became famous for his Latin poetry. His major work, from which this story is taken, was a collection of history, humor, folklore, superstition, and gossip. Map died at Oxford in 1210.

A belief in monsters which feed on human flesh and drink human blood runs deep in Anglo-Saxon literature. One finds it illustrated, for instance, by the man-devouring Grendel, a character in the Old English epic *Beowulf*, which perhaps dates from the eighth century. The poet states that in the king's hall Grendel seized a sleeping man and "drank blood from his veins." Anglo-Saxon vampires were sometimes female, as in the following account.

A knight, having wed a serious, religious society woman, was aghast at a horrible incident on the morning following the birth of his first child. The baby's throat had been slit so that blood stained the cradle. A second child was born a year later, then a

In this French woodcut of 1490, based on paintings in a cloister surrounding a cemetery for infants, a corpse robs an unwilling child from its cradle. (Metropolitan Museum of Art. Harris Brisbane Dick Fund, 1923.)

third. The same horrible thing happened despite the watchings of the knight and the rest of the household. When his wife again announced her pregnancy, she and the knight tried to sway the wrath of God through prayer and sacrifice.

The house and the surrounding area were brightly illuminated when the fourth child was born. This time, they resolved, nothing would enter of a malevolent nature that would escape their notice and vengeance.

It was then that a stranger, tired from his long journey, begged entrance to the house in the name of God. The knight admitted him and told the sad reasons of their vigil. Sympathizing and grateful for their hospitality, the stranger offered to stay up and await the unknown killer of children.

Midnight found the members of the household mysteriously falling asleep. The stranger, shocked and bewildered, managed to resist the compulsion to sleep. Through his heavy eyes he saw the trusted matron [nurse] bend over the cradle. She was about to slit the child's throat. Without hesitation the stranger sprang forward and seized the woman, which resulted in such a commotion that everyone awakened and identified the captured murderess. To their astonishment it was the most trusted and loved matron in the city.

The matron was questioned. But she refused to give her name or any other information. The knight, believing that she was merely too ashamed to speak, let her go. The stranger, however, replied that she was a diabolical vampire. He pressed a key to the nearby church against her face, branding her with its holy impression.

The knight asked how such a well-known woman could have been a demon undetected for so many years. The stranger replied that she was not a woman but a monster in disguise. He sent some members of the household to fetch the real woman whom the vampire resembled. The true matron then looked in bewilderment at her double. Across the face of the matron was a mark identical to the key brand on the vampire's scowling face.

The stranger then remarked, "There can be no doubt that the lady who has now come is very virtuous and very dear to heaven, and that by her good works she has stirred hell and provoked the anger of devils against her, and so this evil messenger of theirs, this loathsome instrument of their wrath, has been fashioned as far as possible in the likeness of this noble lady, that this demon may cause this noble soul to be accused of the guilt for her heinous deeds. And in order that you may believe, see what she will do after I release her."

The vampire stood away from the others. Then howling and screeching like an animal she flew away from the window and, defeated, never returned to the house again.

5

Two
Twelfth-Century
Vampires

From William of Newburgh, *Historia Rerum Anglicarum*, 2
vols., London, Sumptibus Societatis, 1856; Vol. II, chap. XXII,
pp. 182–85. My translation.

William of Newburgh was born in 1135 or 1136, probably in York-
shire, and was educated at the Augustinian Priory of Newburgh. At
age twenty-five or thirty, he married the wealthy Emma de Peri, an
alliance enabling him to collect four "Knight's Fees." William left
his wife in 1182 and reentered the priory where he had been educated, eventually becoming canon there. He died in 1201.

His *Historia Rerum Anglicarum*, which chronicles the history of
England from 1066 to 1198, was the most forceful and polished work
of its kind produced in the twelfth century. In it, William charges
Geoffrey of Monmouth, writer of *Historia Regum Britanniae*, with
disregard of factual truth—for example, his having "lied most idly and
most impudently" about King Arthur and his wizard Merlin. To William the true historian *must* stick to the facts. The reader should keep
that in mind when reading the two following accounts.

I.   THE BUCKINGHAMSHIRE VAMPIRE

*This story tells of "the extraordinary happening when a dead man
wandered abroad out of his grave" in Buckinghamshire in the year
1196. It was told to William of Newburgh by Stephen, archdeacon
of the diocese.*

A certain man having died, according to the course of nature,
was by the seemly care of his wife and relations decently buried
on the Eve of Ascension Day. But on the following night he
suddenly entered the room where his wife lay asleep and, having
awakened her, he not only filled her with the greatest alarm but
almost killed her by leaping upon her with the whole of his weight
and overlying her. On the second night also he tormented the
woman in just the same way. Wherefore in the extremity of dread
she resolved that on the third night she would remain awake and
that then and thenceforth she would protect herself from his
horrible attack by providing a company of persons to watch with
her. Nevertheless, he visited her; but when he was driven away
by the shouts and cries of those who were keeping watch, so that
he could do her no harm, he swiftly departed. Having been thus
baffled and repulsed by his wife, he proceeded in exactly the same
manner to harass and annoy his brothers who resided in the same
town.

The brothers defended themselves from the vampire's visits
by sitting up all night and making a noise. As a result he appeared
to several townspeople in broad daylight. The archdeacon wrote
a letter to the Bishop of Lincoln, requesting his direction in
combating "so intolerable an evil."

When the Bishop heard of this he was greatly amazed, and
forthwith consulted with a number of learned priests and reverend theologians, from certain of whom he learned that similar
occurrences had often taken place in England, and many well-

known instances were quoted to him. They all agreed that the neighborhood would never obtain any peace until the body of this miserable wretch had been disinterred and burned to ashes. However, such a method seemed extremely undesirable and unbecoming to the holy Bishop, who forthwith wrote out with his own hand an absolution and sent this to the archdeacon, ordering that, whatever might be the reason why this man wandered from the grave, the tomb should be opened, and when the absolution had been laid on the breast of the corpse, all should be fastened up as before.

Therefore they opened the tomb, and the body was found therein uncorrupt, just as it had been laid upon the day of his burial. The episcopal absolution was placed upon his breast, and after the grave had again been fast closed, the dead man never wandered abroad, nor had he the power to injure or frighten anybody from that very hour.

II.   THE BERWICK VAMPIRE

This second tale was told to William of Newburgh by a priest from Melrose Abbey who "used to hunt with horse and hounds" like a layman; it concerns the deceased squire of Alnwick Castle in Berwick who was "a stranger to God's grace and whose crimes were many."

In the dark hours [the dead squire] was wont to come forth from his tomb and to wander about all the streets, prowling around the houses, whilst on every side the dogs were howling and yelping the whole night long. . . . The air became foul and tainted as this foetid and corrupting body wandered abroad, so that a terrible plague broke out and there was hardly a house which did not mourn its dead, and presently the town, which a little while before had been thickly populated, seemed to be well-nigh deserted, for those who had survived the pestilence and these hideous attacks hastily removed themselves to other districts lest they also should perish.

The local priest, from whom Newburgh learned the story, called a council of devout men to find a means to rid the place of the vampire. While they were deliberating, the impatient young men of the town decided to exhume and burn him.

They armed themselves, therefore, with sharp spades and betaking themselves to the cemetery, they began to dig. And whilst they yet thought they would have to dig much deeper, suddenly they came upon the body covered with but a thin layer of earth.

It was gorged and swollen with frightful corpulence, and its face was florid and chubby, with huge red puffed cheeks, and the shroud in which he had been wrapped was all soiled and torn. But the young men, who were mad with grief and anger, were not in any way frightened. They at once dealt the corpse a sharp blow with the keen edge of the spade, and immediately there gushed forth such a stream of warm red gore that they realised this *sanguisuga* [bloodsucker] had battened on the blood of many poor folk. Accordingly, they dragged it outside the town, and here they built a large pyre. . . . Now no sooner had that infernal monster been thus destroyed than the plague, which had so sorely ravaged the people, entirely ceased, just as if the polluted air was cleansed by the fire which burned up the hellish brute who had infected the whole atmosphere.

6

Sixteenth-Century
Vampire in Silesia

From Henry More, the famous Cambridge Platonist
(1614–87), *An Anti-dote Against Atheism: or, An Appeal to
the Natural Faculties of the Mind of Man, whether there be
not a God.* First edition, London, 1653; second edition, with
appendix, 1655.

A certain Shoemaker in one of the chief Towns of Silesia, in the
year 1591, Septemb. 20, on a Friday betimes in the morning, in
the further part of his house, where there was adjoining a little
Garden, cut his own Throat with his Shoemaker's knife. The
Family, to cover the foulness of the fact, and that no disgrace
might come upon his Widow, gave out, that he died of an Apo-
plexy, declined all visits of friends and neighbours, in the meantime got him washed, and laid Linens so handsomely about him,
that even they that saw him afterwards, as the Parson, and some
others, had not the least Suspicion but that he did die of that
disease; and so he had honest Burial, with a funeral Sermon, and
other circumstances becoming one of his rank and reputation. Six
weeks had not past, but so strong a rumour broke out, that he died
not of any disease, but had laid violent hands upon himself, that
the Magistracy of the place could not but bring all those that had
seen the corpse, to a strict examination. They shuffled off the
matter as well as they could at first, with many fair Apologies, in
behalf of the deceased, to remove all suspicion of so heinous an

act: but it being pressed more home to their Conscience, at last they confessed, he died a violent death, but desired their favour and clemency to his widow and children, who were in no fault; adding also, that it was uncertain but that he might be slain by some external mishap, or, if by himself, in some irresistible fit of phrency [daemoniacal possession] or madness.

Hereupon the Council deliberate what is to be done, Which the Widow hearing, and fearing they might be determining something that would be harsh, and to the discredit of her Husband, and herself, being also animated thereto by some busie bodies, makes a great complaint against those that raised these reports of her Husband, and resolved to follow the Law upon them, earnestly contending that there was no reason, upon mere rumours and idle defamations of malevolent people, that her Husband's body should be digged up, or dealt with as if he had been either *Magician*, or *Self-murtherer*. Which boldness and pertinacity of the woman, though after the confession of the fact, did in some measure work upon the Council, and put them to a stand.

But while these things are in agitation, to the astonishment of the Inhabitants of the place, there appears a *Spectrum* in the exact shape and habit of the deceased, and that not only in the night, but at mid-day. Those that were asleep it terrified with horrible visions; those that were waking it would strike, pull, or press, lying heavy upon them like an *Ephialtes* [giant in Greek mythology, or a daemon causing a nightmare]: so that there were perpetual complaints every morning of their last night's rest through the whole Town. But the more freaks this *Spectrum* play'd, the more diligent were the friends of the deceased to suppress the rumours of them, or at least to hinder the effects of those rumours; and therefore made their addresses to the President, complaining how unjust a thing it was, that so much credit should be given to idle reports and blind suspicions, and therefore beseech'd him that he would hinder the Council from digging up the corpse of the deceased, and from all ignominious usage of him: adding also, that they intended to appeal to the Emperour's Court, that their Wisdoms might rather decide the Controversy, than that the cause should be determined from the light conjectures of malicious men.

An inventive 16th-century Parisian Dance of Death woodcut shows Death attacking like a wolf—or a vampire. (From Robert Gobin, *Les loups ravissans*, Paris, ca. 1505. Harvard College Library, Department of Printing Arts)

But while by this means the business was still protracted, there were such stirs and tumults all over the Town, that they are hardly to be described. For no sooner did the Sun hide his head, but this *Spectrum* would be sure to appear, so that every body was fain to look about him, and stand upon his guard, which was a sore trouble to those whom the Labours of the Day made more sensible of the want of rest in the night. For this terrible *Apparrition* would sometimes stand by their bed-sides, sometimes cast itself upon the midst of their beds, would lie close to them, would miserably suffocate them, and would so strike them and pinch them, that not only blue marks, but plain impressions of his fingers would be upon sundry parts of their bodies in the morning. Nay, such was the violence and impetuousness of this Ghost, that when men forsook their beds, and kept their dining-rooms, with Candles lighted, and many of them in company together, the better to secure themselves from fear and disturbance; yet he would then appear to them, and have a bout with some of them, notwithstanding all this provision against it. In brief, he was so troublesome, that the people were ready to forsake their houses, and seek other dwellings, and the Magistrates so awakened at the perpetual complaints of them, that at last they resolved, the President agreeing thereto, to dig up the Body.

He had lain in the ground near eight months, viz. from Sept. 22, 1591, to April 18, 1592. When he was digged up, which was in the presence of the Magistracy of the Town, his body was found entire, not at all putrid, no ill smell about him, saving the mustiness of the Grave-cloaths, his joints limber and flexible, as in those that are alive, his skin only flaccid, but a more fresh grown in the room of it, the wound of his throat gaping, but no gear nor corruption in it; there was also observed a Magical mark in the great toe of his right foot, viz. an Excrescency in the form of a Rose. His body was kept out of the earth from April 18, to the 24th, at what time many both of the same town and others came daily to view him. These unquiet stirs did not cease for all this, which they after attempted to appease, by burying the corpse under the Gallows, but in vain; for they were as much as ever, if not more, he now not sparing his own Family: insomuch that his Widow at last went her self to the Magistrate, and told them, that she should be no longer against it, if they thought fit to fall upon some course of more strict proceedings touching her Husband.

Wherefore the seventh of May he was again digged up, and it was observable, that he was grown more sensibly fleshy since his last interment. To be short, they cut off the Head, Arms, and Legs of the Corps, and opening his Back, took out his Heart, which was as fresh and intire as in a Calf new kill'd. These, together with his Body, they put on a pile of wood, and burnt them to Ashes, which they carefully sweeping together, and putting into a Sack (that none might get them for wicked uses) poured them into the River, after which the *Spectrum* was never seen more.

As it also happen'd in his Maid that dy'd after him, who appeared within eight days after her death, to her fellow servant, and lay so heavy upon her, that she brought upon her a great swelling of the eyes. She so grievously handled a Child in the cradle, that if the Nurse had not come to his help, he had been quite spoil'd; but she crossing her self, and calling upon the Name of *Jesus*, the Spectre vanished. The next night she appeared in the shape of an *Hen*, which, when one of the Maids of the house took to be so indeed, and followed her, the Hen grew into an immense bigness, and presently caught the Maid by the throat, and made it swell, so that she could neither eat nor drink of a good while after.

She continued these stirs for a whole month, slapping some so smartly, that the stroke were heard of them that stood by, pulling the bed also from under others, and appearing sometimes in one shape, sometimes in another, as of a Woman, of a Dog, of a Cat, and of a Goat. But at last her body being digged up, and burnt, the Apparition was never seen more.

The original Count Dracula's capital city, Târgoviște, Romania. (Raymond T. McNally)

7

Seventeenth-Century Vampire in an Austrian Province

From Erasmus Franciscus' commentary on Baron Valvasor's *Die Ehre des Herzogthums Krain* (The Honor of the Dukedom of Krain), Ljubljana, 1689. My translation.

The area where the following episode takes place has several names: Carniola, as in the story; Kranj, a German name, as also in the story; and Krain, a Slovene name, which is used in the title of the source. This area was a former province of the Austrian empire. Since 1947 it has been part of northwestern Yugoslavia.

A landowning peasant named Grando who lived in the district of Kranj was a hard-working, well-liked man. His death, however, was followed by the attacks of a vampire which satisfied its thirst on the blood of the villagers. Everyone in Carniola realized, because of the timing, that the vampire had to be Grando.

With the permission of the Church, Grando's body was exhumed, and the body was found as though he slept. The complexion was ruddy like that of a man alive. His face quivered, then curled into a cruel grin, taking in a breath of new air. His eyes popped open. Terrified by the uncanny phenomenon, the people at the grave began to pray, while a priest approached the body, extending a crucifix. Armed with this holy weapon, the priest pronounced these words over the monster:

"Raise thine eyes and look upon Jesus Christ who hath redeemed us from the pains of hell by His most Holy Passion and His precious Death upon the Rood."

Grando's features altered to an expression of utter sorrow. Tears flowed down his cheeks.

Solemnly the priest prayed for the creature's soul, that it might be saved. At last Grando was beheaded and his body gave a final twitch as though alive.

8

An Eighteenth-Century Look at Vampires

Six Selections

From Augustin Calmet, *Traité sur les apparitions des espirits, et sur les vampires, ou Les revenans de Hongrie, de Moravie,* written in 1746 and published in Paris in 1751. My translation.

Augustin Calmet was born February 26, 1672, at Mésnil-la-Horgne in Lorraine. Educated at the priory of Breuil, he joined the Benedictines at Saint Mansuy Abbey at Toril in 1688 and was ordained in 1696. He spent most of his life presiding over an academy at the abbey of Moyen-Moutier preferring to remain in that place despite offers of higher positions elsewhere. He is best known as a scholar and Biblical critic. His works include *Commentaire de la Bible* (1707–16) and *Dictionnaire historique . . . et littéral de la Bible* (1720). Calmet died on October 25, 1757, at the Abbey of Sénones near Saint-Dié.

Voltaire, in his *Dictionnaire philosophique*, expressed his reaction to the publication of Calmet's work as follows:

"What! There have been vampires during our 18th century! After the reign of Locke, Shaftesbury, Trenchard, Collins; and under the reign of d'Alembert, Diderot, Saint-Lambert, Duclos, people believed in vampires and the Reverend Father Augustin Calmet, priest, Benedictine from the congregation of Saint-Vannes and Saint-Hidulphe, abbot of Sénones . . . has published and republished the History of Vampires with the approbation of the Sorbonne, signed Marcilli!

"The result of all this is that a great portion of Europe has been infected with vampires for five or six years, and there are no more; we have had people afflicted by convulsions in France for more than twenty years, and there are no more; we have had the possessed for seventeen years, and there are no more; the dead have always been resuscitated since Hippolytus but one does not resuscitate them any more; we have had Jesuits in Spain, Portugal and France and in the Kingdom of the Two Sicilies and we have them no more."

I. PETER PLOGOSOVITZ OF KISILOVA, 1725

In the village of Kisilova, three leagues from Gradisch, an old man of sixty-two died in September; three days after the funeral he appeared before his son in the night and asked for food. His son gave him some and he disappeared. The next day the son told his neighbors what had happened. That night the old man did not appear; but the following night he appeared and demanded food; no one knows whether his son gave it to him or not, but in the morning the son was found dead in his bed, and on that same day five or six others in the village suddenly fell ill, and they died one after the other a few days later. The governor of the district forwarded a report to the Tribunal in Belgrade, and they sent two officials and an executioner to deal with the matter. The governor who first reported it traveled from Gradisch to see with his own eyes what had happened. All the bodies that had been buried for the last six weeks were disinterred; when they reached the body of the old man, they found his eyes were open and of a red color, and his respiration was normal, though he was quite still and dead. From this they concluded that he undoubtedly was a vampire. The hangman drove a stake through his heart. A great fire was made, and the corpse was reduced to ashes. It is said that "none of the marks of vampirism was found on the body of the son, nor on any of the others."

II.   TESTIMONY OF THE COUNT OF CABRERAS, 1730

The following testimony of the Count of Cabreras, one of the Imperial officers who led vampire investigations, was related to a Freiburg University professor at Brisgaw in 1730. Upon the request of Father Calmet the professor wrote down what the count had told him:

It is now fifteen years since a soldier, who was quartered in the house of a Haidamack peasant, on the frontiers of Hungary, saw as he was at table with his landlord, a stranger come in and sit down with them. The lord of the house and the rest of the company were strangely terrified but the soldier did not know what to make of it. The next day the peasant died, and when the soldier asked about the meaning of it all, he was told that it was the landlord's father, who had been dead and buried for over ten years, who had come and had sat down at the table and given notice to his son of his impending death.

The soldier soon spread the story around through his regiment, and in this way it reached the officers, who commissioned the Count of Cabreras, a captain in Allendetti's Fort Regiment, to conduct an exact inquiry into the facts. The count, attended by several officers, a surgeon, and a notary, went to the house and took depositions from the entire family, who unanimously swore that the spectre was the landlord's father and that all that the soldier had said was completely true. All the inhabitants of the village also attested the same facts.

As a result of this, the body of the spectre was dug up and discovered to be in the same state as if it had just been dead, the blood being that of a living person. The Count of Cabreras ordered that its head be cut off and that the corpse be buried again.

He then proceeded to take depositions against other spectres of the same type, and particularly against a man who had been dead more than thirty years, and yet had appeared several times in his own home at meal time.

During his first visit he had fastened upon the neck of his own brother and sucked his blood; during the second visit he had treated one of his own children in the same way, and during his third visit he had grabbed one of the servants of the family; all three had died instantly.

On the basis of this evidence the count issued orders that the man should be disinterred, and, as he was found to be like the first, with his blood in a fluid state as if alive, a great nail was driven through his temples and he was buried again. The count commanded that a third person, who had been dead for over sixteen years, be burned; and he was found guilty of murdering two of his children by sucking their blood.

The commissioner then made his report to the general officer, who sent a deputation to Emperor Charles VI's court for further instructions, and the Emperor issued an order for a court, consisting of officers, lawyers, physicians, surgeons, and some men of the cloth to go and inquire on the spot into the cause of these extraordinary events.

III.   ARNOLD PAOLE, 1732

About five years ago in Medreiga a certain Haidouk, or Hungarian soldier, called Arnold Paole, was killed when a cartload of hay fell on top of him. Thirty days after his death four persons died suddenly in the manner that was traditionally ascribed to vampirism. It was recalled that this same Arnold Paole had often related how he had been tormented by a Turkish vampire, near Cassova on the frontiers of Turkish Serbia; for he too believed that those who had been passive vampires in life became active ones after death, that is to say, those who had been sucked would suck in their turn; but that he had cured himself by eating earth from the vampire's grave and rubbing himself with its blood; yet this precaution had not prevented him from becoming one after death, for when he was exhumed forty days after his burial he showed all the marks of an arch-vampire. His body was flushed; his hair, nails, and beard had grown, and his veins were full of liquid blood that had splashed all over his winding-sheet. The *Hadnagy,* or governor of the district, who was well versed in the ways of vampires, was present at the exhumation, and he ordered that a sharp stake be driven right through the body as was customary, whereupon the corpse emitted a fearful shriek as though it were still living. Next the head was cut off and the body burnt. After this, the same procedure was followed with the four other persons who had died at the vampire's hands, lest they should cause more deaths. All this dispatch was to no purpose, for towards the end of last year, five years after the original occurrences, these terrible events recommenced, and several inhabitants of the same village perished miserably. Within the space of three months seventeen persons of both sexes and all ages died of vampirism, some without any illness, others after two or three days of illness. Among others, a certain Stanoska, daughter of the Haidouk Jotuitzo, is reported to have gone to bed in good health and to have awakened trembling and shrieking in the middle of the night, saying that the son of Millo, who had died nine weeks before, had nearly strangled her in her sleep. She sickened from this moment and died three days later. This woman's accusation was the first sign that Millo's son was a vampire; he was exhumed, and found to be one indeed. The governors of the district, and the doctors and surgeons, demanded how it was that vampirism had reappeared after all the precautions they had taken several years before.

After careful inquiries they discovered that the deceased Arnold Paole had killed not only these four persons but also several animals, which the new vampires had eaten, among them Millo's son. Therefore they undertook to exhume all the recent dead. Seventeen of them were found with all the signs of vampirism; so they were transfixed with the stake, decapitated, burnt, and the ashes thrown into the river.

All these inquiries and executions were legally and impartially carried out and witnessed by several of the officers garrisoned in the district, by the regimental surgeons, and by many respected local inhabitants. A copy of the proceedings was sent to the Imperial Council of War in Vienna at the end of last January, and they instituted a military commission to investigate the true facts of the case.

IV.   MICHEL RANFT'S ACCOUNT OF THE DIET OF THE DEAD

A German author called Michel Ranft has written a book entitled *De Masticatione Mortuorum in Tumulis* (That Dead Men Chew in Their Coffins). He assumes without question that certain corpses have devoured their winding-sheets and anything else close to their mouths, even their own flesh. He relates that in certain parts of Germany a lump of earth is placed under the corpse's chin in the coffin, to prevent him from biting, and in other parts of the country a small piece of silver and a stone are placed in the mouth, which is then tightly gagged with a handkerchief.

He might also have related the story of Henry, Comte de Salm, who was accidentally buried alive; during the night shrieks

I. N. J.
DISSERTATIO
HISTORICO-PHILOSOPHICA
De
MASTICATIONE
MORTUORUM,
Quam
Dei & Superiorum indultu,
in illuſtri Academ. Lipſ.
ſiſtent
PRÆSES
M. PHILIPPUS Rohr / Marckran-
ſtadio-Miſnic.
&
RESPONDENS
BENJAMIN FRIZSCHIUS, Muſilaviâ-Miſnicus,
Alumni Electorales.
ad diem XVI. Auguſti Ann. M. DC. LXXIX.
H. L. Q. C.

LIPSIÆ,
Typis MICHAELIS VOGTII.
DE MASTICATIONE MORTUORUM
By Philip Rohr

were heard coming from the church of the Abbey of Haute-Seille where he was buried, and the next day when his tomb was opened he was found lying face downwards, although he had been placed in the coffin on his back. Some years ago, at Bar-le-Duc, after a man had been buried in the cemetery, sounds were heard coming from his grave; he was exhumed the next day and was discovered to have eaten the flesh of his own arms; this was attested by several witnesses. He had passed into a stupor after drinking *eau-de-vie* and was buried alive. Ranft mentions a woman in Bohemia who ate half her winding-sheet in the year 1345. In the time of Luther a man and a woman buried at the same time gnawed out each other's vitals. In Moravia a dead man devoured the winding-sheet of the woman buried next to him.

V.   CALMET'S EIGHTEENTH-CENTURY QUESTIONS ABOUT VAMPIRES

These examples and arguments in favor of vampirism may be said to show that the apparitions in Hungary, Moravia, Poland, etc., are not really dead at all, that the fresh scarlet blood, the flexibility of their limbs, their shrieks when pierced through the heart or decapitated, prove that they were in truth entombed alive, but without movement or respiration. This indeed might be possible; but how could they issue from their graves and return to them without disturbing the earth; and how appear in their own clothes, and find food? Why return to their graves? Why not stay among the living? Why harass and torment those who should be dearest to them and have never caused them any harm? If all this is a delusion of the victims, how is it that the vampires are found uncorrupted in their graves, still soft and full of blood, that their feet are muddy soon after they have appeared in the village, and that nothing of the sort is found on the other corpses buried at the same time in the same cemetery? Why do the visitations cease after the bodies have been burnt or impaled on a stake? Might this too be due simply to superstition, if the peasants are reassured by the executions? How is it that these events are so frequent in this part of the world, and that the superstitions do not abate but increase with the familiarity of the experience?

VI.   CALMET'S ENLIGHTENED EXPLANATION OF VAMPIRISM

Many explanations for these occurrences have been advanced. Firstly, some people have declared them to be miracles. Secondly, others have considered them to be no more than the results of a restless imagination or a powerful superstition. Thirdly, others offer a simple and natural explanation: these persons were still alive. Fourthly, others have claimed that this was the work of the Devil; some of these people distinguish harmless devils, authors of practical jokes, from the race of malicious and evil demons, who are the cause of sin and crime and all our woes. Fifthly, others maintain that it is not the dead who eat their own flesh or their winding-sheets, but snakes, rats, moles, wolves, or other voracious beasts, or even what the pagans called *Striges*, which are birds that devour animals and men and suck their blood. Some authors have argued that these cases mostly concern women and occur chiefly in times of pestilence. But there are examples of apparitions of both sexes, more men than women; though indeed those who died of plague, poison, cholera, or drunkenness are more likely to appear and haunt people, doubtless because sometimes they are buried still alive, for fear that they will spread infection if they are left unburied.

It is also maintained that these vampires are only reported in certain countries, such as Hungary, Moravia, and Silesia, where pestilence is common and the people suffer from hunger and bad weather, ignorance, and superstition. As for the belief that the dead chew like pigs in their graves, this is manifestly nonsensical and can only be a superstition.

As I have already said, it is indeed hard to believe that the vampires could move in and out of their graves without disturbing the earth; this has never been accounted for, and never can be. To say that the Devil dematerializes the vampires' bodies is irrational and unwarranted.

The redness and fluidity of the vampires' blood and the pliability of their limbs are nothing extraordinary, nor are the growth of their nails and hair and the failure of their flesh to decay. It is common to see bodies that have not decayed at all and have retained a flushed complexion after death. This may occur after a very sudden death without illness, or after certain illnesses, well known to physicians, which leave the blood liquid and the limbs pliant.

Regarding the growth of the hair and the nails in bodies that have not decayed, this is a natural occurrence. The humors of the body still circulate gradually and cause them to grow, just as bulbs can commonly be seen to continue sprouting without any moisture or nourishment from the earth. The same is true of flowers, and indeed of the vegetative system of both animals and plants.

The belief of the ancient Greeks in the return of departed spirits was no more rational than the belief in ghosts and vampires. Ignorance, prejudice, and fear nourished this foolish fantasy and nourish it still.

The reports of the dead chewing in their graves are so pitifully puerile that they do not deserve serious consideration.

It is widely known that all too often bodies are buried while there is still some life in them. There are examples, too many of them, in ancient times and modern. The discourse of Monsieur Winflou and the additional remarks by Monsieur Bruhier prove beyond doubt that there are no certain signs of death apart from the commencement of putrefaction and odor. There are numberless cases of persons believed dead who have revived, even after burial. In many illnesses the patient may lie for long unconscious, without speaking, moving, or apparently breathing; sometimes a drowned man has been taken for dead, and then revived by bleeding and careful nursing.

This is common knowledge, and it suffices to explain why vampires have been dragged from the grave and made to speak, shout, scream and bleed: they were still alive. They were [then] killed by decapitation, perforation, or burning, and this has been a great wrong; for the allegation that they returned to haunt and destroy the living has never been sufficiently proved to authorize such inhumanity, or to permit innocent beings to be dishonored and ignominiously killed as a result of wild and unproved accusations. For the stories told of these apparitions, and all the distress caused by these supposed vampires, are totally without solid proof. I am not surprised that the Sorbonne has condemned the bloody and violent retribution wrought on these corpses; but it is astonishing that the magistrates and secular bodies have not employed their authority and legal force to put an end to it.

This is a mysterious and difficult matter, and I leave bolder and more proficient minds to resolve it.

9

Hungarian Antidote Against Vampires

From a letter written by a Walloon officer of the Austrian Imperial Army who was stationed in southeastern Hungary; published in *Les Lettres Juives*, 1732. My translation.

As for these Hungarian spectres, the thing generally happens in this manner: a man finds himself fallen into a languid state, loses his appetite, decreases visibly in bulk and, at eight or ten days' end, dies without a fever or any other symptom of illness save anemia and loss of flesh and a dried, withered body.

In Hungary they say that a vampire has attacked him and sucked his blood. Many of those who fall ill in this way declare that a white spectre is following them and sticks to them as close as their own shadow. When we were in our Kalocsa-Bács quarters, in the country of Temesvár, two officers of the regiment in which I was a cornet died from this languor, and several more were attacked and would have perished had not a corporal of our regiment put an end to these maladies by resorting to the remedial ceremonies which are practiced by local people. These are very unusual, and although they are considered an infallible cure I cannot remember ever having seen these in any ritual.

They select a young lad who is innocent of girls, that is to say who has never performed the sexual act. He is placed upon a young stallion who has not yet mounted a mare, who has never stumbled, and who must be pitch-black without a speck of white. The stud is ridden into the cemetery to and fro among the graves, and the grave over which the horse refuses to pass, in spite of blows liberally administered to him, is where the vampire lies.

The tomb is opened and they find a sleek, fat corpse, as healthily colored as though the man were quietly and happily sleeping in calm repose. With one single blow from a sharp spade they cut off the head, whereupon there gushes forth a *warm* stream of blood of rich red color, filling the whole grave. It could easily be surmised that they had just decapitated a big brawny fellow of most sanguine habit and complexion.

When this business is done, they refill the grave with earth and then the ravages of the disease immediately cease, whilst those suffering from this malady gradually recover their strength, just as convalescents recuperate after a long illness.

This is exactly what occurred in the case of our young officers who had sickened. As the colonel of the regiment, the captain, and the lieutenant were absent, I happened to be in command just then and I was very angry to find that the corporal had arranged the affair without my knowledge.

10

The First Great Vampire in Modern Literature

Extract from John Polidori, "The Vampyre," first published in Colburn's *New Monthly Magazine*, London, April 1819.

John Polidori (1795–1821), an Englishman of Italian descent, deserves remembrance as the creator of Lord Ruthven, the first great fictional vampire in modern letters. This character appears in "The Vampyre," and the story of how this story came to be written is itself a remarkable one.

Polidori was twenty-one years old when he composed "The Vampyre." His previous medical training at the University of Edinburgh had brought him appointment as personal physician to Lord Byron. His literary interests had already led him to translate Horace Walpole's Gothic novel *The Castle of Otranto*. In the summer of 1816, Byron, Polidori, Mary Godwin Shelley, her stepsister Claire, and Percy Bysshe Shelley all lived in adjacent villas along the shores of Lake Geneva. During this holiday Byron sketched out a plan for a vampire tale but never finished it. Polidori took over the idea and developed it into "The Vampyre."

The first printing—and several successive reprints—appeared with a preface attributing the story to Byron. Polidori had apparently told the publisher that Byron had originated the idea and that he himself had merely copied it down. When the work appeared to be heading for success, Polidori demanded more money. For many years, the general public still considered "The Vampyre" to be Byron's work. It was translated into French and German, and it almost immediately was made into a play, for dramas with a vampire theme had become the rage of Paris and London. The over-all pattern of "The Vampyre" is quite

John Polidori, personal physician to Lord Byron. (National Portrait Gallery, London)

similar to the "Fragment" which Byron wrote and published at the end of *Mazeppa* in 1819.

Polidori's vampiric Lord Ruthven dresses, speaks, and in general performs in accordance with the mode of those around him, yet from the outset is distinguished by certain traits that suggest a mysterious, even dangerous side to his nature. The combination of the attractive and the repulsive which is found in Lord Ruthven occurs in his literary descendants—certainly in all successful ones. The following extract from "The Vampyre" indicates Polidori's skill in transforming the ancient, one-dimensional bloodsucker who makes nocturnal appearances among the living into a credible, complex being who lives round the clock in the real world.

It happened that in the midst of the dissipations attendant upon a London winter, there appeared at the various parties of the leaders of the town a nobleman, more remarkable for his singularities, than his rank. He gazed upon the mirth around him, as if he could not participate therein. Apparently, the light laughter of the fair only attracted his attention, that he might by a look quell it, and throw fear into those breasts where thoughtlessness reigned. Those who felt this sensation of awe, could not explain whence it arose: some attributed it to the dead grey eye, which fixing upon the object's face, did not seem to penetrate . . . but fell upon the cheek with a leaden ray that weighed upon the skin it could not pass. His peculiarities caused him to be invited to every house; all wished to see him, and those who had been accustomed to violent excitement, and now felt the weight of *ennui*, were pleased at having something in their presence capable of engaging their attention. In spite of the deadly hue of his face, which never gained a warmer tint, either from the blush of modesty, or from the strong emotion of passion, though its form and outline were beautiful, many of the female hunters after notoriety attempted to win his attentions, and gain, at least, some marks of what they might term affection: Lady Mercer, who had been the mockery of every monster shewn in drawing-rooms since her marriage, threw herself in his way, and did all but put on the dress of a mountebank, to attract his notice—though in vain. . . . though the common adultress could not influence even the guidance of his eyes, it was not that the female sex was indifferent to him: yet such was the apparent caution with which he spoke to the virtuous wife and innocent daughter, that few knew he ever addressed himself to females. He had, however, the reputation of a winning tongue; and whether it was that it even overcame the dread of his singular character, or that they were moved by his apparent hatred of vice, he was as often among those females who form the boast of their sex from their domestic virtues, as among those who sully it by their vices.

. . . [Lord Ruthven] was profuse in his liberality—the idle, the vagabond, and the beggar, received from his hand more than enough to relieve their immediate wants. But Aubrey could not avoid remarking, that it was not upon the virtuous, reduced to indigence by the misfortunes attendant ever upon virtue, that he bestowed his alms—these were sent from the door with hardly suppressed sneers; but when the profligate came to ask something, not to relieve his wants, but to allow him to wallow in his lust, or to sink him still deeper in his iniquity, he was sent away with rich charity. This was, however, attributed by him to the greater importunity of the vicious, which generally prevails over the retiring bashfulness of the virtuous indigent. There was one [more] circumstance about the charity of his Lordship . . . all those upon whom it was bestowed, inevitably found that there was a curse upon it, for they were all either led to the scaffold, or sunk to the lowest and the most abject misery. . . . he entered into all the spirit of the faro table. . . . Yet he took no money from the gambling table; but immediately lost, to the ruin of many, the last gilder he had just snatched from the convulsive grasp of the innocent: this might but be the result of a certain degree of knowledge, which was not, however, capable of combating the cunning of the more experienced. Aubrey often wished to represent this to his friend, and beg him to resign that charity and pleasure which proved the ruin of all, and did not tend to his own profit; but he delayed it—for each day he hoped his friend would give him some opportunity of speaking frankly and openly to him; however, this never occurred. Lord Ruthven in his carriage, and amidst the various wild and rich scenes of nature, was always the same: his eye spoke less than his lip; and though Aubrey was near the object of his curiosity, he obtained no greater gratification from it than the constant excitement of vainly wishing to break that mystery, which to his exalted imagination began to assume the appearance of something supernatural. . . .

Joseph Sheridan Le Fanu, author of "Carmilla." (Radio Times Hulton Picture Library)

11

Carmilla

by Joseph Sheridan Le Fanu

First published in the magazine *The Dark Blue*, London, 1871.

Born in Ireland on August 28, 1814, Le Fanu was educated at Trinity College, Dublin. He became a lawyer in 1839 but soon abandoned law in favor of journalism. His *Purcell Papers*, written while he was still a student, demonstrates his proclivity toward the supernatural. Between 1845 and 1873 he published some fourteen novels. Among the best-known are *The House by the Churchyard* (1863) and *Uncle Silas* (1864). *In a Glass Darkly*, published in 1872, contained five long stories which are considered by most critics to be his best; among them was "Carmilla." After the death of his wife in 1858, Le Fanu became a recluse. He died in Dublin on February 7, 1873.

Le Fanu is one of the most talented Gothic novelists of all time. I have decided to reproduce his classic vampire tale here in its entirety, except for the brief prologue, in the hope that a new generation of readers may come to recognize his greatness. "Carmilla" is, indeed, a masterpiece.

The young heroine Laura, who tells the story, is strangely attracted to the female vampire, Carmilla, in a kind of Lesbian relationship. Such sexual deviancy is unusual, for in most vampire stories female vampires seek male companions and vice versa. The story takes place near the city of Gratz in southeastern Austria, an area which is the source of many vampire accounts.

I. AN EARLY FRIGHT

In Styria, we, though by no means magnificent people, inhabit a castle, or schloss. A small income, in that part of the world, goes a great way. Eight or nine hundred a year does wonders. Scantily enough ours would have answered among wealthy people at home. My father is English, and I bear an English name, although I never saw England. But, in this lonely and primitive place, where everything is so marvelously cheap, I really don't see how ever so much more money would at all materially add to our comforts, or even luxuries.

My father was in the Austrian service, and retired upon a pension and his patrimony, and purchased this feudal residence, and the small estate on which it stands, a bargain.

Nothing can be more picturesque or solitary. It stands on a slight eminence in a forest. The road, very old and narrow, passes in front of its drawbridge, never raised in my time, and its moat, stocked with perch, and sailed over by many swans, and floating on its surface white fleets of water-lilies.

Over all this the schloss shows its many-windowed front; its towers, and its Gothic chapel.

The forest opens in an irregular and very picturesque glade before its gate, and at the right a steep Gothic bridge carries the road over a stream that winds in deep shadow through the wood.

I have said that this is a very lonely place. Judge whether I say truth. Looking from the hall door toward the road, the forest in which our castle stands extends fifteen miles to the right, and twelve to the left. The nearest inhabited village is about seven of your English miles to the left. The nearest inhabited schloss of any historic associations, is that of old General Spielsdorf, nearly twenty miles away to the right.

I have said "the nearest *inhabited* village," because there is, only three miles westward, that is to say in the direction of

General Spielsdorf's schloss, a ruined village, with its quaint little church, now roofless, in the aisle of which are the moldering tombs of the proud family of Karnstein, now extinct, who once owned the equally-desolate château which, in the thick of the forest, overlooks the silent ruins of the town.

Respecting the cause of the desertion of this striking and melancholy spot, there is a legend which I shall relate to you another time.

I must tell you now, how very small is the party who constitute the inhabitants of our castle. I don't include servants, or those dependants who occupy rooms in the buildings attached to the schloss. Listen, and wonder! My father, who is the kindest man on earth, but growing old; and I, at the date of my story, only nineteen. Eight years have passed since then. I and my father constituted the family at the schloss. My mother, a Styrian lady, died in my infancy, but I had a good-natured governess, who had been with me from, I might almost say, my infancy. I could not remember the time when her fat, benignant face was not a familiar picture in my memory. This was Madame Perrodon, a native of Berne, whose care and good nature in part supplied to me the loss of my mother, whom I do not even remember, so early I lost her. She made a third at our little dinner party. There was a fourth, Mademoiselle De Lafontaine, a lady such as you term, I believe, a "finishing governess." She spoke French and German, Madame Perrodon French and broken English, to which my father and I added English, which, partly to prevent its becoming a lost language among us, and partly from patriotic motives, we spoke every day. The consequence was a Babel, at which strangers used to laugh, and which I shall make no attempt to reproduce in this narrative. And there were two or three young lady friends besides, pretty nearly of my own age, who were occasional visitors, for longer or shorter terms; and these visits I sometimes returned.

These were our regular social resources; but of course there were chance visits from "neighbors" of only five or six leagues' distance. My life was, notwithstanding, rather a solitary one, I can assure you.

My gouvernantes had just so much control over me as you might conjecture such sage persons would have in the case of a rather spoiled girl, whose only parent allowed her pretty nearly her own way in everything.

The first occurrence in my existence, which produced a terrible impression upon my mind, which, in fact, never has been effaced, was one of the very earliest incidents of my life which I can recollect. Some people will think it so trifling that it should not be recorded here. You will see, however, by-and-by, why I mention it. The nursery, as it was called, though I had it all to myself, was a large room in the upper story of the castle, with a steep oak roof. I can't have been more than six years old, when one night I awoke, and looking round the room from my bed, failed to see the nursery-maid. Neither was my nurse there; and I thought myself alone. I was not frightened, for I was one of those happy children who are studiously kept in ignorance of ghost stories, of fairy tales, and of all such lore as makes us cover up our heads when the door creaks suddenly, or the flicker of an expiring candle makes the shadow of a bed-post dance upon the wall, nearer to our faces. I was vexed and insulted at finding myself, as I conceived, neglected, and I began to whimper, preparatory to a hearty bout of roaring; when to my surprise, I saw a solemn, but very pretty face looking at me from the side of the bed. It was that of a young lady who was kneeling, with her hands under the coverlet. I looked at her with a kind of pleased wonder, and ceased whimpering. She caressed me with her hands, and lay down beside me on the bed, and drew me toward her, smiling; I felt immediately delightfully soothed, and fell asleep again. I was wakened by a sensation as if two needles ran into my breast very deep at the same moment, and I cried loudly. The lady started back, with her eyes fixed on me, and then slipped down upon the floor, and, as I thought, hid herself under the bed.

I was now for the first time frightened, and I yelled with all my might and main. Nurse, nursery-maid, housekeeper, all came running in, and hearing my story, they made light of it, soothing me all they could meanwhile. But, child as I was, I could perceive that their faces were pale with an unwonted look of anxiety, and I saw them look under the bed, and about the room, and peep under tables and pluck open cupboards; and the housekeeper whispered to the nurse: "Lay your hand along that hollow in the bed; some one *did* lie there, so sure as you did not; the place is still warm."

I remember the nursery-maid petting me, and all three examining my chest, where I told them I felt the puncture, and pronouncing that there was no sign visible that any such thing had happened to me.

The housekeeper and the two other servants who were in charge of the nursery, remained sitting up all night; and from that time a servant always sat up in the nursery until I was about fourteen.

I was very nervous for a long time after this. A doctor was called in, he was pallid and elderly. How well I remember his long saturnine face, slightly pitted with smallpox, and his chestnut wig. For a good while, every second day, he came and gave me medicine, which of course I hated.

The morning after I saw this apparition I was in a state of terror, and could not bear to be left alone, daylight though it was, for a moment.

I remember my father coming up and standing at the bedside, and talking cheerfully, and asking the nurse a number of questions, and laughing very heartily at one of the answers; and patting me on the shoulder, and kissing me, and telling me not to be frightened, that it was nothing but a dream and could not hurt me.

But I was not comforted, for I knew the visit of the strange woman was *not* a dream; and I was *awfully* frightened.

I was a little consoled by the nursery-maid's assuring me that it was she who had come and looked at me, and lain down beside me in the bed and that I must have been half-dreaming not to have known her face. But this, though supported by the nurse, did not quite satisfy me.

I remember, in the course of that day, a venerable old man, in a black cassock, coming into the room with the nurse and housekeeper, and talking a little to them, and very kindly to me; his face was very sweet and gentle, and he told me they were going to pray, and joined my hands together, and desired me to say, softly, while they were praying, "Lord, hear all good prayers for us, for Jesus' sake." I think these were the very words, for I often repeated them to myself, and my nurse used for years to make me say them in my prayers.

I remember so well the thoughtful sweet face of that white-haired old man, in his black cassock, as he stood in that rude, lofty, brown room, with the clumsy furniture of a fashion three hundred years old, about him, and the scanty light entering its shadowy atmosphere through the small lattice. He kneeled, and the three women with him, and he prayed aloud with an earnest quavering voice for, what appeared to me, a long time. I forget all my life preceding that event, and for some time after it is all obscure also; but the scenes I have just described stand out vivid as the isolated pictures of the phantasmagoria surrounded by darkness.

II.   A GUEST

I am now going to tell you something so strange that it will require all your faith in my veracity to believe my story. It is not only true, nevertheless, but truth of which I have been an eye-witness.

It was a sweet summer evening, and my father asked me, as he sometimes did, to take a little ramble with him along that beautiful forest vista which I have mentioned as lying in front of the schloss.

"General Spielsdorf cannot come to us so soon as I had hoped," said my father, as we pursued our walk.

He was to have paid us a visit of some weeks, and we had expected his arrival next day. He was to have brought with him a young lady, his niece and ward, Mademoiselle Rheinfeldt, whom I had never seen, but whom I had heard described as a very charming girl, and in whose society I had promised myself many happy days. I was more disappointed than a young lady living in a town, or a bustling neighborhood can possibly imagine. This visit, and the new acquaintance it promised, had furnished my daydream for many weeks.

"And how soon does he come?" I asked.

"Not till autumn. Not for two months, I dare say," he answered. "And I am very glad now, dear, that you never knew Mademoiselle Rheinfeldt."

"And why?" I asked, both mortified and curious.

"Because the poor young lady is dead," he replied. "I quite forgot I had not told you, but you were not in the room when I received the General's letter this evening."

I was very much shocked. General Spielsdorf had mentioned in his first letter, six or seven weeks before, that she was not so well as he would wish her, but there was nothing to suggest the remotest suspicion of danger.

"Here is the General's letter," he said, handing it to me. "I am afraid he is in great affliction; the letter appears to me to have been written very nearly in distraction."

We sat down on a rude bench, under a group of magnificent lime trees. The sun was setting with all its melancholy splendor behind the sylvan horizon, and the stream that flows beside our home, and passes under the steep old bridge I have mentioned, wound through many a group of noble trees, almost at our feet, reflecting in its current the fading crimson of the sky. General Spielsdorf's letter was so extraordinary, so vehement, and in some places so self-contradictory, that I read it twice over—the second time aloud to my father—and was still unable to account for it, except by supposing that grief had unsettled his mind.

It said, "I have lost my darling daughter, for as such I loved her. During the last days of dear Bertha's illness I was not able to write to you. Before then I had no idea of her danger. I have lost her, and now learn *all*, too late. She died in the peace of innocence, and in the glorious hope of a blessed futurity. The fiend who betrayed our infatuated hospitality has done it all. I thought I was receiving into my house innocence, gaiety, a charming companion for my lost Bertha. Heavens! What a fool have I been! I thank God my child died without a suspicion of the cause of her sufferings. She is gone without so much as conjecturing the nature of her illness, and the accursed passion of the agent of all this misery. I devote my remaining days to tracking and extinguishing a monster. I am told I may hope to accomplish my righteous and merciful purpose. At present there is scarcely a gleam of light to guide me. I curse my conceited incredulity, my despicable affectation of superiority, my blindness, my obstinacy —all—too late. I cannot write or talk collectedly now. I am distracted. So soon as I shall have a little recovered, I mean to devote myself for a time to inquiry, which may possibly lead me as far as Vienna. Some time in the autumn, two months hence, or earlier if I live, I will see you—that is, if you permit me; I will then tell you all that I scarce dare put upon paper now. Farewell. Pray for me, dear friend."

In these terms ended this strange letter. Though I had never seen Bertha Rheinfeldt, my eyes filled with tears at the sudden intelligence; I was startled, as well as profoundly disappointed.

The sun had now set, and it was twilight by the time I had returned the General's letter to my father.

It was a soft clear evening, and we loitered, speculating upon the possible meanings of the violent and incoherent sentences which I had just been reading. We had nearly a mile to walk before reaching the road that passes the schloss in front, and by that time the moon was shining brilliantly. At the drawbridge we met Madame Perrodon and Mademoiselle De Lafontaine, who had come out, without their bonnets, to enjoy the exquisite moonlight.

We heard their voices gabbling in animated dialogue as we approached. We joined them at the drawbridge, and turned about to admire with them the beautiful scene.

The glade through which we had just walked lay before us. At our left the narrow road wound away under clumps of lordly trees, and was lost to sight amid the thickening forest. At the right the same road crosses the steep and picturesque bridge, near which stands a ruined tower, which once guarded that pass; and beyond the bridge an abrupt eminence rises, covered with trees, and showing in the shadow some gray ivy-clustered rocks.

Over the sward and low grounds, a thin film of mist was stealing, like smoke, marking the distances with a transparent veil; and here and there we could see the river faintly flashing in the moonlight.

No softer, sweeter scene could be imagined. The news I had just heard made it melancholy; but nothing could disturb its character of profound serenity, and the enchanted glory and vagueness of the prospect.

My father, who enjoyed the picturesque, and I, stood looking in silence over the expanse beneath us. The two good governesses, standing a little way behind us, discoursed upon the scene, and were eloquent upon the moon.

Madame Perrodon was fat, middle-aged, and romantic, and talked and sighed poetically. Mademoiselle De Lafontaine—in right of her father, who was a German, assumed to be psychological, metaphysical, and something of a mystic—now declared that when the moon shone with a light so intense it was well known that it indicated a special spiritual activity. The effect of the full moon in such a state of brilliancy was manifold. It acted on dreams, it acted on lunacy, it acted on nervous people; it had marvelous physical influences connected with life. Mademoiselle related that her cousin, who was mate of a merchant ship, having taken a nap on deck on such a night, lying on his back, with his face full in the light of the moon, had wakened, after a dream of an old woman clawing him by the cheek, with his features horribly drawn to one side; and his countenance had never quite recovered its equilibrium.

"The moon, this night," she said, "is full of odylic and magnetic influence—and see, when you look behind you at the front of the schloss, how all its windows flash and twinkle with that silvery splendor, as if unseen hands had lighted up the rooms to receive fairy guests."

There are indolent states of the spirits in which, indisposed to talk ourselves, the talk of others is pleasant to our listless ears; and I gazed on, pleased with the tinkle of the ladies' conversation.

"I have got into one of my moping moods to-night," said my father, after a silence, and quoting Shakespeare, whom, by way of keeping up our English, he used to read aloud, he said:—

> " 'In truth I know not why I am so sad:
> It wearies me; you say it wearies you;
> But how I got it—came by it.'

"I forget the rest. But I feel as if some great misfortune were hanging over us. I suppose the poor General's afflicted letter has had something to do with it."

At this moment the unwonted sound of carriage wheels and many hoofs upon the road, arrested our attention.

They seemed to be approaching from the high ground overlooking the bridge, and very soon the equipage emerged from that point. Two horsemen first crossed the bridge, then came a carriage drawn by four horses, and two men rode behind.

It seemed to be a traveling carriage of a person of rank; and we were all immediately absorbed in watching that very unusual spectacle. It became, in a few moments, greatly more interesting, for just as the carriage had passed the summit of the steep bridge, one of the leaders, taking fright, communicated his panic to the rest, and, after a plunge or two, the whole team broke into a wild gallop together, and dashing between the horsemen who rode in front, came thundering along the road toward us with the speed of a hurricane.

The excitement of the scene was made more painful by the clear, long-drawn screams of a female voice from the carriage window.

We all advanced in curiosity and horror; my father in silence, the rest with various ejaculations of terror.

Our suspense did not last long. Just before you reach the castle drawbridge, on the route they were coming, there stands by the roadside a magnificent lime tree, on the other stands an ancient stone cross, at sight of which the horses, now going at a pace that was perfectly frightful, swerved so as to bring the wheel over the projecting roots of the tree.

I knew what was coming. I covered my eyes, unable to see it out, and turned my head away; at the same moment I heard a cry from my lady friends, who had gone on a little.

Curiosity opened my eyes, and I saw a scene of utter confusion. Two of the horses were on the ground, the carriage lay upon its side, with two wheels in the air; the men were busy removing the traces, and a lady, with a commanding air and figure had got out, and stood with clasped hands, raising the handkerchief that was in them every now and then to her eyes. Through the carriage door was now lifted a young lady, who appeared to be lifeless. My dear old father was already beside the elder lady, with his hat in his hand, evidently tendering his aid and the resources of his schloss. The lady did not appear to hear him, or to have eyes for anything but the slender girl who was being placed against the slope of the bank.

I approached; the young lady was apparently stunned, but she was certainly not dead. My father, who piqued himself on being something of a physician, had just had his fingers to her wrist and assured the lady, who declared herself her mother, that her pulse, though faint and irregular, was undoubtedly still distinguishable. The lady clasped her hands and looked upward, as if in a momentary transport of gratitude; but immediately she broke out again in that theatrical way which is, I believe, natural to some people.

She was what is called a fine-looking woman for her time of life, and must have been handsome; she was tall, but not thin, and dressed in black velvet, and looked rather pale, but with a proud and commanding countenance, though now agitated strangely.

"Was ever being so born to calamity?" I heard her say, with clasped hands, as I came up. "Here am I, on a journey of life and death, in prosecuting which to lose an hour is possibly to lose all. My child will not have recovered sufficiently to resume her route for who can say how long. I must leave her; I cannot, dare not, delay. How far on, sir, can you tell, is the nearest village? I must leave her there; and shall not see my darling, or even hear of her till my return, three months hence."

I plucked my father by the coat, and whispered earnestly in his ear, "Oh! papa, pray ask her to let her stay with us—it would be so delightful. Do, pray."

"If madame will entrust her child to the care of my daughter, and of her good gouvernante, Madame Perrodon, and permit her to remain as our guest, under my charge, until her return, it will confer a distinction and an obligation upon us, and we shall treat her with all the care and devotion which so sacred a trust deserves."

"I cannot do that, sir, it would be to task your kindness and chivalry too cruelly," said the lady, distractedly.

"It would, on the contrary, be to confer on us a very great kindness at the moment when we most need it. My daughter has just been disappointed by a cruel misfortune, in a visit from which she had long anticipated a great deal of happiness. If you confide this young lady to our care it will be her best consolation. The nearest village on your route is distant, and affords no such inn as you think of placing your daughter at; you cannot allow her to continue her journey for any considerable distance without danger. If, as you say, you cannot suspend your journey, you must part with her to-night, and nowhere could you do so with more honest assurances of care and tenderness than here."

There was something in this lady's air and appearance so distinguished, and even imposing, and in her manner so engaging, as to impress one, quite apart from the dignity of her equipage, with a conviction that she was a person of consequence.

By this time the carriage was replaced in its upright position, and the horses, quite tractable, in the traces again.

The lady threw on her daughter a glance which I fancied was not quite so affectionate as one might have anticipated from the beginning of the scene; then she beckoned slightly to my father, and withdrew two or three steps with him out of hearing; and talked to him with a fixed and stern countenance, not at all like that with which she had hitherto spoken.

I was filled with wonder that my father did not seem to perceive the change, and also unspeakably curious to learn what it could be that she was speaking, almost in his ear, with so much earnestness and rapidity.

Two or three minutes at most, I think, she remained thus employed, then she turned and a few steps brought her to where her daughter lay, supported by Madame Perrodon. She kneeled beside her for a moment and whispered, as madame supposed, a little benediction in her ear; then hastily kissing her, she stepped into her carriage, the door was closed, the footmen in stately liveries jumped up behind, the outriders spurred on, the postilions cracked their whips, the horses plunged and broke suddenly into a furious canter that threatened soon again to become a gallop, and the carriage whirled away, followed at the same rapid pace by the two horsemen in the rear.

III.   WE COMPARE NOTES

We followed the *cortége* with our eyes until it was swiftly lost to sight in the misty wood; and the very sound of the hoofs and wheels died away in the silent night air.

Nothing remained to assure us that the adventure had not been an illusion of a moment but the young lady, who just at that moment opened her eyes. I could not see, for her face was turned from me, but she raised her head, evidently looking about her, and I heard a very sweet voice ask complainingly, "Where is mamma?"

Our good Madame Perrodon answered tenderly, and added some comfortable assurances.

I then heard her ask:

"Where am I? What is this place?" and after that she said, "I don't see the carriage; and Matska, where is she?"

Madame answered all her questions in so far as she understood them; and gradually the young lady remembered how the misadventure came about, and was glad to hear that no one in, or in attendance on, the carriage was hurt; and on learning that her mamma had left her here, till her return in about three months, she wept.

I was going to add my consolations to those of Madame Perrodon when Mademoiselle De Lafontaine placed her hand upon my arm, saying:

"Don't approach, one at a time is as much as she can at present converse with; a very little excitement would possibly overpower her now."

As soon as she is comfortably in bed, I thought, I will run up to her room and see her.

My father in the meantime had sent a servant on horseback for the physician, who lived about two leagues away; and a bedroom was being prepared for the young lady's reception.

The stranger now rose, and leaning on madame's arm, walked slowly over the drawbridge and into the castle gate.

In the hall, servants waited to receive her, and she was conducted forthwith to her room.

The room we usually sat in as our drawing-room is long, having four windows, that looked over the moat and drawbridge, upon the forest scene I have just described.

It is furnished in old carved oak, with large carved cabinets, and the chairs are cushioned with crimson Utrecht velvet. The walls are covered with tapestry, and surrounded with great gold frames, the figures being as large as life, in ancient and very curious costume, and the subjects represented are hunting, hawking and generally festive. It is not too stately to be extremely comfortable; and here we had our tea, for with his usual patriotic leanings he insisted that the national beverage should make its appearance regularly with our coffee and chocolate.

We sat here this night, and with candles lighted, were talking over the adventure of the evening.

Madame Perrodon and Mademoiselle De Lafontaine were both of our party. The young stranger had hardly lain down in her bed when she sank into a deep sleep; and those ladies had left her in the care of a servant.

"How do you like our guest?" I asked, as soon as madame entered. "Tell me all about her?"

"I like her extremely," answered madame, "she is, I almost think the prettiest creature I ever saw; about your age, and so gentle and nice."

"She is absolutely beautiful," threw in mademoiselle, who had peeped for a moment into the stranger's room.

Scene from Carl Dreyer's *Vampyr* (1932), freely adapted
from "Carmilla." The distant, grainy quality of the film
helped create a suggestion of horror and a mood that remains unique among vampire films. (The Museum of
Modern Art/Film Stills Archive)

"And such a sweet voice!" added Madame Perrodon.

"Did you remark a woman in the carriage, after it was set up again, who did not get out," inquired mademoiselle, "but only looked from the window?"

No, we had not seen her.

Then she described a hideous black woman, with a sort of colored turban on her head, who was gazing all the time from the carriage window, nodding and grinning derisively toward the ladies, with gleaming eyes and large white eyeballs, and her teeth set as if in fury.

"Did you remark what an ill-looking pack of men the servants were?" asked madame.

"Yes," said my father, who had just come in, "ugly, hang-dog looking fellows, as ever I beheld in my life. I hope they mayn't rob the poor lady in the forest. They are clever rogues, however; they got everything to rights in a minute."

"I dare say they are worn out with too long traveling," said madame. "Besides looking wicked, their faces were so strangely lean, and dark, and sullen. I am very curious, I own; but I dare say the young lady will tell us all about it to-morrow, if she is sufficiently recovered."

"I don't think she will," said my father, with a mysterious smile, and a little nod of his head, as if he knew more about it than he cared to tell us.

This made me all the more inquisitive as to what had passed between him and the lady in the black velvet, in the brief but earnest interview that had immediately preceded her departure.

We were scarcely alone, when I entreated him to tell me. He did not need much pressing.

"There is no particular reason why I should not tell you. She expressed a reluctance to trouble us with the care of her daughter, saying she was in delicate health, and nervous, but not subject to any kind of seizure—she volunteered that—nor to any illusion; being, in fact, perfectly sane."

"How very odd to say all that!" I interpolated. "It was so unnecessary."

"At all events it was *said*," he laughed, "and as you wish to know all that passed, which was indeed very little, I tell you. She then said, 'I am making a long journey of *vital* importance'—she emphasized the word—'rapid and secret; I shall return for my child in three months; in the meantime, she will be silent as to who we are, whence we come, and whither we are traveling.' That is all she said. She spoke very pure French. When she said the word 'secret,' she paused for a few seconds, looking sternly, her eyes fixed on mine. I fancy she makes a great point of that. You saw how quickly she was gone. I hope I have not done a very foolish thing, in taking charge of the young lady."

For my part, I was delighted. I was longing to see and talk to her; and only waiting till the doctor should give me leave. You, who live in towns, can have no idea how great an event the introduction of a new friend is, in such a solitude as surrounded us.

The doctor did not arrive till nearly one o'clock; but I could no more have gone to my bed and slept, than I could have overtaken, on foot, the carriage in which the princess in black velvet had driven away.

When the physician came down to the drawing-room, it was to report very favorably upon his patient. She was now sitting up, her pulse quite regular, apparently perfectly well. She had sustained no injury, and the little shock to her nerves had passed away quite harmlessly. There could be no harm certainly in my seeing her, if we both wished it; and, with this permission, I sent, forthwith, to know whether she would allow me to visit her for a few minutes in her room.

The servant returned immediately to say that she desired nothing more.

You may be sure I was not long in availing myself of this permission.

Our visitor lay in one of the handsomest rooms in the schloss. It was, perhaps, a little stately. There was a somber piece of tapestry opposite the foot of the bed, representing Cleopatra with the asps to her bosom; and other solemn classic scenes were displayed, a little faded, upon the other walls. But there was gold carving, and rich and varied color enough in the other decorations of the room, to more than redeem the gloom of the old tapestry.

There were candles at the bedside. She was sitting up; her slender pretty figure enveloped in the soft silk dressing-gown, embroidered with flowers, and lined with thick quilted silk, which her mother had thrown over her feet as she lay upon the ground.

What was it that, as I reached the bedside and had just begun my little greeting, struck me dumb in a moment, and made me recoil a step or two from before her? I will tell you.

I saw the very face which had visited me in my childhood at night, which remained so fixed in my memory, and on which I had for so many years so often ruminated with horror, when no one suspected of what I was thinking.

It was pretty, even beautiful; and when I first beheld it, wore the same melancholy expression.

But this almost instantly lighted into a strange fixed smile of recognition.

There was a silence of fully a minute, and then at length *she* spoke; *I* could not.

"How wonderful!" she exclaimed. "Twelve years ago, I saw your face in a dream, and it has haunted me ever since."

"Wonderful indeed!" I repeated, overcoming with an effort the horror that had for a time suspended my utterances. "Twelve years ago, in vision or reality, *I* certainly saw you. I could not forget your face. It has remained before my eyes ever since."

Her smile had softened. Whatever I had fancied strange in it, was gone, and it and her dimpling cheeks were now delightfully pretty and intelligent.

I felt reassured, and continued more in the vein which hospitality indicated, to bid her welcome, and to tell her how much pleasure her accidental arrival had given us all, and especially what a happiness it was to me.

I took her hand as I spoke. I was a little shy, as lonely people are, but the situation made me eloquent, and even bold. She pressed my hand, she laid hers upon it, and her eyes glowed, as, looking hastily into mine, she smiled again, and blushed.

She answered my welcome very prettily. I sat down beside her, still wondering; and she said:

"I must tell you my vision about you; it is so very strange that you and I should have had, each of the other so vivid a dream, that each should have seen, I you and you me, looking as we do now, when of course we both were mere children. I was a child, about six years old, and I awoke from a confused and troubled dream, and found myself in a room, unlike my nursery, wainscoted clumsily in some dark wood, and with cupboards and bedsteads, and chairs, and benches placed about it. The beds were, I thought, all empty, and the room itself without any one but myself in it; and I, after looking about me for some time, and admiring especially an iron candlestick, with two branches, which I should certainly know again, crept under one of the beds to reach the window; but as I got from under the bed, I heard some one crying; and looking up, while I was still upon my knees, I saw *you*—most assuredly you—as I see you now; a beautiful young lady, with golden hair and large blue eyes, and lips—your lips—you, as you are here. Your looks won me; I climbed on the bed and put my arms about you, and I think we both fell asleep. I was aroused by a scream; you were sitting up screaming. I was frightened, and slipped down upon the ground, and, it seemed to me, lost consciousness for a moment; and when I came to myself, I was again in my nursery at home. Your face I have never forgotten since. I could not be misled by mere resemblance. You *are* the lady whom I then saw."

It was now my turn to relate my corresponding vision, which I did, to the undisguised wonder of my new acquaintance.

"I don't know which should be most afraid of the other," she said, again smiling. "If you were less pretty I think I should be very much afraid of you, but being as you are, and you and I both so young, I feel only that I have made your acquaintance twelve years ago, and have already a right to your intimacy; at all events, it does seem as if we were destined, from our earliest childhood, to be friends. I wonder whether you feel as strangely drawn toward me as I do to you; I have never had a friend—shall I find one now?" She sighed, and her fine dark eyes gazed passionately on me.

Now the truth is, I felt rather unaccountably toward the beautiful stranger. I did feel, as she said, "drawn toward her," but there was also something of repulsion. In this ambiguous feeling, however, the sense of attraction immensely prevailed. She interested and won me, she was so beautiful and so indescribably engaging.

I perceived now something of languor and exhaustion stealing over her, and hastened to bid her good-night.

"The doctor thinks," I added, "that you ought to have a maid to sit up with you to-night; one of ours is waiting, and you will find her a very useful and quiet creature."

"How kind of you, but I could not sleep, I never could with an attendant in the room. I shan't require any assistance—and, shall I confess my weakness, I am haunted with a terror of robbers. Our house was robbed once, and two servants murdered, so I always lock my door. It has become a habit—and you look so kind I know you will forgive me. I see there is a key in the lock."

She held me close in her pretty arms for a moment and whispered in my ear, "Good-night, darling, it is very hard to part with you, but good-night; to-morrow, but not early, I shall see you again."

She sank back on the pillow with a sigh, and her fine eyes followed me with a fond and melancholy gaze, and she murmured again, "Good-night, dear friend."

Young people like, and even love, on impulse. I was flattered by the evident, though as yet undeserved, fondness she showed me. I liked the confidence with which she at once received me. She was determined that we should be very dear friends.

Next day came and we met again. I was delighted with my companion; that is to say, in many respects.

Her looks lost nothing in daylight—she was certainly the most beautiful creature I had ever seen, and the unpleasant remembrance of the face presented in my early dream, had lost the effect of the first unexpected recognition.

She confessed that she had experienced a similar shock on seeing me, and precisely the same faint antipathy that had mingled with my admiration of her. We now laughed together over our momentary horrors.

IV.   HER HABITS—A SAUNTER

I told you that I was charmed with her in most particulars.

There were some that did not please me so well.

She was above the middle height of women. I shall begin by describing her. She was slender, and wonderfully graceful. Except that her movements were languid—*very* languid—indeed, there was nothing in her appearance to indicate an invalid. Her complexion was rich and brilliant; her features were small and beautifully formed; her eyes large, dark, and lustrous; her hair was quite wonderful, I never saw hair so magnificently thick and long when it was down about her shoulders; I have often placed my hands under it, and laughed with wonder at its weight. It was exquisitely fine and soft, and in color a rich very dark brown, with something of gold. I loved to let it down, tumbling with its own weight, as, in her room, she lay back in her chair talking in her sweet low voice, I used to fold and braid it, and spread it out and play with it. Heavens! If I had but known all!

I said there were particulars which did not please me. I have told you that her confidence won me the first night I saw her; but I found that she exercised with respect to herself, her mother, her history, everything in fact connected with her life, plans, and people, an ever-wakeful reserve. I dare say I was unreasonable, perhaps I was wrong; I dare say I ought to have respected the solemn injunction laid upon my father by the stately lady in black velvet. But curiosity is a restless and unscrupulous passion, and no one girl can endure, with patience, that hers should be baffled by another. What harm could it do anyone to tell me what I so ardently desired to know? Had she no trust in my good sense or honor? Why would she not believe me when I assured her, so solemnly, that I would not divulge one syllable of what she told me to any mortal breathing.

There was a coldness, it seemed to me, beyond her years, in her smiling melancholy persistent refusal to afford me the least ray of light.

I cannot say we quarreled upon this point, for she would not quarrel upon any. It was, of course, very unfair of me to press her, very ill-bred, but I really could not help it; and I might just as well have let it alone.

What she did tell me amounted, in my unconscionable estimation—to nothing.

It was all summed up in three very vague disclosures:

First.—Her name was Carmilla.

Second.—Her family was very ancient and noble.

Third.—Her home lay in the direction of the west.

She would not tell me the name of her family, nor their armorial bearings, nor the name of their estate, nor even that of the country they lived in.

You are not to suppose that I worried her incessantly on these subjects. I watched opportunity, and rather insinuated than urged my inquiries. Once or twice, indeed, I did attack her more directly. But no matter what my tactics, utter failure was invariably the result. Reproaches and caresses were all lost upon her. But I must add this, that her evasion was conducted with so pretty a melancholy and deprecation, with so many, and even passionate declarations of her liking for me, and trust in my honor, and with so many promises that I should at last know all, that I could not find it in my heart long to be offended with her.

She used to place her pretty arms about my neck, draw me to her, and laying her cheek to mine, murmur with her lips near my ear, "Dearest, your little heart is wounded; think me not cruel because I obey the irresistible law of my strength and weakness; if your dear heart is wounded, my wild heart bleeds with yours. In the rapture of my enormous humiliation I live in your warm life, and you shall die—die, sweetly die—into mine. I cannot help it; as I draw near to you, you, in your turn, will draw near to others, and learn the rapture of that cruelty, which yet is love; so, for a while, seek to know no more of me and mine, but trust me with all your loving spirit."

And when she had spoken such a rhapsody, she would press me more closely in her trembling embrace, and her lips in soft kisses gently glow upon my cheek.

Her agitations and her language were unintelligible to me.

From these foolish embraces, which were not of very frequent occurrence, I must allow, I used to wish to extricate myself; but my energies seemed to fail me. Her murmured words sounded like a lullaby in my ear, and soothed my resistance into a trance, from which I only seemed to recover myself when she withdrew her arms.

In these mysterious moods I did not like her. I experienced a strange tumultuous excitement that was pleasurable, ever and anon, mingled with a vague sense of fear and disgust. I had no distinct thoughts about her while such scenes lasted, but I was conscious of a love growing into adoration, and also of abhorrence. This I know is paradox, but I can make no other attempt to explain the feeling.

I now write, after an interval of more than ten years, with a trembling hand, with a confused and horrible recollection of certain occurrences and situations, in the ordeal through which I was unconsciously passing; though with a vivid and very sharp remembrance of the main current of my story. But, I suspect, in all lives there are certain emotional scenes, those in which our passions have been most wildly and terribly roused, that are of all others the most vaguely and dimly remembered.

Sometimes after an hour of apathy, my strange and beautiful companion would take my hand and hold it with a fond pressure, renewed again and again; blushing softly, gazing in my face with languid and burning eyes, and breathing so fast that her dress rose and fell with the tumultuous respiration. It was like the ardor of a lover; it embarrassed me; it was hateful and yet overpowering; and with gloating eyes she drew me to her, and her hot lips traveled along my cheek in kisses; and she would whisper, almost in sobs, "You are mine, you *shall* be mine, and you and I are one forever." Then she has thrown herself back in her chair, with her small hands over her eyes, leaving me trembling.

"Are we related," I used to ask; "what can you mean by all this? I remind you perhaps of some one whom you love; but you must not, I hate it; I don't know you—I don't know myself when you look so and talk so."

She used to sigh at my vehemence, then turn away and drop my hand.

Respecting these very extraordinary manifestations I strove in vain to form any satisfactory theory—I could not refer them to affection or trick. It was unmistakably the momentary breaking out of suppressed instinct and emotion. Was she, notwithstanding her mother's volunteered denial, subject to brief visitations of insanity; or was there here a disguise and a romance? I had read in old story books of such things. What if a boyish lover had found his way into the house, and sought to prosecute his suit in masquerade, with the assistance of a clever old adventuress. But there were many things against this hypothesis, highly interesting as it was to my vanity.

I could boast of no little attentions such as masculine gallantry delights to offer. Between these passionate moments there were long intervals of commonplace, of gaiety, of brooding melancholy, during which, except that I detected her eyes so full of melancholy fire, following me, at times I might have been as nothing to her. Except in their brief periods of mysterious excitement her ways were girlish; and there was always a languor about her, quite incompatible with a masculine system in a state of health.

In some respects her habits were odd. Perhaps not so singular in the opinion of a town lady like you, as they appeared to us rustic people. She used to come down very late, generally not till one o'clock, she would then take a cup of chocolate, but eat nothing; we then went out for a walk, which was a mere saunter, and she seemed, almost immediately, exhausted, and either returned to the schloss or sat on one of the benches that were placed, here and there, among the trees. This was a bodily languor in which her mind did not sympathize. She was always an animated talker, and very intelligent.

She sometimes alluded for a moment to her own home, or mentioned an adventure or situation, or an early recollection, which indicated a people of strange manners, and described customs of which we knew nothing. I gathered from these chance hints that her native country was much more remote than I had at first fancied.

As we sat thus one afternoon under the trees a funeral passed us by. It was that of a pretty young girl, whom I had often seen, the daughter of one of the rangers of the forest. The poor man was walking behind the coffin of his darling; she was his only child, and he looked quite heartbroken. Peasants walking two-and-two came behind, they were singing a funeral hymn.

I rose to mark my respect as they passed, and joined in the hymn they were very sweetly singing.

My companion shook me a little roughly, and I turned surprised.

She said brusquely, "Don't you perceive how discordant that is?"

"I think it very sweet, on the contrary," I answered, vexed at the interruption, and very uncomfortable, lest the people who composed the little procession should observe and resent what was passing.

I resumed, therefore, instantly, and was again interrupted. "You pierce my ears," said Carmilla, almost angrily, and stopping her ears with her tiny fingers. "Besides, how can you tell that your religion and mine are the same; your forms wound me, and I hate funerals. What a fuss! Why, *you* must die—*everyone* must die; and all are happier when they do. Come home."

"My father has gone on with the clergyman to the church-yard. I thought you knew she was to be buried to-day."

"*She?* I don't trouble my head about peasants. I don't know who she is," answered Carmilla, with a flash from her fine eyes.

"She is the poor girl who fancied she saw a ghost a fortnight ago, and has been dying ever since, till yesterday, when she expired."

"Tell me nothing about ghosts. I shan't sleep to-night if you do."

"I hope there is no plague or fever coming; all this looks very like it," I continued. "The swineherd's young wife died only a week ago, and she thought something seized her by the throat as she lay in her bed, and nearly strangled her. Papa says such horrible fancies do accompany some forms of fever. She was quite well the day before. She sank afterward, and died before a week."

"Well, *her* funeral is over, I hope, and *her* hymn sung; and our ears shan't be tortured with that discord and jargon. It has made me nervous. Sit down here, beside me; sit close; hold my hand; press it hard—hard—harder."

We had moved a little back, and had come to another seat.

She sat down. Her face underwent a change that alarmed and even terrified me for a moment. It darkened, and became horribly livid; her teeth and hands were clenched, and she frowned and compressed her lips, while she stared down upon the ground at her feet, and trembled all over with a continued shudder as irrepressible as ague. All her energies seemed strained to suppress a fit, with which she was then breathlessly tugging; and at length a low convulsive cry of suffering broke from her, and gradually the hysteria subsided. "There! That comes of strangling people with hymns!" she said at last. "Hold me, hold me still. It is passing away."

And so gradually it did; and perhaps to dissipate the somber impression which the spectacle had left upon me, she became unusually animated and chatty; and so we got home.

This was the first time I had seen her exhibit any definable symptoms of that delicacy of health which her mother had spoken of. It was the first time, also, I had seen her exhibit anything like temper.

Both passed away like a summer cloud; and never but once afterward did I witness on her part a momentary sign of anger. I will tell you how it happened.

She and I were looking out of one of the long drawing-room windows, when there entered the courtyard, over the drawbridge, a figure of a wanderer whom I knew very well. He used to visit the schloss generally twice a year.

It was the figure of a hunchback, with the sharp lean features that generally accompany deformity. He wore a pointed black beard, and he was smiling from ear to ear, showing his white fangs. He was dressed in buff, black, and scarlet, and crossed with more straps and belts than I could count, from which hung all manner of things. Behind, he carried a magic-lantern, and two boxes, which I well knew, in one of which was a salamander, and in the other a mandrake. These monsters used to make my father laugh. They were compounded of parts of monkeys, parrots, squirrels, fish, and hedgehogs, dried and stitched together with great neatness and startling effect. He had a fiddle, a box of conjuring apparatus, a pair of foils and masks attached to his belt, several other mysterious cases dangling about him, and a black staff with copper ferrules in his hand. His companion was a rough spare dog, that followed at his heels, but stopped short, suspiciously at the drawbridge, and in a little while began to howl dismally.

In the meantime, the mountebank, standing in the midst of the courtyard, raised his grotesque hat, and made us a very ceremonious bow, paying his compliments very volubly in execrable French, and German not much better. Then, disengaging his fiddle, he began to scrape a lively air, to which he sang with a merry discord, dancing with ludicrous airs and activity, that made me laugh, in spite of the dog's howling.

Then he advanced to the window with many smiles and salutations, and his hat in his left hand, his fiddle under his arm, and with a fluency that never took breath, he grabbed a long advertisement of all his accomplishments, and the resources of the various arts which he placed at our service, and the curiosities and entertainments which it was in his power, at our bidding, to display.

"Will your ladyships be pleased to buy an amulet against the oupire, which is going like the wolf, I hear, through these woods," he said, dropping his hat on the pavement. "They are dying of it right and left, and here is a charm that never fails; only pinned to the pillow, and you may laugh in his face."

These charms consisted of oblong slips of vellum, with cabalistic ciphers and diagrams upon them.

Carmilla instantly purchased one, and so did I.

He was looking up, and we were smiling down upon him,

amused; at least, I can answer for myself. His piercing black eye, as he looked up in our faces, seemed to detect something that fixed for a moment his curiosity.

In an instant he unrolled a leather case, full of all manner of odd little steel instruments.

"See here, my lady," he said, displaying it, and addressing me, "I profess, among other things less useful, the art of dentistry. Plague take the dog!" he interpolated. "Silence, beast! He howls so that your ladyships can scarcely hear a word. Your noble friend, the young lady at your right, has the sharpest tooth—long, thin, pointed, like an awl, like a needle; ha, ha! With my sharp and long sight, as I look up, I have seen it distinctly; now if it happens to hurt the young lady, and I think it must, here am I, here are my file, my punch, my nippers; I will make it round and blunt, if her ladyship pleases; no longer the tooth of a fish, but of a beautiful young lady as she is. Hey? Is the young lady displeased? Have I been too bold? Have I offended her?"

The young lady, indeed, looked very angry as she drew back from the window.

"How dares that mountebank insult us so? Where is your father? I shall demand redress from him. My father would have had the wretch tied up to the pump, and flogged with a cartwhip, and burnt to the bones with the castle brand!"

She retired from the window a step or two, and sat down, and had hardly lost sight of the offender, when her wrath subsided as suddenly as it had risen, and she gradually recovered her usual tone, and seemed to forget the little hunchback and his follies.

My father was out of spirits that evening. On coming in he told us that there had been another case very similar to the two fatal ones which had lately occurred. The sister of a young peasant on his estate, only a mile away, was very ill, had been, as she described it, attacked very nearly in the same way, and was now slowly but steadily sinking.

"All this," said my father, "is strictly referable to natural causes. These poor people infect one another with their superstitions, and so repeat in imagination the images of terror that have infested their neighbors."

"But that very circumstance frightens one horribly," said Carmilla.

"How so?" inquired my father.

"I am so afraid of fancying I see such things; I think it would be as bad as reality."

"We are in God's hands; nothing can happen without His permission, and all will end well for those who love Him. He is our faithful creator; He has made us all, and will take care of us."

"Creator! *Nature!*" said the young lady in answer to my gentle father. "And this disease that invades the country is natural. Nature. All things spring from nature—don't they? All things in the Heaven, in the earth, and under the earth, act and live as nature ordains? I think so."

"The doctor said he would come here to-day," said my father, after a silence. "I want to know what he thinks about it, and what he thinks we had better do."

"Doctors never did me any good," said Carmilla.

"Then you have been ill?" I asked.

"More ill than ever you were," she answered.

"Long ago?"

"Yes, a long time. I suffered from this very illness; but I forget all but my pain and weaknesses, and they were not so bad as are suffered in other diseases."

"You were very young then?"

"I dare say; let us talk no more of it. You would not wound a friend?" She looked languidly in my eyes, and passed her arm round my waist lovingly, and led me out of the room. My father was busy over some papers near the window.

"Why does your papa like to frighten us?" said the pretty girl, with a sigh and a little shudder.

"He doesn't, dear Carmilla, it is the very furthest thing from his mind."

"Are you afraid, dearest?"

"I should be very much if I fancied there was any real danger of my being attacked as those poor people were."

"You are afraid to die?"

"Yes, every one is."

"But to die as lovers may—to die together, so that they may live together. Girls are caterpillars while they live in the world, to be finally butterflies when the summer comes; but in the meantime there are grubs and larvæ, don't you see—each with their peculiar propensities, necessities, and structure. So says Monsieur Buffon, in his big book, in the next room."

Later in the day the doctor came, and was closeted with papa for some time. He was a skilful man, of sixty and upwards, he wore powder, and shaved his pale face as smooth as a pumpkin. He and papa emerged from the room together, and I heard papa laugh, and say as they came out:

"Well, I do wonder at a wise man like you. What do you say to hippogriffs and dragons?"

The doctor was smiling, and made answer, shaking his head—

"Nevertheless, life and death are mysterious states, and we know little of the resources of either."

And so they walked on, and I heard no more. I did not then know what the doctor had been broaching, but I think I guess it now.

V.   A WONDERFUL LIKENESS

This evening there arrived from Gratz the grave, dark-faced son
of the picture-cleaner, with a horse and cart laden with two large
packing-cases, having many pictures in each. It was a journey of
ten leagues, and whenever a messenger arrived at the schloss from
our little capital of Gratz, we used to crowd about him in the hall,
to hear the news.

This arrival created in our secluded quarters quite a sensation.
The cases remained in the hall, and the messenger was taken
charge of by the servants till he had eaten his supper. Then with
assistants, and armed with hammer, ripping chisel, and turnscrew,
he met us in the hall, where we had assembled to witness the
unpacking of the cases.

Carmilla sat looking listlessly on, while one after the other the
old pictures, nearly all portraits, which had undergone the process
of renovation, were brought to light. My mother was of an old
Hungarian family, and most of these pictures, which were about
to be restored to their places, had come to us through her.

My father had a list in his hand, from which he read, as the
artist rummaged out the corresponding numbers. I don't know
that the pictures were very good, but they were undoubtedly very
old, and some of them very curious also. They had, for the most
part, the merit of being now seen by me, I may say, for the first
time; for the smoke and dust of time had all but obliterated them.

"There is a picture that I have not seen yet," said my father.
"In one corner, at the top of it, is the name, as well as I could
read, 'Marcia Karnstein,' and the date '1698'; and I am curious
to see how it has turned out."

I remembered it; it was a small picture, about a foot and a
half high, and nearly square, without a frame; but it was so
blackened by age that I could not make it out.

The artist now produced it, with evident pride. It was quite beautiful; it was startling; it seemed to live. It was the effigy of Carmilla!

"Carmilla, dear, here is an absolute miracle. Here you are, living, smiling, ready to speak, in this picture. Isn't it beautiful, papa? And see, even the little mole on her throat."

My father laughed, and said "Certainly it is a wonderful likeness," but he looked away, and to my surprise seemed but little struck by it, went on talking to the picture-cleaner, who was also something of an artist, and discoursed with intelligence about the portraits or other works, which his art had just brought into light and color, while *I* was more and more lost in wonder the more I looked at the picture.

"Will you let me hang this picture in my room, papa?" I asked.

"Certainly, dear," said he, smiling, "I'm very glad you think it so like. It must be prettier even than I thought it, if it is."

The young lady did not acknowledge this pretty speech, did not seem to hear it. She was leaning back in her seat, her fine eyes under their long lashes gazing on me in contemplation, and she smiled in a kind of rapture.

"And now you can read quite plainly the name that is written in the corner. It is not Marcia; it looks as if it was done in gold. The name is Mircalla, Countess Karnstein, and this is a little coronet over it, and underneath A.D. 1698. I am descended from the Karnsteins; that is, mamma was."

"Ah!" said the lady, languidly, "so am I, I think, a very long descent, very ancient. Are there any Karnsteins living now?"

"None who bear the name, I believe. The family were ruined, I believe, in some civil wars, long ago, but the ruins of the castle are only about three miles away."

"How interesting!" she said, languidly. "But see what beautiful moonlight!" She glanced through the hall door, which stood a little open. "Suppose you take a little ramble round the court, and look down at the road and river."

"It is so like the night you came to us," I said.

She sighed, smiling.

She rose, and each with her arm about the other's waist, we walked out upon the pavement.

In silence, slowly we walked down to the drawbridge, where the beautiful landscape opened before us.

"And so you were thinking of the night I came here?" she almost whispered. "Are you glad I came?"

"Delighted, dear Carmilla," I answered.

"And you ask for the picture you think like me, to hang in your room," she murmured with a sigh, as she drew her arm closer about my waist, and let her pretty head sink upon my shoulder.

"How romantic you are, Carmilla," I said. "Whenever you tell me your story, it will be made up chiefly of some one great romance."

She kissed me silently.

"I am sure, Carmilla, you have been in love; that there is, at this moment, an affair of the heart going on."

"I have been in love with no one, and never shall," she whispered, "unless it should be with you."

How beautiful she looked in the moonlight!

Shy and strange was the look with which she quickly hid her face in my neck and hair, with tumultuous sighs, that seemed almost to sob, and pressed in mine a hand that trembled.

Her soft cheek was glowing against mine. "Darling, darling," she murmured, "I live in you; and you would die for me, I love you so."

I started from her.

She was gazing on me with eyes from which all fire, all meaning had flown, and a face colorless and apathetic.

"Is there a chill in the air, dear?" she said drowsily. "I almost shiver; have I been dreaming? Let us come in. Come, come; come in."

"You look ill, Carmilla; a little faint. You certainly must take some wine," I said.

"Yes, I will. I'm better now. I shall be quite well in a few minutes. Yes, do give me a little wine," answered Carmilla, as we approached the door. "Let us look again for a moment; it is the last time, perhaps, I shall see the moonlight with you."

"How do you feel now, dear Carmilla? Are you really better?" I asked.

I was beginning to take alarm, lest she should have been stricken with the strange epidemic that they said had invaded the country about us.

"Papa would be grieved beyond measure," I added, "if he thought you were ever so little ill, without immediately letting us know. We have a very skilful doctor near this, the physician who was with papa today."

"I'm sure he is. I know how kind you all are; but, dear child, I am quite well again. There is nothing ever wrong with me, but a little weakness. People say I am languid; I am incapable of exertion; I can scarcely walk as far as a child of three years old; and every now and then the little strength I have falters, and I become as you have just seen me. But after all I am very easily set up again; in a moment I am perfectly myself. See how I have recovered."

So, indeed, she had; and she and I talked a great deal, and very animated she was; and the remainder of that evening passed without any recurrence of what I called her infatuations. I mean her crazy talk and looks, which embarrassed, and even frightened me.

But there occurred that night an event which gave my thoughts quite a new turn, and seemed to startle even Carmilla's languid nature into momentary energy.

VI.   A VERY STRANGE AGONY

When we got into the drawing-room, and had sat down to our coffee and chocolate, although Carmilla did not take any, she seemed quite herself again and madame, and Mademoiselle De Lafontaine, joined us, and made a little card party, in the course of which papa came in for what he called his "dish of tea."

When the game was over he sat down beside Carmilla on the sofa, and asked her, a little anxiously, whether she had heard from her mother since her arrival.

She answered "No."

He then asked her whether she knew where a letter would reach her at present.

"I cannot tell," she answered, ambiguously, "but I have been thinking of leaving you; you have been already too hospitable and too kind to me. I have given you an infinity of trouble, and I should wish to take a carriage to-morrow, and post in pursuit of her; I know where I shall ultimately find her, although I dare not tell you."

"But you must not dream of any such thing," exclaimed my father, to my great relief. "We can't afford to lose you so, and I won't consent to your leaving us, except under the care of your mother, who was so good as to consent to your remaining with us till she should herself return. I should be quite happy if I knew that you heard from her; but this evening the accounts of the progress of the mysterious disease that has invaded our neighborhood, grow even more alarming; and my beautiful guest, I do feel the responsibility, unaided by advice from your mother, very much. But I shall do my best; and one thing is certain, that you must not think of leaving us without her distinct direction to that effect. We should suffer too much in parting from you to consent to it easily."

"Thank you, sir, a thousand times for your hospitality," she answered, smiling bashfully. "You have all been too kind to me; I have seldom been so happy in all my life before, as in your beautiful château, under your care, and in the society of your dear daughter."

So he gallantly, in his old-fashioned way, kissed her hand, smiling, and pleased at her little speech.

I accompanied Carmilla as usual to her room, and sat and chatted with her while she was preparing for bed.

"Do you think," I said, at length, "that you will ever confide fully in me?"

She turned round smiling, but made no answer, only continued to smile on me.

"You won't answer that?" I said. "You can't answer pleasantly; I ought not to have asked you."

"You were quite right to ask me that, or anything. You do not know how dear you are to me, or you could not think any confidence too great to look for. But I am under vows, no nun half so awfully, and I dare not tell my story yet, even to you. The time is very near when you shall know everything. You will think me cruel, very selfish, but love is always selfish; the more ardent the more selfish. How jealous I am you cannot know. You must come with me, loving me, to death; or else hate me, and still come with me, and *hating* me through death and after. There is no such word as indifference in my apathetic nature."

"Now, Carmilla, you are going to talk your wild nonsense again," I said hastily.

"Not I, silly little fool as I am, and full of whims and fancies; for your sake I'll talk like a sage. Were you ever at a ball?"

"No; how you do run on. What is it like? How charming it must be."

"I almost forget, it is years ago."

I laughed.

"You are not so old. Your first ball can hardly be forgotten yet."

Edvard Munch, *Harpy*, lithograph, 1900. (Timm, *The Graphic Art of Edvard Munch*)

"I remember everything about it—with an effort. I see it all, as divers see what is going on above them, through a medium, dense, rippling, but transparent. There occurred that night what has confused the picture, and made its colors faint. I was all but assassinated in my bed, wounded *here*," she touched her breast, "and never was the same since."

"Were you near dying?"

"Yes, very—a cruel love—strange love, that would have taken my life. Love will have its sacrifices. No sacrifice without blood. Let us go to sleep now; I feel so lazy. How can I get up just now and lock my door?"

She was lying with her tiny hands buried in her rich wavy hair, under her cheek, her little head upon the pillow, and her glittering eyes followed me wherever I moved, with a kind of shy smile that I could not decipher.

I bid her good-night, and crept from the room with an uncomfortable sensation.

I often wondered whether our pretty guest ever said her prayers. *I* certainly had never seen her upon her knees. In the morning she never came down until long after our family prayers were over, and at night she never left the drawing-room to attend our brief evening prayers in the hall.

If it had not been that it had casually come out in one of our careless talks that she had been baptised, I should have doubted her being a Christian. Religion was a subject on which I had never heard her speak a word. If I had known the world better, this particular neglect or antipathy would not have so much surprised me.

The precautions of nervous people are infectious, and persons of a like temperament are pretty sure, after a time, to imitate them. I had adopted Carmilla's habit of locking her bedroom door, having taken into my head all her whimsical alarms about midnight invaders, and prowling assassins. I had also adopted her precaution of making a brief search through her room, to satisfy herself that no lurking assassin or robber was "ensconced."

These wise measures taken, I got into my bed and fell asleep. A light was burning in my room. This was an old habit, of very early date, and which nothing could have tempted me to dispense with.

Thus fortified I might take my rest in peace. But dreams come through stone walls, light up dark rooms, or darken light ones, and their persons make their exits and their entrances as they please, and laugh at locksmiths.

I had a dream that night that was the beginning of a very strange agony.

I cannot call it a nightmare, for I was quite conscious of being asleep. But I was equally conscious of being in my room, and lying in bed, precisely as I actually was. I saw, or fancied I saw, the room and its furniture just as I had seen it last, except that it was very dark, and I saw something moving round the foot of the bed, which at first I could not accurately distinguish. But I soon saw that it was a sooty-black animal that resembled a monstrous cat. It appeared to me about four or five feet long, for it measured fully the length of the hearth-rug as it passed over it; and it continued to-ing and fro-ing with the lithe sinister restlessness of a beast in a cage. I could not cry out, although as you may suppose, I was terrified. Its pace was growing faster, and the room rapidly darker and darker, and at length so dark that I could no longer see anything of it but its eyes. I felt it spring lightly on the bed. The two broad eyes approached my face, and suddenly I felt a stinging pain as if two large needles darted, an inch or two apart, deep into my breast. I waked with a scream. The room was lighted by the candle that burned there all through the night, and I saw a female figure standing at the foot of the bed, a little at the right side. It was in a dark loose dress, and its hair was down and covered its shoulders. A block of stone could not have been more still. There was not the slightest stir of respiration. As I stared at it, the figure appeared to have changed its place, and was now nearer the door;

then, close to it, the door opened, and it passed out.

I was now relieved, and able to breathe and move. My first thought was that Carmilla had been playing me a trick, and that I had forgotten to secure my door. I hastened to it, and found it locked as usual on the inside. I was afraid to open it—I was horrified. I sprang into my bed and covered my head up in the bedclothes, and lay there more dead than alive till morning.

VII.   DESCENDING

It would be vain my attempting to tell you the horror with which, even now, I recall the occurrence of that night. It was no such transitory terror as a dream leaves behind it. It seemed to deepen by time, and communicated itself to the room and the very furniture that had encompassed the apparition.

I could not bear next day to be alone for a moment. I should have told papa, but for two opposite reasons. At one time I thought he would laugh at my story, and I could not bear its being treated as a jest; and at another, I thought he might fancy that I had been attacked by the mysterious complaint which had invaded our neighborhood. I had myself no misgivings of the kind, and as he had been rather an invalid for some time, I was afraid of alarming him.

I was comfortable enough with my good-natured companions, Madame Perrodon, and the vivacious Mademoiselle Lafontaine. They both perceived that I was out of spirits and nervous, and at length I told them what lay so heavy at my heart.

Mademoiselle laughed, but I fancied that Madame Perrodon looked anxious.

"By-the-by," said mademoiselle, laughing, "the long lime tree walk, behind Carmilla's bedroom window, is haunted!"

"Nonsense!" exclaimed madame, who probably thought the theme rather inopportune, "and who tells that story, my dear?"

"Martin says that he came up twice, when the old yard-gate was being repaired before sunrise, and twice saw the same female figure walking down the lime tree avenue."

"So he well might, as long as there are cows to milk in the river fields," said madame.

"I daresay; but Martin chooses to be frightened, and never did I see fool *more* frightened."

"You must not say a word about it to Carmilla, because she can see down that walk from her room window," I interposed, "and she is, if possible, a greater coward than I."

Carmilla came down rather later than usual that day.

"I was so frightened last night," she said, so soon as we were together, "and I am sure I should have seen something dreadful if it had not been for that charm I bought from the poor little hunchback whom I called such hard names. I had a dream of something black coming round my bed, and I awoke in a perfect horror, and I really thought, for some seconds, I saw a dark figure near the chimney piece, but I felt under my pillow for my charm, and the moment my fingers touched it, the figure disappeared, and I felt quite certain, only that I had it by me, that something frightful would have made its appearance, and, perhaps, throttled me, as it did those poor people we heard of."

"Well, listen to me," I began, and recounted my adventure, at the recital of which she appeared horrified.

"And had you the charm near you?" she asked earnestly.

"No, I had dropped it into a china vase in the drawing-room, but I shall certainly take it with me to-night, as you have so much faith in it."

At this distance of time I cannot tell you, or even understand, how I overcame my horror so effectually as to lie alone in my room that night. I remember distinctly that I pinned the charm to my pillow. I fell asleep almost immediately, and slept even more soundly than usual all night.

Next night I passed as well. My sleep was delightfully deep

and dreamless. But I wakened with a sense of lassitude and melancholy, which, however, did not exceed a degree that was almost luxurious.

"Well, I told you so," said Carmilla, when I described my quiet sleep, "I had such delightful sleep myself last night; I pinned the charm to the breast of my nightdress. It was too far away the night before. I am quite sure it was all fancy, except the dreams. I used to think that evil spirits made dreams, but our doctor told me it is no such thing. Only a fever passing by, or some other malady, as they often do, he said, knocks at the door, and not being able to get in, passes on, with that alarm."

"And what do you think the charm is?" said I.

"It has been fumigated or immersed in some drug, and is an antidote against the malaria," she answered.

"Then it acts only on the body?"

"Certainly; you don't suppose that evil spirits are frightened by bits of ribbon, or the perfumes of a druggist's shop? No, these complaints, wandering in the air, begin by trying the nerves, and so infect the brain; but before they can seize upon you, the antidote repels them. That I am sure is what the charm has done for us. It is nothing magical, it is simply natural."

I should have been happier if I could quite have agreed with Carmilla, but I did my best, and the impression was a little losing its force.

For some nights I slept profoundly; but still every morning I felt the same lassitude, and a languor weighed upon me all day. I felt myself a changed girl. A strange melancholy was stealing over me, a melancholy that I would not have interrupted. Dim thoughts of death began to open, and an idea that I was slowly sinking took gentle, and, somehow, not unwelcome possession of me. If it was sad, the tone of mind which this induced was also sweet. Whatever it might be, my soul acquiesced in it.

I would not admit that I was ill, I would not consent to tell my papa, or to have the doctor sent for.

Carmilla became more devoted to me than ever, and her strange paroxysms of languid adoration more frequent. She used to gloat on me with increasing ardor the more my strength and spirits waned. This always shocked me like a momentary glare of insanity.

Without knowing it, I was now in a pretty advanced stage of the strangest illness under which mortal ever suffered. There was an unaccountable fascination in its earlier symptoms that more than reconciled me to the incapacitating effect of that stage of the malady. This fascination increased for a time, until it reached a certain point, when gradually a sense of the horrible mingled itself with it, deepening as you shall hear, until it discolored and perverted the whole state of my life.

The first change I experienced was rather agreeable. It was very near the turning point from which began the descent of Avernus.

Certain vague and strange sensations visited me in my sleep. The prevailing one was of that pleasant, peculiar cold thrill which we feel in bathing, when we move against the current of a river. This was soon accompanied by dreams that seemed interminable, and were so vague that I could never recollect their scenery and persons, or any one connected portion of their action. But they left an awful impression, and a sense of exhaustion, as if I had passed through a long period of great mental exertion and danger. After all these dreams there remained on waking a remembrance of having been in a place very nearly dark, and of having spoken to people whom I could not see; and especially of one clear voice, of a female's, very deep, that spoke as if at a distance, slowly, and producing always the same sensation of indescribable solemnity and fear. Sometimes there came a sensation as if a hand was drawn softly along my cheek and neck. Sometimes it was as if warm lips kissed me, and longer and more lovingly as they reached my throat, but there the caress fixed itself. My heart beat faster, my breathing rose and fell rapidly and full drawn; a sobbing, that rose into a sense of strangulation, supervened, and turned into a dreadful convulsion, in which my sense left me, and I became unconscious.

It was now three weeks since the commencement of this unaccountable state. My sufferings had, during the last week, told upon my appearance. I had grown pale, my eyes were dilated and darkened underneath, and the languor which I had long felt began to display itself in my countenance.

My father asked me often whether I was ill; but, with an obstinacy which now seems to me unaccountable, I persisted in assuring him that I was quite well.

In a sense this was true. I had no pain, I could complain of no bodily derangement. My complaint seemed to be one of the imagination, or the nerves, and, horrible as my sufferings were, I kept them, with a morbid reserve, very nearly to myself.

It could not be that terrible complaint which the peasants call the oupire, for I had now been suffering for three weeks, and they were seldom ill for much more than three days, when death put an end to their miseries.

Carmilla complained of dreams and feverish sensations, but by no means of so alarming a kind as mine. I say that mine were extremely alarming. Had I been capable of comprehending my condition, I would have invoked aid and advice on my knees. The narcotic of an unsuspected influence was acting upon me, and my perceptions were benumbed.

I am going to tell you now of a dream that led immediately to an odd discovery.

One night, instead of the voice I was accustomed to hear in the dark, I heard one, sweet and tender, and at the same time terrible, which said, "Your mother warns you to beware of the assassin." At the same time a light unexpectedly sprang up, and I saw Carmilla, standing near the foot of my bed, in her white nightdress, bathed, from her chin to her feet, in one great stain of blood.

I wakened with a shriek, possessed with the one idea that Carmilla was being murdered. I remember springing from my bed, and my next recollection is that of standing on the lobby, crying for help.

Madame and mademoiselle came scurrying out of their rooms in alarm; a lamp burned always in the lobby, and seeing me, they soon learned the cause of my terror.

I insisted on our knocking at Carmilla's door. Our knocking was unanswered. It soon became a pounding and an uproar. We shrieked her name, but all was vain.

We all grew frightened, for the door was locked. We hurried back, in panic, to my room. There we rang the bell long and furiously. If my father's room had been at that side of the house, we would have called him up at once to our aid. But, alas! he was quite out of hearing, and to reach him involved an excursion for which we none of us had courage.

Servants, however, soon came running up the stairs; I had got on my dressing-gown and slippers meanwhile, and my companions were already similarly furnished. Recognizing the voices of the servants on the lobby, we sallied out together; and having renewed, as fruitlessly, our summons at Carmilla's door, I ordered the men to force the lock. They did so, and we stood, holding our lights aloft, in the doorway, and so stared into the room.

We called her by name; but there was still no reply. We looked round the room. Everything was undisturbed. It was exactly in the state in which I left it on bidding her good night. But Carmilla was gone.

VIII.   SEARCH

At sight of the room, perfectly undisturbed except for our violent entrance, we began to cool a little, and soon recovered our senses sufficiently to dismiss the men. It had struck mademoiselle that possibly Carmilla had been wakened by the uproar at her door, and in her first panic had jumped from her bed, and hid herself in a press, or behind a curtain, from which she could not, of course, emerge until the majordomo and his myrmidons had withdrawn. We now recommenced our search, and began to call her by name again.

It was all to no purpose. Our perplexity and agitation increased. We examined the windows, but they were secured. I implored of Carmilla, if she had concealed herself, to play this cruel trick no longer—to come out, and to end our anxieties. It was all useless. I was by this time convinced that she was not in the room, nor in the dressing-room, the door of which was still locked on this side. She could not have passed it. I was utterly puzzled. Had Carmilla discovered one of those secret passages which the old housekeeper said were known to exist in the schloss, although the tradition of their exact situation had been lost. A little time would, no doubt, explain all—utterly perplexed as, for the present, we were.

It was past four o'clock, and I preferred passing the remaining hours of darkness in madame's room. Daylight brought no solution of the difficulty.

The whole household, with my father at its head, was in a state of agitation next morning. Every part of the château was searched. The grounds were explored. Not a trace of the missing lady could be discovered. The stream was about to be dragged; my father was in distraction; what a tale to have to tell the poor girl's mother on her return. I, too, was almost beside myself, though my grief was quite of a different kind.

The morning was passed in alarm and excitement. It was now one o'clock, and still no tidings. I ran up to Carmilla's room, and found her standing at her dressing-table. I was astounded. I could not believe my eyes. She beckoned me to her with her pretty finger, in silence. Her face expressed extreme fear.

I ran to her in an ecstasy of joy; I kissed and embraced her again and again. I ran to the bell and rang it vehemently, to bring others to the spot, who might at once relieve my father's anxiety.

"Dear Carmilla, what has become of you all this time? We have been in agonies of anxiety about you," I exclaimed. "Where have you been? How did you come back?"

"Last night has been a night of wonders," she said.

"For mercy's sake, explain all you can."

"It was past two last night," she said, "when I went to sleep as usual in my bed, with my doors locked, that of the dressing-room, and that opening upon the gallery. My sleep was uninter-rupted, and, so far as I know, dreamless; but I awoke just now on the sofa in the dressing-room there, and I found the door between the rooms open, and the other door forced. How could all this have happened without my being wakened? It must have been accompanied with a great deal of noise, and I am particularly easily wakened; and how could I have been carried out of my bed without my sleep having been interrupted, I whom the slightest stir startles?"

By this time, madame, mademoiselle, my father, and a num-ber of the servants were in the room. Carmilla was, of course, overwhelmed with inquiries, congratulations, and welcomes. She had but one story to tell, and seemed the least able of all the party to suggest any way of accounting for what had happened.

My father took a turn up and down the room, thinking. I saw Carmilla's eye follow him for a moment with a sly, dark glance.

When my father had sent the servants away, mademoiselle having gone in search of a little bottle of valerian and sal-volatile, and there being no one now in the room with Carmilla except my father, madame, and myself, he came to her thoughtfully, took her hand very kindly, led her to the sofa, and sat down beside her.

"Will you forgive me, my dear, if I risk a conjecture, and ask a question?"

"Who can have a better right?" she said. "Ask what you please, and I will tell you everything. But my story is simply one of bewilderment and darkness. I know absolutely nothing. Put any question you please. But you know, of course, the limitations mamma has placed me under."

"Perfectly, my dear child. I need not approach the topics on which she desires our silence. Now, the marvel of last night consists in your having been removed from your bed and your room without being wakened, and this removal having occurred apparently while the windows were still secured, and the two doors locked upon the inside. I will tell you my theory, and first ask you a question."

Carmilla was leaning on her hand dejectedly; madame and I were listening breathlessly.

"Now, my question is this. Have you ever been suspected of walking in your sleep?"

"Never since I was very young indeed."

"But you did walk in your sleep when you were young?"

"Yes; I know I did. I have been told so often by my old nurse."

My father smiled and nodded.

"Well, what has happened is this. You got up in your sleep, unlocked the door, not leaving the key, as usual, in the lock, but taking it out and locking it on the outside; you again took the key out, and carried it away with you to some one of the five-and-twenty rooms on this floor, or perhaps upstairs or downstairs. There are so many rooms and closets, so much heavy furniture, and such accumulations of lumber [old household stuff], that it would require a week to search this old house thoroughly. Do you see, now, what I mean?"

"I do, but not all," she answered.

"And how, papa, do you account for her finding herself on the sofa in the dressing-room, which we had searched so carefully?"

"She came there after you had searched it, still in her sleep, and at last awoke spontaneously, and was as much surprised to find herself where she was as any one else. I wish all mysteries were as easily and innocently explained as yours, Carmilla," he said, laughing. "And so we may congratulate ourselves on the certainty that the most natural explanation of the occurrence is one that involves no drugging, no tampering with locks, no burglars, or poisoners, or witches—nothing that need alarm Carmilla, or any one else, for our safety."

Carmilla was looking charmingly. Nothing could be more beautiful than her tints. Her beauty was, I think, enhanced by that graceful languor that was peculiar to her. I think my father was silently contrasting her looks with mine, for he said:—

"I wish my poor Laura was looking more like herself," and he sighed.

So our alarms were happily ended, and Carmilla restored to her friends.

IX.   THE DOCTOR

As Carmilla would not hear of an attendant sleeping in her room, my father arranged that a servant should sleep outside her door, so that she could not attempt to make another such excursion without being arrested at her own door.

That night passed quietly; and next morning early, the doctor, whom my father had sent for without telling me a word about it, arrived to see me.

Madame accompanied me to the library; and there the grave little doctor, with white hair and spectacles, whom I mentioned before, was waiting to receive me.

I told him my story, and as I proceeded he grew graver and graver.

We were standing, he and I, in the recess of one of the windows, facing one another. When my statement was over, he leaned with his shoulders against the wall, and with his eyes fixed on me earnestly, with an interest in which was a dash of horror.

After a minute's reflection, he asked madame if he could see my father.

He was sent for accordingly, and as he entered, smiling, he said:

"I dare say, doctor, you are going to tell me that I am an old fool for having brought you here; I hope I am."

But his smile faded into shadow as the doctor, with a very grave face, beckoned him to him.

He and the doctor talked for some time in the same recess where I had just conferred with the physician. It seemed an earnest and argumentative conversation. The room is very large, and I and madame stood together, burning with curiosity, at the further end. Not a word could we hear, however, for they spoke in a very low tone, and the deep recess of the window quite concealed the doctor from view, and very nearly my father, whose foot, arm, and shoulder only could we see; and the voices were, I suppose, all the less audible for the sort of closet which the thick wall and window formed.

After a time my father's face looked into the room; it was pale, thoughtful, and, I fancied, agitated.

"Laura, dear, come here for a moment. Madame, we shan't trouble you, the doctor says, at present."

Accordingly I approached, for the first time a little alarmed; for, although I felt very weak, I did not feel ill; and strength, one always fancies, is a thing that may be picked up when we please.

My father held out his hand to me as I drew near, but he was looking at the doctor, and he said:

"It certainly *is* very odd; I don't understand it quite. Laura, come here, dear; now attend to Doctor Spielsberg, and recollect yourself."

"You mentioned a sensation like that of two needles piercing the skin, somewhere about your neck, on the night when you experienced your first horrible dream. Is there still any soreness?"

"None at all," I answered.

"Can you indicate with your finger about the point at which you think this occurred?"

"Very little below my throat—*here,*" I answered.

I wore a morning dress, which covered the place I pointed to.

"Now you can satisfy yourself," said the doctor. "You won't mind your papa's lowering your dress a very little. It is necessary, to detect a symptom of the complaint under which you have been suffering."

I acquiesced. It was only an inch or two below the edge of my collar.

"God bless me!—so it is," exclaimed my father, growing pale.

"You see it now with your own eyes," said the doctor, with a gloomy triumph.

"What is it?" I exclaimed, beginning to be frightened.

"Nothing, my dear young lady, but a small blue spot, about the size of the tip of your little finger; and now," he continued, turning to papa, "the question is what is best to be done?"

"Is there any danger?" I urged, in great trepidation.

"I trust not, my dear," answered the doctor. "I don't see why you should not recover. I don't see why you should not begin *immediately* to get better. That is the point at which the sense of strangulation begins?"

"Yes," I answered.

"And—recollect as well as you can—the same point was a kind of center of that thrill which you described just now, like the current of a cold stream running against you?"

"It may have been; I think it was."

"Ay, you see?" he added, turning to my father. "Shall I say a word to madame?"

"Certainly," said my father.

He called madame to him, and said:

"I find my young friend here far from well. It won't be of any great consequence, I hope; but it will be necessary that some steps be taken, which I will explain by-and-by; but in the meantime, madame, you will be so good as not to let Miss Laura be alone for one moment. That is the only direction I need give for the present. It is indispensable."

"We may rely upon your kindness, madame, I know," added my father.

Madame satisfied him eagerly.

"And you, dear Laura, I know you will observe the doctor's direction."

"I shall have to ask your opinion upon another patient, whose symptoms slightly resemble those of my daughter, that have just been detailed to you—very much milder in degree, but I believe quite of the same sort. She is a young lady—our guest; but as you say you will be passing this way again this evening, you can't do better than take your supper here, and you can then see her. She does not come down till the afternoon."

"I thank you," said the doctor. "I shall be with you, then, at about seven this evening."

And then they repeated their directions to me and to madame, and with this parting charge my father left us, and walked out with the doctor; and I saw them pacing together up and down between the road and the moat, on the grassy platform in front of the castle, evidently absorbed in earnest conversation.

The doctor did not return. I saw him mount his horse there, take his leave, and ride away eastward through the forest. Nearly at the same time I saw the man arrive from Dranfeld with the letters, and dismount and hand the bag to my father.

In the meantime, madame and I were both busy, lost in conjecture as to the reasons of the singular and earnest direction which the doctor and my father had concurred in imposing. Madame, as she afterward told me, was afraid the doctor apprehended a sudden seizure, and that, without prompt assistance, I might either lose my life in a fit, or at least be seriously hurt.

This interpretation did not strike me; and I fancied, perhaps luckily for my nerves, that the arrangement was prescribed simply to secure a companion, who would prevent my taking too much exercise, or eating unripe fruit, or doing any of the fifty foolish things to which young people are supposed to be prone.

About half-an-hour after my father came in—he had a letter in his hand—and said:

"This letter had been delayed; it is from General Spielsdorf. He might have been here yesterday, he may not come till tomorrow, or he may be here today."

He put the open letter into my hand; but he did not look pleased, as he used when a guest, especially one so much loved as the General, was coming. On the contrary, he looked as if he wished him at the bottom of the Red Sea. There was plainly something on his mind which he did not choose to divulge.

"Papa, darling, will you tell me this?" said I, suddenly laying my hand on his arm, and looking, I am sure, imploringly in his face.

"Perhaps," he answered, smoothing my hair caressingly over my eyes.

"Does the doctor think me very ill?"

"No, dear; he thinks, if right steps are taken, you will be quite well again, at least on the high road to a complete recovery, in a day or two," he answered, a little drily. "I wish our good friend, the General, had chosen any other time; that is, I wish you had been perfectly well to receive him."

"But do tell me, Papa," I insisted, "*what* does he think is the matter with me?"

"Nothing; you must not plague me with questions," he answered, with more irritation than I ever remember him to have displayed before; and seeing that I looked wounded, I suppose, he kissed me, and added, "You shall know all about it in a day or two; that is, all that *I* know. In the meantime, you are not to trouble your head about it."

He turned and left the room, but came back before I had

done wondering and puzzling over the oddity of all this; it was merely to say that he was going to Karnstein, and had ordered the carriage to be ready at twelve, and that I and madame should accompany him; he was going to see the priest who lived near those picturesque grounds upon business, and as Carmilla had never seen them, she could follow, when she came down, with mademoiselle, who would bring materials for what you call a pic-nic, which might be laid for us in the ruined castle.

At twelve o'clock, accordingly, I was ready, and not long after, my father, madame and I set out upon our projected drive. Passing the drawbridge we turn to the right, and follow the road over the steep Gothic bridge, westward, to reach the deserted village and ruined castle of Karnstein.

No sylvan drive can be fancied prettier. The ground breaks into gentle hills and hollows, all clothed with beautiful wood, totally destitute of the comparative formality which artificial planting and early culture and pruning impart.

The irregularities of the ground often lead the road out of its course, and cause it to wind beautifully round the sides of broken hollows and the steeper sides of the hills, among varieties of ground almost inexhaustible.

Turning one of these points, we suddenly encountered our old friend, the General, riding toward us, attended by a mounted servant. His portmanteaus were following in a hired wagon, such as we term a cart.

The General dismounted as we pulled up, and, after the usual greetings, was easily persuaded to accept the vacant seat in the carriage, and send his horse on with his servant to the schloss.

X.   BEREAVED

It was about ten months since we had last seen him; but that time had sufficed to make an alteration of years in his appearance. He had grown thinner; something of gloom and anxiety had taken the place of that cordial serenity which used to characterize his features. His dark blue eyes, always penetrating, now gleamed with a sterner light from under his shaggy gray eyebrows. It was not such a change as grief alone usually induces, and angrier passions seemed to have had their share in bringing it about.

We had not long resumed our drive, when the General began to talk, with his usual soldierly directness, of the bereavement, as he termed it, which he had sustained in the death of his beloved niece and ward; and he then broke out in a tone of intense bitterness and fury, inveighing against the "hellish arts" to which she had fallen a victim, and expressing, with more exasperation than piety, his wonder that Heaven should tolerate so monstrous an indulgence of the lusts and malignity of Hell.

My father, who saw at once that something very extraordinary had befallen, asked him, if not too painful to him, to retail the circumstances which he thought justified the strong terms in which he expressed himself.

"I should tell you all with pleasure," said the General, "but you would not believe me."

"Why should I not?" he asked.

"Because," he answered testily, "you believe in nothing but what consists with your own prejudices and illusions. I remember when I was like you, but I have learned better."

"Try me," said my father; "I am not such a dogmatist as you suppose. Besides which, I very well know that you generally require proof for what you believe, and am, therefore, very strongly predisposed to respect your conclusions."

"You are right in supposing that I have not been led lightly into a belief in the marvelous—for what I have experienced *is* marvelous—and I have been forced by extraordinary evidence to credit that which ran counter, diametrically, to all my theories. I have been made the dupe of a preternatural conspiracy."

Notwithstanding his professions of confidence in the General's penetration, I saw my father, at this point, glance at the General, with, as I thought, a marked suspicion of his sanity.

The General did not see it, luckily. He was looking gloomily and curiously into the glades and vistas of the woods that were opening before us.

"You are going to the Ruins of Karnstein?" he said. "Yes, it is a lucky coincidence; do you know I was going to ask you to bring me there to inspect them. I have a special object in exploring. There is a ruined chapel, ain't there, with a great many tombs of that extinct family?"

"So there are—highly interesting," said my father. "I hope you are thinking of claiming the title and estates?"

My father said this gaily, but the General did not recollect the laugh, or even the smile, which courtesy exacts for a friend's joke; on the contrary, he looked grave and even fierce, ruminating on a matter that stirred his anger and horror.

"Something very different," he said, gruffly. "I mean to unearth some of those fine people. I hope, by God's blessing, to accomplish a pious sacrilege here, which will relieve our earth of certain monsters, and enable honest people to sleep in their beds without being assailed by murderers. I have strange things to tell you, my dear friend, such as I myself would have scouted as incredible a few months since."

My father looked at him again, but this time not with a glance of suspicion—with an eye, rather, of keen intelligence and alarm.

"The house of Karnstein," he said, "has been long extinct: a hundred years at least. My dear wife was maternally descended from the Karnsteins. But the name and title have long ceased to exist. The castle is a ruin; the very village is deserted; it is fifty years since the smoke of a chimney was seen there; not a roof left."

"Quite true. I have heard a great deal about that since I last saw you; a great deal that will astonish you. But I had better relate everything in the order in which it occurred," said the General.

"You saw my dear ward—my child, I may call her. No creature could have been more beautiful, and only three months ago none more blooming."

"Yes, poor thing! When I saw her last she certainly was quite lovely," said my father. "I was grieved and shocked more than I can tell you, my dear friend; I knew what a blow it was to you."

He took the General's hand, and they exchanged a kind pressure. Tears gathered in the old soldier's eyes. He did not seek to conceal them. He said:

"We have been very old friends; I knew you would feel for me, childless as I am. She had become an object of very dear interest to me, and repaid my care by an affection that cheered my home and made my life happy. That is all gone. The years that remain to me on earth may not be very long; but by God's mercy I hope to accomplish a service to mankind before I die, and to subserve the vengeance of Heaven upon the fiends who have murdered my poor child in the spring of her hopes and beauty!"

"You said, just now, that you intended relating everything as it occurred," said my father. "Pray do; I assure you that it is not mere curiosity that prompts me."

By this time we had reached the point at which the Drunstall road, by which the General had come, diverges from the road which we were traveling to Karnstein.

"How far is it to the ruins?" inquired the General, looking anxiously forward.

"About half a league," answered my father. "Pray let us hear the story you were so good as to promise."

XI.   THE STORY

"With all my heart," said the General, with an effort; and after a short pause in which to arrange his subject, he commenced one of the strangest narratives I ever heard.

"My dear child was looking forward with great pleasure to the visit you had been so good as to arrange for her to your charming daughter." Here he made me a gallant but melancholy bow. "In the meantime we had an invitation to my old friend the Count Carlsfeld, whose schloss is about six leagues to the other side of Karnstein. It was to attend the series of fêtes which, you remember, were given by him in honor of his illustrious visitor, the Grand Duke Charles."

"Yes; and very splendid, I believe, they were," said my father.

"Princely! But then his hospitalities are quite regal. He has Aladdin's lamp. The night from which my sorrow dates was devoted to a magnificent masquerade. The grounds were thrown open, the trees hung with colored lamps. There was such a display of fireworks as Paris itself had never witnessed. And such music —music, you know, is my weakness—such ravishing music! The finest instrumental band, perhaps, in the world, and the finest singers who could be collected from all the great operas in Europe. As you wandered through these fantastically illuminated grounds, the moon-lighted château throwing a rosy light from its long rows of windows, you would suddenly hear these ravishing voices stealing from the silence of some grove, or rising from boats upon the lake. I felt myself, as I looked and listened, carried back into the romance and poetry of my early youth.

"When the fireworks were ended, and the ball beginning, we returned to the noble suite of rooms that were thrown open to the dancers. A masked ball, you know, is a beautiful sight; but so brilliant a spectacle of the kind I never saw before.

"It was a very aristocratic assembly. I was myself almost the only 'nobody' present.

"My dear child was looking quite beautiful. She wore no mask. Her excitement and delight added an unspeakable charm to her features, always lovely. I remarked a young lady, dressed magnificently, but wearing a mask, who appeared to me to be observing my ward with extraordinary interest. I had seen her, earlier in the evening, in the great hall, and again, for a few minutes, walking near us, on the terrace under the castle windows, similarly employed. A lady, also masked, richly and gravely dressed, and with a stately air, like a person of rank, accompanied her as a chaperon. Had the young lady not worn a mask, I could, of course, have been much more certain upon the question whether she was really watching my poor darling. I am now well assured that she was.

"We were now in one of the *salons*. My poor dear child had been dancing, and was resting a little in one of the chairs near the door; I was standing near. The two ladies I have mentioned had approached, and the younger took the chair next my ward; while her companion stood beside me, and for a little time addressed herself, in a low tone, to her charge.

"Availing herself of the privilege of her mask, she turned to me, and in the tone of an old friend, and calling me by my name, opened a conversation with me, which piqued my curiosity a good deal. She referred to many scenes where she had met me—at Court, and at distinguished houses. She alluded to little incidents which I had long ceased to think of, but which, I found, had only lain in abeyance in my memory, for they instantly started into life at her touch.

"I became more and more curious to ascertain who she was, every moment. She parried my attempts to discover very adroitly and pleasantly. The knowledge she showed of many passages in my life seemed to me all but unaccountable; and she appeared to take a not unnatural pleasure in foiling my curiosity, and in seeing me flounder in my eager perplexity, from one conjecture to another.

"In the meantime the young lady, whom her mother called by the odd name of Millarca, when she once or twice addressed her, had, with the same ease and grace, got into conversation with my ward.

"She introduced herself by saying that her mother was a very old acquaintance of mine. She spoke of the agreeable audacity which a mask rendered practicable; she talked like a friend; she admired her dress, and insinuated very prettily her admiration of her beauty. She amused her with laughing criticisms upon the people who crowded the ballroom, and laughed at my poor child's fun. She was very witty and lively when she pleased, and after a time they had grown very good friends, and the young stranger lowered her mask, displaying a remarkably beautiful face. I had never seen it before, neither had my dear child. But though it was new to us, the features were so engaging, as well as lovely, that it was impossible not to feel the attraction powerfully. My poor child did so. I never saw anyone more taken with another at first sight, unless, indeed, it was the stranger herself, who seemed quite to have lost her heart to her.

"In the meantime, availing myself of the license of a masquerade, I put not a few questions to the elder lady.

" 'You have puzzled me utterly,' I said, laughing. 'Is that not enough? Won't you, now, consent to stand on equal terms, and do me the kindness to remove your mask?'

" 'Can any request be more unreasonable?' she replied. 'Ask a lady to yield an advantage! Beside, how do you know you should recognize me? Years make changes.'

" 'As you see,' I said, with a bow, and, I suppose, a rather melancholy little laugh.

" 'As philosophers tell us,' she said; 'and how do you know that a sight of my face would help you?'

" 'I should take chance for that,' I answered. 'It is vain trying to make yourself out an old woman; your figure betrays you.'

" 'Years, nevertheless, have passed since I saw you, rather since you saw me, for that is what I am considering. Millarca, there, is my daughter; I cannot then be young, even in the opinion of people whom time has taught to be indulgent, and I may not like to be compared with what you remember me. You have no mask to remove. You can offer me nothing in exchange.'

" 'My petition is to your pity, to remove it.'

" 'And mine to yours, to let it stay where it is,' she replied.

" 'Well, then, at least you will tell me whether you are French or German; you speak both languages so perfectly.'

" 'I don't think I shall tell you that, General; you intend a surprise, and are meditating the particular point of attack.'

" 'At all events, you won't deny this,' I said, 'that being honored by your permission to converse, I ought to know how to address you. Shall I say Madame la Comtesse?'

"She laughed, and she would, no doubt, have met me with another evasion—if, indeed, I can treat any occurrence in an interview every circumstance of which was prearranged, as I now believe, with the profoundest cunning, as liable to be modified by accident.

" 'As to that,' she began; but she was interrupted, almost as she opened her lips, by a gentleman, dressed in black, who looked particularly elegant and distinguished, with this drawback, that his face was the most deadly pale I ever saw, except in death. He was in no masquerade—in the plain evening dress of a gentleman; and he said without a smile, but with a courtly and unusually low bow:—

" 'Will Madame la Comtesse permit me to say a very few words which may interest her?'

"The lady turned quickly to him, and touched her lip in token of silence; she then said to me, 'Keep my place for me, General; I shall return when I have said a few words.'

"And with this injunction, playfully given, she walked a little aside with the gentleman in black, and talked for some minutes, apparently very earnestly. They then walked away slowly together in the crowd, and I lost them for some minutes.

"I spent the interval in cudgeling my brains for conjecture as to the identity of the lady who seemed to remember me so kindly, and I was thinking of turning about and joining in the conversation between my pretty ward and the Countess's daughter, and

Castle Anif, near Salzburg, in which a portrait of the original Count Dracula was said to have hung in the 1880s. The painting has now disappeared. (Raymond T. McNally)

trying whether, by the time she returned, I might not have a surprise in store for her, by having her name, title, château, and estates at my fingers' ends. But at this moment she returned, accompanied by the pale man in black, who said:

" 'I shall return and inform Madame la Comtesse when her carriage is at the door.'

"He withdrew with a bow."

XII.   A PETITION

" 'Then we are to lose Madame la Comtesse, but I hope only for a few hours,' I said, with a low bow.

" 'It may be that only, or it may be a few weeks. It was very unlucky his speaking to me just now as he did. Do you now know me?'

"I assured her I did not.

" 'You shall know me,' she said, 'but not at present. We are older and better friends than, perhaps, you suspect. I cannot yet declare myself. I shall in three weeks pass your beautiful schloss about which I have been making inquiries. I shall then look in upon you for an hour or two, and renew a friendship which I never think of without a thousand pleasant recollections. This moment a piece of news has reached me like a thunderbolt. I must set out now, and travel by a devious route, nearly a hundred miles, with all the dispatch I can possibly make. My perplexities multiply. I am only deterred by the compulsory reserve I practice as to my name from making a very singular request of you. My poor child has not quite recovered her strength. Her horse fell with her, at a hunt which she had ridden out to witness, her nerves have not yet recovered the shock, and our physician says that she must on no account exert herself for some time to come. We came here, in consequence, by very easy stages—hardly six leagues a day. I must now travel day and night, on a mission of life and death—

a mission the critical and momentous nature of which I shall be able to explain to you when we meet, as I hope we shall, in a few weeks, without the necessity of any concealment.'

"She went on to make her petition, and it was in the tone of a person from whom such a request amounted to conferring, rather than seeking a favor. This was only in manner, and, as it seemed, quite unconsciously. Than the terms in which it was expressed, nothing could be more deprecatory. It was simply that I would consent to take charge of her daughter during her absence.

"This was, all things considered, a strange, not to say, an audacious request. She in some sort disarmed me, by stating and admitting everything that could be urged against it, and throwing herself entirely upon my chivalry. At the same moment, by a fatality that seems to have predetermined all that happened, my poor child came to my side, and, in an undertone, besought me to invite her new friend, Millarca, to pay us a visit. She had just been sounding her, and thought, if her mamma would allow her, she would like it extremely.

"At another time I should have told her to wait a little, until, at least, we knew who they were. But I had not a moment to think in. The two ladies assailed me together, and I must confess the refined and beautiful face of the young lady, about which there was something extremely engaging, as well as the elegance and fire of high birth, determined me; and quite overpowered, I submitted, and undertook too easily, the care of the young lady, whom her mother called Millarca.

"The Countess beckoned to her daughter, who listened with grave attention while she told her, in general terms, how suddenly and peremptorily she had been summoned, and also of the arrangement she had made for her under my care, adding that I was one of her earliest and most valued friends.

"I made, of course, such speeches as the case seemed to call for, and found myself, on reflection, in a position which I did not half like.

"The gentleman in black returned, and very ceremoniously conducted the lady from the room.

"The demeanor of this gentleman was such as to impress me with the conviction that the Countess was a lady of very much more importance than her modest title alone might have led me to assume.

"Her last charge to me was that no attempt was to be made to learn more about her than I might have already guessed, until her return. Our distinguished host, whose guest she was, knew her reasons.

" 'But here,' she said, 'neither I nor my daughter could safely remain for more than a day. I removed my mask imprudently for a moment, about an hour ago, and, too late, I fancied you saw me. So I resolved to seek an opportunity of talking a little to you. Had I found that you *had* seen me, I should have thrown myself on your high sense of honor to keep my secret for some weeks. As it is, I am satisfied that you did not see me; but if you now *suspect*, or, on reflection, *should* suspect, who I am, I commit myself, in like manner, entirely to your honor. My daughter will observe the same secrecy, and I well know that you will, from time to time, remind her, lest she should thoughtlessly disclose it.'

"She whispered a few words to her daughter, kissed her hurriedly twice, and went away, accompanied by the pale gentleman in black, and disappeared in the crowd.

" 'In the next room,' said Millarca, 'there is a window that looks upon the hall door. I should like to see the last of mamma, and to kiss my hand to her.'

"We assented, of course, and accompanied her to the window. We looked out, and saw a handsome old-fashioned carriage, with a troop of couriers and footmen. We saw the slim figure of the pale gentleman in black, as he held a thick velvet cloak, and placed it about her shoulders and threw the hood over her head. She nodded to him, and just touched his hand with hers. He bowed low repeatedly as the door closed, and the carriage began to move.

" 'She is gone,' said Millarca, with a sigh.

" 'She is gone,' I repeated to myself, for the first time—in the hurried moments that had elapsed since my consent—reflecting upon the folly of my act.

" 'She did not look up,' said the young lady, plaintively.

" 'The Countess had taken off her mask, perhaps, and did not care to show her face,' I said; 'and she could not know that you were in the window.'

"She sighed and looked in my face. She was so beautiful that I relented. I was sorry I had for a moment repented of my hospitality, and I determined to make her amends for the una-vowed churlishness of my reception.

"The young lady, replacing her mask, joined my ward in persuading me to return to the grounds, where the concert was soon to be renewed. We did so, and walked up and down the terrace that lies under the castle windows. Millarca became very intimate with us, and amused us with lively descriptions and stories of most of her great people whom we saw upon the terrace. I liked her more and more every minute. Her gossip, without being ill-natured, was extremely diverting to me, who had been so long out of the great world. I thought what life she would give to our sometimes lonely evenings at home.

"This ball was not over until the morning sun had almost reached the horizon. It pleased the Grand Duke to dance till then, so loyal people could not go away, or think of bed.

"We had just got through a crowded saloon, when my ward asked me what had become of Millarca. I thought she had been by her side, and she fancied she was by mine. The fact was, we had lost her.

"All my efforts to find her were vain. I feared that she had mistaken, in the confusion of a momentary separation from us, other people for her new friends, and had, possibly, pursued and lost them in the extensive grounds which were thrown open to us.

"Now, in its full force, I recognized a new folly in my having undertaken the charge of a young lady without so much as knowing her name; and fettered as I was by promises, of the reasons for imposing which I knew nothing, I could not even point my inquiries by saying that the missing young lady was the daughter of the Countess who had taken her departure a few hours before.

"Morning broke. It was clear daylight before I gave up my search. It was not till near two o'clock next day that we heard anything of my missing charge.

"At about that time a servant knocked at my niece's door, to say that he had been earnestly requested by a young lady, who appeared to be in great distress, to make out where she could find the General Baron Spielsdorf and the young lady, his daughter, in whose charge she had been left by her mother.

"There could be no doubt, notwithstanding the slight inaccuracy, that our young friend had turned up; and so she had. Would to Heaven we had lost her!

"She told my poor child a story to account for her having failed to recover us for so long. Very late, she said, she had got into the housekeeper's bedroom in despair of finding us, and had then fallen into a deep sleep which, long as it was, had hardly sufficed to recruit her strength after the fatigues of the ball.

"That day Millarca came home with us. I was only too happy, after all, to have secured so charming a companion for my dear girl.

XIII. THE WOODMAN

"There soon, however, appeared some drawbacks. In the first place, Millarca complained of extreme languor—the weakness that remained after her late illness—and she never emerged from her room till the afternoon was pretty far advanced. In the next place, it was accidentally discovered, although she always locked her door on the inside, and never disturbed the key from its place, till she admitted the maid to assist at her toilet, that she was undoubtedly sometimes absent from her room in the very early morning, and at various times later in the day, before she wished it to be understood that she was stirring. She was repeatedly seen from the windows of the schloss, in the first faint gray of the morning, walking through the trees, in an easterly direction, and looking like a person in a trance. This convinced me that she walked in her sleep. But this hypothesis did not solve the puzzle. How did she pass out from her room, leaving the door locked on the inside. How did she escape from the house without unbarring door or window?

"In the midst of my perplexities, an anxiety of a far more urgent kind presented itself.

"My dear child began to lose her looks and health, and that in a manner so mysterious, and even horrible, that I became thoroughly frightened.

"She was at first visited by appalling dreams; then, as she fancied, by a specter sometimes resembling Millarca, sometimes in the shape of a beast, indistinctly seen, walking round the foot of her bed, from side to side. Lastly came sensations. One, not unpleasant, but very peculiar, she said, resembled the flow of an icy stream against her breast. At a later time, she felt something like a pair of large needles pierce her, a little below the throat, with a very sharp pain. A few nights after, followed a gradual and convulsive sense of strangulation; then came unconsciousness."

I could hear distinctly every word the kind old General was saying, because by this time we were driving upon the short grass that spreads on either side of the road as you approach the roofless village which had not shown the smoke of a chimney for more than half a century.

You may guess how strangely I felt as I heard my own symptoms so exactly described in those which had been experienced by the poor girl who, but for the catastrophe which followed, would have been at that moment a visitor at my father's château. You may suppose, also, how I felt as I heard him detail habits and mysterious peculiarities which were, in fact, those of our beautiful guest, Carmilla!

A vista opened in the forest; we were on a sudden under the chimneys and gables of the ruined village, and the towers and battlements of the dismantled castle, round which gigantic trees are grouped, overhung us from a slight eminence.

In a frightened dream I got down from the carriage, and in silence, for we had each abundant matter for thinking; we soon mounted the ascent, and were among the spacious chambers, winding stairs, and dark corridors of the castle.

"And this was once the palatial residence of the Karnsteins!" said the old General at length, as from a great window he looked out across the village, and saw the wide, undulating expanse of forest. "It was a bad family, and here its bloodstained annals were written," he continued. "It is hard that they should, after death, continue to plague the human race with their atrocious lusts. That is the chapel of the Karnsteins, down there."

He pointed down to the gray walls of the Gothic building, partly visible through the foliage, a little way down the steep. "And I hear the axe of a woodman," he added, "busy among the trees that surround it; he possibly may give us the information of which I am in search, and point out the grave of Mircalla, Countess of Karnstein. These rustics preserve the local traditions of great families, whose stories die out among the rich and titled so soon as the families themselves become extinct."

"We have a portrait, at home, of Mircalla, the Countess Karnstein; should you like to see it?" asked my father.

"Time enough, dear friend," replied the General. "I believe that I have seen the original; and one motive which has led me to you earlier than I at first intended, was to explore the chapel which we are now approaching."

"What! See the Countess Mircalla," exclaimed my father. "Why, she has been dead more than a century!"

"Not so dead as you fancy, I am told," answered the General.

"I confess, General, you puzzle me utterly," replied my father, looking at him, I fancied, for a moment with a return of the suspicion I detected before. But although there was anger and detestation, at times, in the old General's manner, there was nothing flighty.

"There remains to me," he said, as we passed under the heavy arch of the Gothic church—for its dimensions would have justified its being so styled—"but one object which can interest me during the few years that remain to me on earth, and that is to wreak on her the vengeance which, I thank God, may still be accomplished by a mortal arm."

"What vengeance can you mean?" asked my father, in increasing amazement.

"I mean, to decapitate the monster," he answered, with a fierce flush, and a stamp that echoed mournfully through the hollow ruin, and his clenched hand was at the same moment raised, as if it grasped the handle of an axe, while he shook it ferociously in the air.

"What!" exclaimed my father, more than ever bewildered.

"To strike her head off."

"Cut her head off?"

"Aye, with a hatchet, with a spade, or with anything that can cleave through her murderous throat. You shall hear," he answered, trembling with rage. And hurrying forward he said:

"That beam will answer for a seat; your dear child is fatigued; let her be seated, and I will, in a few sentences, close my dreadful story."

The squared block of wood, which lay on the grass-grown pavement of the chapel, formed a bench on which I was very glad to seat myself, and in the meantime the General called to the woodman, who had been removing some boughs which leaned upon the old walls; and, axe in hand, the hardy old fellow stood before us.

He could not tell us anything of these monuments; but there was an old man, he said, a ranger of this forest, at present sojourning in the house of the priest, about two miles away, who could point out every monument of the old Karnstein family; and, for a trifle, he undertook to bring him back with him, if we would lend him one of our horses, in little more than half-an-hour.

"Have you been long employed about this forest?" asked my father of the old man.

"I have been a woodman here," he answered in his *patois*, "under the forester, all my days; so has my father before me, and so on, as many generations as I can count up. I could show you the very house in the village here, in which my ancestors lived."

"How came the village to be deserted?" asked the General.

"It was troubled by *revenants*, sir; several were tracked to their graves, there detected by the usual tests, and extinguished in the usual way, by decapitation, by the stake, and by burning; but not until many of the villagers were killed.

"But after all these proceedings according to law," he continued—"so many graves opened, and so many vampires deprived of their horrible animation—the village was not relieved. But a Moravian nobleman, who happened to be traveling this way, heard how matters were, and being skilled—as many people are in his country—in such affairs, he offered to deliver the village from its tormentor. He did so thus: There being a bright moon that night, he ascended, shortly after sunset, the tower of the chapel here, from whence he could distinctly see the churchyard beneath him; you can see it from that window. From this point he watched until he saw the vampire come out of his grave, and place near it the linen clothes in which he had been folded, and glide away toward the village to plague its inhabitants.

"The stranger, having seen all this, came down from the steeple, took the linen wrappings of the vampire, and carried them up to the top of the tower, which he again mounted. When the vampire returned from his prowlings and missed his clothes, he cried furiously to the Moravian, whom he saw at the summit of the tower, and who, in reply, beckoned him to ascend and take them. Whereupon the vampire, accepting his invitation, began to climb the steeple, and so soon as he had reached the battlements, the Moravian, with a stroke of his sword, clove his skull in twain, hurling him down to the churchyard, whither, descending by the winding stairs, the stranger followed and cut his head off, and next day delivered it and the body to the villagers, who duly impaled and burned them.

"This Moravian nobleman had authority from the then head of the family to remove the tomb of Mircalla, Countess Karnstein, which he did effectually, so that in a little while its site was quite forgotten."

"Can you point out where it stood?" asked the General, eagerly.

The forester shook his head and smiled.

"Not a soul living could tell you that now," he said; "besides, they say her body was removed; but no one is sure of that either."

Having thus spoken, as time pressed, he dropped his axe and departed, leaving us to hear the remainder of the General's strange story.

XIV.   THE MEETING

"My beloved child," he resumed, "was now growing rapidly worse. The physician who attended her had failed to produce the slightest impression upon her disease, for such I then supposed it to be. He saw my alarm, and suggested a consultation. I called in an abler physician, from Gratz. Several days elapsed before he arrived. He was a good and pious, as well as a learned man. Having seen my poor ward together, they withdrew to my library to confer and discuss. I, from the adjoining room, where I waited their summons, heard these two gentlemen's voices raised in something sharper than a strictly philosophical discussion. I knocked at the door and entered. I found the old physician from Gratz maintaining his theory. His rival was combating it with undisguised ridicule, accompanied with bursts of laughter. This unseemly manifestation subsided and the altercation ended on my entrance.

" 'Sir,' said my first physician, 'my learned brother seems to think that you want a conjuror, and not a doctor.'

" 'Pardon me,' said the old physician from Gratz, looking displeased, 'I shall state my own view of the case in my own way another time. I grieve, Monsieur le General, that by my skill and science I can be of no use. Before I go I shall do myself the honor to suggest something to you.'

"He seemed thoughtful, and sat down at a table, and began to write. Profoundly disappointed, I made my bow, and as I turned to go, the other doctor pointed over his shoulder to his companion who was writing, and then, with a shrug, significantly touched his forehead.

"This consultation, then, left me precisely where I was. I walked out into the grounds, all but distracted. The doctor from Gratz, in ten or fifteen minutes, overtook me. He apologized for having followed me, but said that he could not conscientiously take his leave without a few words more. He told me that he could not be mistaken; no natural disease exhibited the same symptoms; and that death was already very near. There remained, however, a day, or possibly two, of life. If the fatal seizure were at once arrested, with great care and skill her strength might possibly return. But all hung now upon the confines of the irrevocable. One more assault might extinguish the last spark of vitality which is, every moment, ready to die.

" 'And what is the nature of the seizure you speak of?' I entreated.

" 'I have stated all fully in this note, which I place in your hands, upon the distinct condition that you send for the nearest clergyman, and open my letter in his presence, and on no account read it till he is with you; you would despise it else, and it is a matter of life and death. Should the priest fail you, then, indeed, you may read it.'

"He asked me, before taking his leave finally, whether I would wish to see a man curiously learned upon the very subject, which, after I had read his letter, would probably interest me above all others, and he urged me earnestly to invite him to visit him there; and so took his leave.

"The ecclesiastic was absent, and I read the letter by myself. At another time, or in another case, it might have excited my ridicule. But into what quackeries will not people rush for a last chance, where all accustomed means have failed, and the life of a beloved object is at stake?

"Nothing, you will say, could be more absurd than the learned man's letter. It was monstrous enough to have consigned him to a madhouse. He said that the patient was suffering from the visits of a vampire! The punctures which she described as having oc-curred near the throat were, he insisted, the insertion of those two long, thin, and sharp teeth which, it is well known, are peculiar to vampires; and there could be no doubt, he added, as to the well-defined presence of the small livid mark which all concurred in describing as that induced by the demon's lips, and every symptom described by the sufferer was in exact conformity with those recorded in every case of a similar visitation.

"Being myself wholly skeptical as to the existence of any such portent as the vampire, the supernatural theory of the good doctor furnished, in my opinion, but another instance of learning and intelligence oddly associated with some one hallucination. I was so miserable, however, that, rather than try nothing, I acted upon the instructions of the letter.

"I concealed myself in the dark dressing-room, that opened upon the poor patient's room, in which a candle was burning, and watched there till she was fast asleep. I stood at the door, peeping through the small crevice, my sword laid on the table beside me, as my directions prescribed, until, a little after one, I saw a large black object, very ill-defined, crawl, as it seemed to me, over the foot of the bed, and swiftly spread itself up to the poor girl's throat, where it swelled, in a moment, into a great, palpitating mass.

"For a few moments I had stood petrified. I now sprang forward, with my sword in my hand. The black creature suddenly contracted toward the foot of the bed, glided over it, and, standing on the floor about a yard below the foot of the bed, with a glare of skulking ferocity and horror fixed on me, I saw Millarca. Speculating I know not what, I struck at her instantly with my sword; but I saw her standing near the door, unscathed. Horrified, I pursued, and struck again. She was gone! And my sword flew to shivers against the door.

"I can't describe to you all that passed on that horrible night. The whole house was up and stirring. The specter Millarca was gone. But her victim was sinking fast, and before the morning dawned, she died."

The old General was agitated. We did not speak to him. My father walked to some little distance, and began reading the inscriptions on the tombstones; and thus occupied, he strolled into the door of a side chapel to prosecute his researches. The General leaned against the wall, dried his eyes, and sighed heavily. I was relieved on hearing the voices of Carmilla and madame, who were at that moment approaching. The voices died away.

In this solitude, having just listened to so strange a story, connected, as it was, with the great and titled dead, whose monuments were moldering among the dust and ivy round us, and every incident of which bore so awfully upon my own mysterious case —in this haunted spot, darkened by the towering foliage that rose on every side, dense and high above its noiseless walls—a horror began to steal over me, and my heart sank as I thought that my friends were, after all, not about to enter and disturb this triste and ominous scene.

The old General's eyes were fixed on the ground, as he leaned with his hand upon the basement of a shattered monument.

Under a narrow, arched doorway, surmounted by one of those demoniacal grotesques in which the cynical and ghastly fancy of old Gothic carving delights, I saw very gladly the beautiful face and figure of Carmilla enter the shadowy chapel.

I was just about to rise and speak, and nodded smiling, in answer to her peculiarly engaging smile; when with a cry, the old man by my side caught up the woodman's hatchet, and started forward. On seeing him a brutalized change came over her features. It was an instantaneous and horrible transformation, as she made a crouching step backward. Before I could utter a scream, he struck at her with all his force, but she dived under his blow, and unscathed, caught him in her tiny grasp by the wrist. He struggled for a moment to release his arm, but his hand opened, the axe fell to the ground, and the girl was gone.

He staggered against the wall. His gray hair stood upon his head, a moisture shone over his face, as if he were at the point of death.

The frightful scene had passed in a moment. The first thing I recollect after, is madame standing before me, and impatiently repeating again and again, the question, "Where is Mademoiselle Carmilla?"

I answered at length, "I don't know—I can't tell—she went there," and I pointed to the door through which madame had just entered; "only a minute or two since."

"But I have been standing there, in the passage, ever since Mademoiselle Carmilla entered; and she did not return."

She then began to call "Carmilla" through every door and passage and from the windows, but no answer came.

"She called herself Carmilla?" asked the General, still agitated.

"Carmilla, yes," I answered.

"Aye," he said, "that is Millarca. That is the same person who long ago was called Mircalla, Countess Karnstein. Depart from this accursed ground, my poor child, as quickly as you can. Drive to the clergyman's house, and stay there till we come. Begone! May you never behold Carmilla more; you will not find her here."

XV.   ORDEAL AND EXECUTION

As he spoke one of the strangest-looking men I ever beheld, entered the chapel at the door through which Carmilla had made her entrance and her exit. He was tall, narrow-chested, stooping, with high shoulders, and dressed in black. His face was brown and dried in with deep furrows; he wore an oddly-shaped hat with a broad leaf. His hair, long and grizzled, hung on his shoulders. He wore a pair of gold spectacles, and walked slowly, with an odd shambling gait, with his face sometimes turned up to the sky, and sometimes bowed down toward the ground, seemed to wear a perpetual smile; his long thin arms were swinging, and his lank hands, in old black gloves ever so much too wide for them, waving and gesticulating in utter abstraction.

"The very man!" exclaimed the General, advancing with

manifest delight. "My dear baron, how happy I am to see you, I had no hope of meeting you so soon." He signed to my father, who had by this time returned, and leading the fantastic old gentleman, whom he called the baron, to meet him, he introduced him formally, and they at once entered into earnest conversation. The stranger took a roll of paper from his pocket, and spread it on the worn surface of a tomb that stood by. He had a pencil case in his fingers, with which he traced imaginary lines from point to point on the paper, which from their often glancing from it, together, at certain points of the building, I concluded to be a plan of the chapel. He accompanied, what I may term his lecture, with occasional readings from a dirty little book, whose yellow leaves were closely written over.

They sauntered together down the side aisle, opposite to the spot where I was standing, conversing as they went; then they began measuring distances by paces, and finally they all stood together, facing a piece of the side-wall, which they began to examine with great minuteness; pulling off the ivy that clung over it, and rapping the plaster with the ends of their sticks, scraping here, and knocking there. At length they ascertained the existence of a broad marble tablet, with letters carved in relief upon it.

With the assistance of the woodman, who soon returned, a monumental inscription, and carved escutcheon, were disclosed. They proved to be those of the long lost monument of Mircalla, Countess Karnstein.

The old General, though not I fear given to the praying mood, raised his hands and eyes to Heaven, in mute thanksgiving for some moments.

"Tomorrow," I heard him say, "the commissioner will be here, and the inquisition will be held according to law."

Then turning to the old man with the gold spectacles, whom I have described, he shook him warmly by both hands and said:

"Baron, how can I thank you? How can we all thank you? You will have delivered this region from a plague that has scourged its inhabitants for more than a century. The horrible enemy, thank God, is at last tracked."

My father led the stranger aside, and the General followed. I knew that he had led them out of hearing, that he might relate my case, and I saw them glance often quickly at me, as the discussion proceeded.

My father came to me, kissed me again and again, and leading me from the chapel, said:

"It is time to return, but before we go home, we must add to our party the good priest, who lives but a little way from this; and persuade him to accompany us to the schloss."

In this quest we were successful: and I was glad, being unspeakably fatigued when we reached home. But my satisfaction was changed to dismay, on discovering that there were no tidings of Carmilla. Of the scene that had occurred in the ruined chapel, no explanation was offered to me, and it was clear that it was a secret which my father for the present determined to keep from me.

The sinister absence of Carmilla made the remembrance of the scene more horrible to me. The arrangements for that night were singular. Two servants and madame were to sit up in my room that night; and the ecclesiastic with my father kept watch in the adjoining dressing-room.

The priest had performed certain solemn rites that night, the purport of which I did not understand any more than I comprehended the reason of this extraordinary precaution taken for my safety during sleep.

I saw all clearly a few days later.

The disappearance of Carmilla was followed by the discontinuance of my nightly sufferings.

You have heard, no doubt, of the appalling superstition that prevails in Upper and Lower Styria, in Moravia, Silesia, in Turkish Servia, in Poland, even in Russia; the superstition, so we must call it, of the vampire.

If human testimony, taken with every care and solemnity, judicially, before commissions innumerable, each consisting of many members, all chosen for integrity and intelligence, and constituting reports more voluminous perhaps than exist upon any one other class of cases, is worth anything, it is difficult to deny, or even to doubt the existence of such a phenomenon as the vampire.

For my part I have heard no theory by which to explain what I myself have witnessed and experienced, other than that supplied by the ancient and well-attested belief of the country.

The next day the formal proceedings took place in the Chapel of Karnstein. The grave of the Countess Mircalla was opened; and the General and my father recognized each his perfidious and beautiful guest, in the face now disclosed to view. The features, though a hundred and fifty years had passed since her funeral, were tinted with the warmth of life. Her eyes were open; no cadaverous smell exhaled from the coffin. The two medical men, one officially present, the other on the part of the promotor of the inquiry, attested the marvelous fact, that there was a faint but appreciable respiration, and a corresponding action of the heart. The limbs were perfectly flexible, the flesh elastic; and the leaden coffin floated with blood, in which to a depth of seven inches, the body lay immersed. Here then, were all the admitted signs and proofs of vampirism. The body, therefore, in accordance with the ancient practice, was raised, and a sharp stake driven through the heart of the vampire, who uttered a piercing shriek at the moment, in all respects such as might escape from a living person in the last agony. Then the head was struck off, and a torrent of blood flowed from the severed neck. The body and head were next placed on a pile of wood, and reduced to ashes, which were thrown upon the river and borne away, and that territory has never since been plagued by the visits of a vampire.

My father has a copy of the report of the Imperial Commission, with the signatures of all who were present at these proceedings, attached in verification of the statement. It is from this official paper that I have summarized my account of this last shocking scene.

XVI.   CONCLUSION

I write all this you suppose with composure. But far from it; I cannot think of it without agitation. Nothing but your earnest desire so repeatedly expressed, could have induced me to sit down to a task that has unstrung my nerves for months to come, and reinduced a shadow of the unspeakable horror which years after my deliverance continued to make my days and nights dreadful, and solitude insupportably terrific.

Let me add a word or two about that quaint Baron Vordenburg, to whose curious lore we are indebted for the discovery of the Countess Mircalla's grave.

He had taken up his abode in Gratz, where, living upon a mere pittance, which was all that remained to him of the once princely estates of his family, in Upper Styria, he devoted himself to the minute and laborious investigation of the marvelously authenticated tradition of vampirism. He had at his fingers' ends all the great and little works upon the subject. *Magia Posthuma, Phlegon de Mirabilibus, Augustinus de curâ pro Mortuis, Philosophicae et Christianae Cogitationes de Vampiris*, by John Christofer Herenberg; and a thousand others, among which I remember only a few of those which he lent to my father. He had a voluminous digest of all the judicial cases, from which he had extracted a system of principles that appear to govern—some always, and others occasionally only—the condition of the vampire. I may mention, in passing, that the deadly pallor attributed to that sort of *revenants*, is a mere melodramatic fiction. They present, in the grave, and when they show themselves in human society, the appearance of healthy life. When disclosed to light in their coffins, they exhibit all the symptoms that are enumerated as those which proved the vampire-life of the long-dead Countess Karnstein.

How they escape from their graves and return to them for certain hours every day, without displacing the clay or leaving any trace of disturbance in the state of the coffin or the cerements, has always been admitted to be utterly inexplicable. The amphibious existence of the vampire is sustained by daily renewed slumber in the grave. Its horrible lust for living blood supplies the vigor of its waking existence. The vampire is prone to be fascinated with an engrossing vehemence, resembling the passion of love, by particular persons. In pursuit of these it will exercise inexhaustible patience and stratagem, for access to a particular object may be obstructed in a hundred ways. It will never desist until it has satiated its passion, and drained the very life of its coveted victim. But it will, in these cases, husband and protract its murderous enjoyment with the refinement of an epicure, and heighten it by the gradual approaches of an artful courtship. In these cases it seems to yearn for something like sympathy and consent. In ordinary ones it goes direct to its object, overpowers with violence, and strangles and exhausts often at a single feast.

The vampire is, apparently, subject, in certain situations, to special conditions. In the particular instance of which I have given you a relation, Mircalla seemed to be limited to a name which, if not her real one, should at least reproduce, without the omission or addition of a single letter, those, as we say, anagrammatically, which compose it. *Carmilla* did this; so did *Millarca*.

My father related to the Baron Vordenburg, who remained with us for two or three weeks after the expulsion of Carmilla, the story about the Moravian nobleman and the vampire at Karnstein churchyard, and then he asked the Baron how he had discovered the exact position of the long-concealed tomb of the Countess Mircalla? The Baron's grotesque features puckered up into a mysterious smile; he looked down, still smiling on his worn spectacle-case and fumbled with it. Then looking up, he said:

"I have many journals, and other papers, written by that remarkable man; the most curious among them is one treating of the visit of which you speak, to Karnstein. The tradition, of course, discolors and distorts a little. He might have been termed a Moravian nobleman, for he had changed his abode to that territory, and was, beside, a noble. But he was, in truth, a native of Upper Styria. It is enough to say that in very early youth he had been a passionate and favored lover of the beautiful Mircalla, Countess Karnstein. Her early death plunged him into inconsolable grief. It is the nature of vampires to increase and multiply, but according to an ascertained and ghostly law.

"Assume, at starting, a territory perfectly free from the pest. How does it begin, and how does it multiply itself? I will tell you. A person, more or less wicked, puts an end to himself. A suicide, under certain circumstances, becomes a vampire. That specter visits living people in their slumbers; *they* die, and almost invariably, in the grave, develop into vampires. This happened in the case of the beautiful Mircalla, who was haunted by one of those demons. My ancestor, Vordenburg, whose title I still bear, soon discovered this, and in the course of the studies to which he devoted himself, learned a great deal more.

"Among other things, he concluded that suspicion of vampirism would probably fall, sooner or later, upon the dead Countess, who in life had been his idol. He conceived a horror, be she what she might, of her remains being profaned by the outrage of a posthumous execution. He has left a curious paper to prove that the vampire, on its expulsion from its amphibious existence, is projected into a far more horrible life; and he resolved to save his once beloved Mircalla from this.

"He adopted the stratagem of a journey here, a pretended

removal of her remains, and a real obliteration of her monument. When age had stolen upon him, and from the vale of years he looked back on the scenes he was leaving, he considered, in a different spirit, what he had done, and a horror took possession of him. He made the tracings and notes which have guided me to the very spot, and drew up a confession of the deception that he had practiced. If he had intended any further action in this matter, death prevented him; and the hand of a remote descendant has, too late for many, directed the pursuit to the lair of the beast."

We talked a little more, and among other things he said was this:

"One sign of the vampire is the power of the hand. The slender hand of Mircalla closed like a vise of steel on the General's wrist when he raised the hatchet to strike. But its power is not confined to its grasp; it leaves a numbness in the limb it seizes, which is slowly, if ever, recovered from."

The following spring my father took me on a tour through Italy. We remained away for more than a year. It was long before the terror of recent events subsided; and to this hour the image of Carmilla returns to memory with ambiguous alternations— sometimes the playful, languid, beautiful girl; sometimes the writhing fiend I saw in the ruined church; and often from a reverie I have started, fancying I heard the light step of Carmilla at the drawing-room door.

12

Croglin Grange Vampire

From Augustus Hare, *Story of My Life*, 4 vols., London, Allen, 1896–1901

Charles G. Harper in his book *Haunted Houses* (1924) claimed that there was no place known as Croglin Grange and that neither of two buildings known as Croglin Low and Croglin High Hall accorded with the house described in Augustus Hare's report. In the June 1967 issue of *Fate* magazine D. Scott pointed out the resemblance of one portion of Hare's report to a section in Prest's novel *Varney the Vampire* (1847) and suggested the possibility of plagiarism.

But F. Clive Ross in the Spring 1963 issue of *Tomorrow* magazine described how he had visited the area in Britain where the events reported by Hare took place. On the porch of a church there, Mr. Ross had found a printed sheet which read: "Croglin Low Hall is the ancient Manor House of Little Croglin. It belonged to the Dacre Family until 1589. There was a second church in Croglin here, probably serving as a private chapel to the house. Nothing of this church now exists. The house is now a farm." In addition, Mr. Ross had interviewed a Mrs. Parkin at Slack Cottage, Ainstable, who had known a member of the Fisher family—the family who, according to the story, owned Croglin Grange. This gentleman, born in the 1860s, had heard the vampire story from his grandparents. Mrs. Parkin also stated that according to the deeds of Croglin Low Hall, it was commonly called Croglin Grange until 1720. The following account should be dated between 1680 and 1690, rather than 1875 as indicated by Hare in his book.

"Fisher," said the Captain, "may sound a very plebeian name, but this family is of a very ancient lineage, and for many hundreds of years they have possessed a very curious old place in Cumberland, which bears the weird name of Croglin Grange. The great characteristic of the house is that never at any period of its very long existence has it been more than one storey high, but it has a terrace from which large grounds sweep away towards the church in the hollow, and a fine distant view.

"When, in lapse of years, the Fishers outgrew Croglin Grange in family and fortune, they were wise enough not to destroy the long-standing characteristic of the place by adding another storey to the house, but they went away to the south to reside at Thorncombe near Guildford, and they let Croglin Grange.

"They were extremely fortunate in their tenants, two brothers and a sister. They heard their praises from all quarters. To their poorer neighbours they were all that is most kind and beneficent, and their neighbours of a higher class spoke of them as a most welcome addition to the little society of the neighbourhood. On their part, the tenants were greatly delighted with their new residence. The arrangement of the house, which would have been a trial to many, was not so to them. In every respect Croglin Grange was exactly suited to them.

"The winter was spent most happily by the new inmates of Croglin Grange, who shared in all the little social pleasures of the district, and made themselves very popular. In the following summer there was one day which was dreadfully, annihilatingly hot. The brothers lay under the trees with their books, for it was too hot for any active occupation. The sister sat on the veranda and worked, or tried to work, for in the intense sultriness of that summer day, work was next to impossible. They dined early, and after dinner they still sat out on the veranda, enjoying the cool air which came with the evening, and they watched the sun set, and the moon rise over the belt of trees which separated the grounds from the churchyard, seeing it mount the heavens till the whole lawn was bathed in silver light, across which the long shadows from the shrubbery fell as if embossed, so vivid and distinct were they.

"When they separated for the night, all retiring to their rooms on the ground floor (for, as I said, there was no upstairs in that house), the sister felt that the heat was still so great that she could not sleep, and having fastened her window, she did not close the shutters—in that very quiet place it was not necessary —and, propped against the pillows, she still watched the wonderful, the marvellous beauty of that summer night. Gradually she became aware of two lights, two lights which flickered in and out in the belt of trees which separated the lawn from the churchyard, and, as her gaze became fixed upon them, she saw them emerge, fixed in a dark substance, a definite ghastly something, which seemed every moment to become nearer, increasing in size and substance as it approached. Every now and then it was lost for a moment in the long shadows which stretched cross the lawn from the trees, and then it emerged larger than ever, and still coming on. As she watched it, the most uncontrollable horror seized her. She longed to get away, but the door was close to the window, and the door was locked on the inside, and while she was unlocking it she must be for an instant nearer to it. She longed to scream, but her voice seemed paralysed, her tongue glued to the roof of her mouth.

"Suddenly—she could never explain why afterwards—the terrible object seemed to turn to one side, seemed to be going round the house, not to be coming to her at all, and immediately she jumped out of bed and rushed to the door, but as she was unlocking it she heard scratch, scratch, scratch upon the window. She felt a sort of mental comfort in the knowledge that the window was securely fastened on the inside. Suddenly the scratching sound ceased, and a kind of pecking sound took its place. Then, in her agony, she became aware that the creature was

Edward Gorey, drop curtain for the Nantucket Stage
Company's 1973 production of *Dracula*, Nantucket, Mass.
The play was adapted from Bram Stoker's novel by John
Balderston and Hamilton Deane, and directed by Dennis
Rosa. (Theatre Collection, The New York Public Library at
Lincoln Center)

Stage setting for the Alliance Theater Company's production of Ted Tiller's play *Count Dracula* in Atlanta, Ga.,
1974. The play, based on Bram Stoker's novel, was directed
by Robert J. Farley; production designer was Lewis S.
Greenleaf III. It was first performed in 1971 by Stage West,
Springfield, Mass., under the production of Stephen E.
Hays. (Alliance Theater Company)

unpicking the lead! The noise continued, and a diamond pane of glass fell into the room. Then a long bony finger of the creature came in and turned the handle of the window, and the window opened, and the creature came in; and it came across the room, and her terror was so great that she could not scream, and it came up to the bed, and it twisted its long, bony fingers into her hair, and it dragged her head over the side of the bed, and—it bit her violently in the throat.

"As it bit her, her voice was released, and she screamed with all her might and main. Her brothers rushed out of their rooms, but the door was locked on the inside. A moment was lost while they got a poker and broke it open. Then the creature had already escaped through the window, and the sister, bleeding violently from a wound in the throat, was lying unconscious over the side of the bed. One brother pursued the creature, which fled before him through the moonlight with gigantic strides, and eventually seemed to disappear over the wall into the churchyard. Then he rejoined his brother by the sister's bedside. She was dreadfully hurt, and her wound was a very definite one, but she was of strong disposition, not ever given to romance or superstition, and when she came to herself she said, 'What has happened is most extraordinary and I am very much hurt. It seems inexplicable, but of course there is an explanation, and we must wait for it. It will turn out that a lunatic has escaped from some asylum and found his way here.' The wound healed, and she appeared to get well, but the doctor who was sent for to her would not believe that she could bear so terrible a shock so easily, and insisted that she must have change, mental and physical; so her brothers took her to Switzerland.

"Being a sensible girl, when she went abroad she threw herself at once into the interests of the country she was in. She dried plants, she made sketches, she went up mountains, and, as autumn came on, she was the person who urged that they should return to Croglin Grange. 'We have taken it,' she said, 'for seven years, and we have only been there one; and we shall always find it difficult to let a house which is only one storey high, so we had better return there; lunatics do not escape every day.' As she urged it, her brothers wished nothing better, and the family returned to Cumberland. From there being no upstairs in the house it was impossible to make any great change in their arrangements. The sister occupied the same room, but it is unnecessary to say she always closed the shutters, which, however, as in many old houses, always left one top pane of the window uncovered. The brothers moved, and occupied a room together, exactly opposite that of their sister, and they always kept loaded pistols in their room.

"The winter passed most peacefully and happily. In the following March, the sister was suddenly awakened by a sound she remembered only too well—scratch, scratch, scratch upon the window, and, looking up, she saw climbed up to the topmost pane of the window, the same hideous brown shrivelled face, with glaring eyes, looking in at her. This time she screamed as loud as she could. Her brothers rushed out of their room with pistols, and out of the front door. The creature was already scudding away across the lawn. One of the brothers fired and hit it in the leg, but still with the other leg it continued to make way, scrambled over the wall into the churchyard, and seemed to disappear into a vault which belonged to a family long extinct.

"The next day the brothers summoned all the tenants of Croglin Grange, and in their presence the vault was opened. A horrible scene revealed itself. The vault was full of coffins; they had been broken open, and their contents, horribly mangled and distorted, were scattered over the floor. One coffin alone remained intact. Of that the lid had been lifted, but still lay loose upon the coffin. They raised it, and there—brown, withered, shrivelled, mummified, but quite entire—was the same hideous figure which had looked in at the windows of Croglin Grange, with the marks of a recent pistol-shot in the leg: and they did the only thing that can lay a vampire—they burnt it."

13

Vampires in and near Newport, Rhode Island

From the *New York World*, February 2, 1896

The Sunday newspaper feature from which the following passages are taken is important in at least two respects. I found it among Bram Stoker's working papers for *Dracula* (1897), and to my knowledge it has never previously been reprinted in whole or in part by any other vampire devotee. Moreover, since it is the only news clipping among the *Dracula* papers, it seems safe to assume that Stoker's notions about vampires were to some degree influenced by it.

VAMPIRES IN NEW ENGLAND

Dead Bodies Dug Up and Their Hearts
Burned to Prevent Disease.

STRANGE SUPERSTITION OF LONG AGO.

The Old Belief Was that Ghostly Monsters
Sucked the Blood of Their Living Relatives.

Recent ethnological research has disclosed something very extraordinary in Rhode Island. It appears that the ancient vampire superstition still survives in that State, and within the last few years many people have been digging up the dead bodies of relatives for the purpose of burning their hearts.

Near Newport scores of such exhumations have been made, the purpose being to prevent the dead from preying upon the living. The belief entertained is that a person who has died of consumption is likely to rise from the grave at night and suck the blood of surviving members of his or her family, thus dooming them to a similar fate.

The discovery of the survival in highly educated New England of a superstition dating back to the days of Sardanapalus and Nebuchadnezzar has been made by George R. Stetson, an ethnologist of repute. He has found it rampant in a district which includes the towns of Exeter, Foster, Kingstown, East Greenwich and many scattered hamlets. This region, where abandoned farms are numerous, is the tramping-ground of the book agent, the chromo peddler and the patent medicine man. The social isolation is as complete as it was two centuries ago. . . .

TWO TYPICAL CASES

There is one small village distant fifteen miles from Newport, where within the last few years there have been at least half a dozen resurrections on this account. The most recent was made two years ago in a family where the mother and four children had already succumbed to consumption. The last of these children was exhumed and the heart was burned.

Another instance was noted in a seashore town, not far from Newport, possessing a summer hotel and a few cottages of hot-weather residents. An intelligent man, by trade a mason, informed Mr. Stetson that he had lost two brothers by consumption. On the death of the second brother, his father was advised to take up the body and burn the heart. He refused to do so, and consequently he was attacked by the disease. Finally he died of it. His heart was burned, and in this way the rest of the family escaped.

This frightful superstition is said to prevail in all of the isolated districts of Southern Rhode Island, and it survives to some extent in the large centres of population. Sometimes the body is burned, not merely the heart, and the ashes are scattered.

In some parts of Europe the belief still has a hold on the popular mind. On the Continent from 1727 to 1735 there prevailed an epidemic of vampires. Thousands of people died, as was supposed, from having their blood sucked by creatures that came to their bedsides at night with goggling eyes and lips eager for the life fluid of the victim. In Servia it was understood that the demon might be destroyed by digging up the body and piercing it through with a sharp instrument, after which it was decapitated and burned. Relief was found in eating the earth of the vampire's grave. In the Levant the corpse was cut to pieces and boiled in wine.

VAMPIRISM A PLAGUE

. . . Vampirism became a plague, more dreaded than any form of disease. Everywhere people were dying from the attacks of the blood-sucking monsters, each victim becoming in turn a night-prowler in pursuit of human prey. Terror of the mysterious and unearthly peril filled all hearts. . . .

The contents of every suspected grave were investigated, and many corpses. . . were promptly subjected to "treatment." This meant that a stake was driven through the chest, and the heart, being taken out, was either burned or chopped into small pieces. For in this way only could a vampire be deprived of power to do mischief. In one case a man who was unburied sat up in his coffin, with fresh blood on his lips. The official in charge of the ceremonies held a crucifix before his face and, saying, "Do you recognize your Saviour?" chopped the unfortunate's head off. This person presumably had been buried alive in a cataleptic trance.

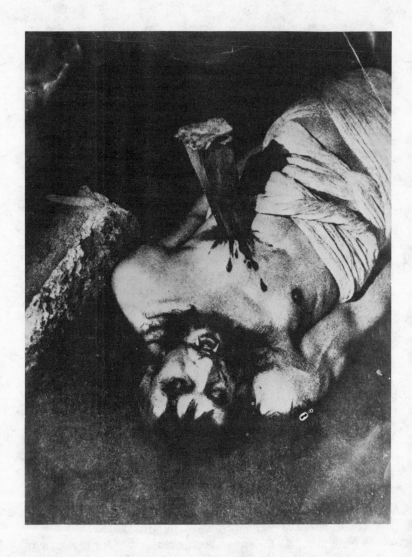

Anonymous lithograph. Driving a stake through the heart of a corpse suspected of vampirism was reported in Rhode Island in the last century. (The Bettmann Archive)

WERE THEY BURIED ALIVE?

How is the phenomenon to be accounted for? Nobody can say with certainty, but it may be that the fright into which people were thrown by the epidemic had the effect of predisposing nervous persons to catalepsy. In a word, people were buried alive in a condition where, the vital functions being suspended, they remained as it were dead for a while. It is a common thing for a cataleptic to bleed at the mouth just before returning to consciousness. According to the popular superstition, the vampire left his or her body in the grave while engaged in nocturnal prowls.

The epidemic prevailed all over southeastern Europe, being at its worst in Hungary and Servia. It is supposed to have originated in Greece, where a belief was entertained to the effect that Latin Christians buried in that country could not decay in their graves being under the ban of the Greek Church. The cheerful notion was that they got out of their graves at night and pursued the occupation of ghouls. The superstition as to ghouls is very ancient and undoubtedly of Oriental origin. Generally speaking, however, a ghoul is just the opposite of a vampire, being a living person who preys on dead bodies, while a vampire is a dead person that feeds on the blood of the living. If you had your choice, which would you rather be a vampire or a ghoul? . . .

Among the numerous folk tales about vampires is one relating to a fiend named Dakanavar, who dwelt in a cave in Armenia. He would not permit anybody to penetrate into the mountains of Ulmish Altotem or to count their valleys. Every one who attempted this had in the night the blood sucked by the monster from the soles of his feet until he died.

At last, however, he was outwitted by two cunning fellows. They began to count the valleys, and when night came they lay down to sleep, taking care to place themselves with the feet of each under the head of the other. In the night the monster came, felt as usual and found a head. Then he felt at the other end and found a head there also.

"Well!" cried he, "I have gone through all of the three hundred and sixty-six valleys of these mountains and have sucked the blood of people without end, but never yet did I find one with two heads and no feet!" So saying he ran away, and never more was seen in that country, but ever since people have known that the mountains have three hundred and sixty-six valleys. . . .

14

Vampire from Brooklyn, N.Y.

From William Seabrook, *Witchcraft*, New York, Harcourt
Brace & Co., Inc., 1940

This extract reports an experience that Seabrook had in 1932. The
bloodsucking female presented here is not undead, hence is not a true
vampire, but I think that Seabrook's enlightened interest in "the thirst
for blood" ranks him as a worthy successor of Calmet and Summers.

I'd been walking in the hills behind Le Trayas, on the Riviera,
with Eugene Bagger, the stocky little Austrian journalist who
worked for the New York *Times* some years ago and later wrote
Eminent Europeans. We'd returned to the town, where he had
a house and where I was staying in the hotel, which contained
that summer a number of other writers, painters, musicians, including some Americans.

It was late afternoon. I was hot, and went down to the shore
for a swim. There was a rocky, pebbled cove, a sort of inlet deep
among the pine trees, closer than the sand beach. Seated on the
pebbles, alone and with her hands clasped round her knees, was
the girl I knew as Mary Lensfield. She painted a little, and translated children's books. She sat all alone there, staring out toward
Porquerolles where the steamers passed. She was a queer type,
striking without being beautiful. She was extremely thin and pale,

with flaming hair and the sort of greenish eyes which frequently go with pale skin and hair that is naturally red. I had known her off and on for quite a time, but never very well. I'm not sure anybody knew her very well. She was friendly enough, but never very gay, and apparently not very strong. She said hello in an absent-minded sort of way. I dived from the top of a rock. In making the turn of the cove, I swam a bit too close to another rock just under water, and scraped my shoulder on the barnacles. It wasn't scraped badly, but when I came out there was a streak of bright, shiny blood glistening on my wet shoulder.

"You've cut yourself," said the girl. I sat down beside her, twisting my head to look at the scratch, and said, "It doesn't amount to much. I doubt if I'll need to put iodine on it." I asked her how her work was going. She was translating some of Comtesse de Segur's juveniles. When she made no answer, I glanced at her. She had bent closer and was staring with wide, dilated eyes at the scarlet abrasion. Then she jerked convulsively toward me, and her teeth were in my shoulder, and she was sucking like a leech there—not like a leech either, but more like a greedy half-grown kitten with sharp-pointed teeth. It hurt sharply, but astonishment held me motionless for a second, and then a mixture of surprise, curiosity, and sheer amazement made me grit my own teeth and let it ride. She had deepened the abrasion, and was literally drinking blood! I am properly ashamed of it, but I sat there tense, perversely fascinated, and let her slake her thirst.

A big truck roared past on the Corniche road above us, behind the trees, and it was this noise, I think, that brought her out of it. She slumped back, terrified, her nerves torn to pieces, sobbing, shaking all over, with her face buried in her hands. I said nothing. I had been frightened too by the glimpse of her smeared, red mouth. But I said nothing. When she quieted a little and realized that I was silent, she said,

"Seabrook, what shall I do? Shall I have myself locked up? Shall I kill myself? Or what?"

Everything I'd ever known about the girl had been racing in that silence through my mind, and some of the things, which had seemed pointless when they occurred, seemed now to have a possible new significance. I'd met her first a couple of years before at a party in Bob Chanler's weird house, off Gramercy Park, in New York. She lived in Brooklyn Heights, and seldom came to Manhattan, but Bob wanted to paint her portrait, so she returned several subsequent times to his house, which I was then frequenting, and once or twice stayed over in the evening. On one of the evenings a queer episode had occurred. Bob never went in deeply for the esoteric, in fact had a slight contempt for it, but his friend Stanislaus Ivorsky was a student of the occult, and had brought there a certain Madame Ludovescu, who claimed to possess supernormal powers, physical rather than psychic, including the ability to heal cuts and burns, and to staunch the flow of blood. She was a dowdy woman, dressed pretentiously—velvet, a big picture hat, long, black kid gloves and bangles. Stanislaus had brought a medical friend to the party, and the doctor had consented to be the subject for the blood-staunching experiment, but Bob, whose skepticism was mixed with a vast, Gargantuan curiosity and childish egoism, roared,

"I want to be the goat in this miracle!"

So it was agreed. The doctor got a saucer, turned back the sleeve from Bob's left wrist, held it over the saucer, dabbed the skin with alcohol and nicked the transverse superficial vein with a small scalpel. It wasn't any pinprick either. The blood trickled in a slight but steady stream, as we all crowded round the table. Madame Ludovescu bent her head, as if nearsightedly studying the puncture, wiping her unrouged lips meanwhile with a handkerchief, which she kept held to her mouth for an appreciable moment. I guess she thought we had our attention safely fixed on Bob's wrist. Then she pressed her lips tight to the wound, seemed to breathe upon it precisely as I had seen Hindu fakirs do. We heard a faint mumbling as if of muttered prayer or incantation,

Edvard Munch, *Vampire*, etching, 1894. (Timm, *The Graphic Art of Edvard Munch*)

and the muscles of her mouth were moving. It took fully a minute or more, and seemed longer. Then she raised her head, saying, "It has ceased. You can see."

It was then the queer interruption had occurred which now brought the whole thing back to me in memory. The woman's mouth and cheek were reddened, a tiny thread of scarlet trickled from the corner of her mouth, and as she lifted her face, saying, "It has ceased," Mary Lensfield, who had been watching with the rest of us, moaned and keeled over in a dead faint. "It's nothing serious," said the doctor in a moment, lifting her to a couch. "She'll come round in a minute or two. The sight of any blood sometimes affects people that way." And she did, and we thought nothing more of it.

The flow from Chanler's wrist had ceased completely, and the others had exclaimed now in awe and admiration, when Bob had shouted,

"Didn't you see? Prayers my eye! She licked it like a puppy! I licked it myself just now, and that's what's caught her cold! I might as well have been licking green persimmons! Make her give you that handkerchief, if she dares. You'll find it stinks of tannic acid, and probably Adrenalin. Hey, Paul! Give this bitch ten dollars and a drink of gin, and throw her out!"

I'd forgotten all about the Rumanian woman and her cheap tricks. It was only the memory now of how Mary Lensfield had moaned, shuddered, and dropped to the floor that brought the episode flashing back. And it made me remember another episode which had occurred more recently at Antibes. It had a queer angle too, which had seemed merely a casual coincidence at the time. The Lensfield girl had shared a room there with a friend, also an American girl, and the two had seemed to be inseparable. The friendship had suddenly been broken for reasons that nobody knew. The girl had moved to another *pension*. And I now sharply recalled that at the time of the quarrel, or of whatever had happened, this second girl had cut herself with an ice pick, or said she had. At Chanler's, Mary Lensfield had gone to pieces and fainted at the sight of blood on another woman's lips. In this second instance, I began to wonder if there had been an accident with an ice pick, and if so, whose lips might afterward have been stained.

For here was Mary Lensfield now, her own pallid mouth smeared with blood—afraid that she was going mad. I said, "Has it ever happened to you before?"

She said, "I was visiting a friend at Vassar. She cut herself on broken glass. I helped bandage it. She slept soundly that night. I had persuaded her to take a triple bromide. I wanted to kill myself next morning."

I said, "Was it something like that when you had the quarrel, if it was a quarrel, with that girl—I don't recall her name—at Antibes a couple of years ago?"

"Yes," she said, "it's as bad as that. *I am what you think.* It has happened more than once."

I said, "What did you mean by saying you were 'what I think'? I don't think anything except that you're a sick girl who ought to see a doctor."

And then it was she, mind you, who whispered the old, ugly word "vampire." While she talked on now, as if a floodgate were opened, spilling out her sick and tortured soul, I think I realized for the first time a truth which has never been clearly stated, so far as I know, by any body: that the persistence and bolstering of superstition not only fosters fear (and cruelty) in the public mass mind, but also helps spawn and foster the very horrors it attacks. Let me explain exactly what I mean, with reference to the vampire. The unsuperstitious individual who becomes afflicted with this craving for blood either sees a doctor or goes out and commits crimes easily dealt with by the police. Which of those two simple things he does depends simply on his moral balance. But the superstitious man or woman, so afflicted and superstition-ridden besides, reacts entirely differently. If he, or she, is a morally bad type, the next step is "Ooooooooh! I'm a vampire!" or "Wooow! I'm a werewolf! I'm superman now, and nothing but a silver bullet or a stake driven through my heart can stop me! So I'll go to town!" He or she, superstition-ridden, but with a moral conscience, as in the case of the wretched young lady with whom I was now talking, says, "Woe is me! I have become a horrible and awful thing. And I can do nothing to resist it. Better I were dead! Better I had never been born!"

It made me sick to learn, as we sat there and talked, of how this otherwise mentally normal girl, afflicted with blood-craving and inclined toward a belief in heaven and hell inherited from overly religious parents, had wallowed in the obsessed reading of everything she could find on the subject of vampires. There's a vast bibliography, containing lots of honest stuff of course, but cluttered with learned, stupid, pious, horrid fantasy and supernatural doctrine, written by professors, esoterics, cultists, crack-brained preachers and priests, including also certain celebrated modern doctors of theology. She had read them all absorbedly, and in three fourths of the medieval stuff she had found that among the marks of the female vampire were pallor, thinness to the point of emaciation, red hair, and green eyes! Pure, crazy coincidence! Yet you can imagine how she must have stared in her own mirror. She knew, since the coincidence hadn't driven her completely crazy—though it might easily have done so in conjunction with her secret knowledge of her own blood lust— that she'd never been dead and buried, and that she didn't crawl back at night to sleep in a vault or coffin like Lady Vere or Dracula. But that hadn't helped her any, because part of the learned, superstitious hogwash on the "nature of vampires" explains that if you're bitten by one (and this, of course, can occur in your sleep without your knowing it), you're in danger of becoming one yourself, before you die, in your own natural lifetime—

just as a person bitten by a mad dog is in danger of hydrophobia. She asked me whether I believed what all those learned writers did, or whether I thought she was crazy.

I gradually realized that she was not only pouring out her fears to me, but was close on the edge of confessing her complete belief in all that horrid nonsense, "confessing" herself to be of that unholy kin.

And I realized too as we sat there in the twilight that if this same misadventure had happened in this same Mediterranean cove a couple of hundred years before instead of in the twentieth century, not only would the man have fled in terror and reported her to the ecclesiastical authorities, but the girl would have made a full confession, voluntarily without need of any torture, that she was a true vampire. She would have died believing in the justice of her condemnation, and would have been buried at a crossroads with a stake driven through her heart. I came out of those reflections angry—but not at her.

I said, "For Christ's sake, forget all that crazy nonsense. *You're* not crazy, but all those goddamned supernaturalists are as crazy as hell. Agreed, you're a 'vampire' if you insist on calling it that—you're a sort of baby vampire who *could* grow up into a monster, but you're not a supernaturally doomed creature, and you're not a criminal either, yet. You're not even wicked, yet. You're just an ill, hallucinated girl, and you ought to see a doctor. See a doctor first, and get him to find you a good psychiatrist, one who is an M.D. too . . . here or back home in America."

My advice was sound enough, but it came too late. Miss Lensfield followed it literally, returned to America, and put herself in the hands of doctors, specialists. She never succumbed again to her tragic craving, but within a year she was dead— of pernicious anemia. The red blood cells in her body, the erythrocytes, had been disintegrating. Her whole chemical organism had been involved in a terrific struggle to balance itself and survive, and it had been discovered too late for transfusion or anything to save her. This desperate physiological maladjustment had been at the bottom of her mental maladjustment, of her awful craving, and she'd been no more morally responsible for her monstrous yearnings than midgets, dwarfs, and giants (innocent victims of their pineal and thyroid glands) are for their monstrous shapes. It all makes part of the picture tied up with the now commonplace certainty discovered in the twentieth-century merging of clinical medicine and psychiatry, that anomalies in the realm of psychology and behavior are often traceable to chemical-organic causes.

Edward Gorey, drawing, 1973.

15

Vampires in
Modern Greece

From Montague Summers, *The Vampire in Europe*, London, Routledge and Kegan Paul, 1928; reprint Hyde Park, N.Y., University Books, Inc., 1968

Montague Summers (1880–1948), English expert on demonology, wrote *The History of Witchcraft and Demonology* (1926), *The Geography of Witchcraft* (1927), *The Vampire, His Kith and Kin* (1928), *The Gothic Quest* (1938), and *A Gothic Bibliography* (1940); he also edited many Gothic novels.

The following extracts indicate the variety of vampiric data that Summers assembled relating to Greece, especially during his visits in 1906 and 1907 to Crete and the so-called "vampire island" of Santorini.

Even to-day the island of Santorini, the most southerly of the Cyclades, is notorious for its vampires, and I myself, when I visited it in 1906–07 heard many a gruesome legend of vampire events which were said to have taken place there quite recently. (p. 220)

As we say "to carry coals to Newcastle", so in Greece at the present day they talk of "sending vampires to Santorini." (p. 223)

In Greece one still hears that the island of Hydra was "once upon a time" infested by vampires, but a zealous primate by his prayers and exorcisms banished them all to Therasia in the Santorini group, and here they walk up and down all night long, since they are unable to cross the salt water to seek their prey. (p. 267)

Summers presents in translation numerous passages from the book Relation de l'Isle de Saint-erini *(Paris, 1657) by the Jesuit priest Father François Richard; among them is this one:*

The following facts entirely persuade me that these cases are instances of a particular kind of demoniacal possession. When the Greeks are molested and disturbed by these monsters, their priests, having applied to the Bishop for formal permission assemble on a Saturday, since they believe that on no other day will they find in the grave the body which serves as a retreat and a covert for the demon. They then recite certain prayers, after which they exhume the body of the person who is suspected of having become a *vrykolakas*. And when they find it whole, fresh and gorged with new blood, they take it for certain that it was serving as an instrument of the Devil. Therefore they conjure the foul spirit with many holy exorcisms to leave this body, and they do not cease to continue their prayers and ceremonies until the Devil has departed, and as he departs the body begins rapidly to decompose, little by little to lose its colour and plumpness, and finally it is left a ghastly and stinking mass of corrupted matter. It was only a few years ago in this very city that there was a remarkable instance of this in the case of a maiden named Caliste, the daughter of a Greek priest. The body of this maid being found whole and entire was exorcized by a Greek priest, who was believed to be orthodox, and in the presence of all the assistants it began to deflate and decay, suddenly falling to putrefaction and emitting so fetid and noisome a stench that nobody could remain in the Church. So they buried the thing immediately, after which the girl never again appeared. (pp. 230–31)

The teaching of the Orthodox Church also had great influence in its effect upon the modern tradition of the Vampire in Greece.

It has already been shown at some length that the incorruptibility of the body of any person bound by a curse, were that curse parental or ecclesiastical, was established as a definite doctrine, and the offender who passed away under the ban of excommunication was doomed to remain whole and undissolved after death until the body was set free by an official and equipollent absolution being pronounced over it and the sentence of excommunication thus revoked. . . .

Very ample accounts of the tradition of the Vampire in Greece and of the various methods which were practised by the Greeks in order to secure themselves against and rid themselves of these demoniacal pests are to be found in many excellent writers of the seventeenth century. To-day the Vampire still ravages the villages, and the tale of his exploits may often be heard from the peasants, but as may be readily supposed in modern times cases of vampirism are much less common than they were two hundred, or even fifty years ago, and it is comparatively rarely that a stranger may witness the traditional ceremonies by which a district rids itself of a vampire, concluding the cremation of the body. This is not to say that the practice is in any way discontinued or out of date, but such an operation constitutes a breach of the law and therefore must necessarily be conducted under conditions of strictest secrecy. (pp. 220–21)

The Slavonic method employed to dispose of a vampire was to drive at one blow a stake of aspen or of whitethorn through the heart. The Greeks knew a yet securer way. Some tradition of the ancient manner of incinerating the dead in old Hellas lingered, although not in actual practise. When more modern descendants were faced by a terrible and threatening danger they remembered the antique practice which by ensuring the immediate and complete dissolution of the body, would at once put an end to all connexion between the living and the deceased, who after cremation would no longer be able to return and molest them. Nor does it appear that in these extreme cases their remedy encountered any serious ecclesiastical opposition. The people argued that since the Christian rite had proved to a certain extent ineffectual, for the vampire returned from his grave, it was surely permissible to employ other and more drastic measures, even if such might be tainted with heathenism. In the case of an epidemic or a plague it was allowable to burn the bodies lest the pestilence should be spread. Assuredly it was equally allowable to burn the body of a monster who would sparge the infection of vampirism. And this argument was tacitly conceded. Indeed, the priests in the remoter villages and lone country districts would, no doubt, be as anxious as the people to rid themselves of the *vrykolakas*, and almost any means would be considered legitimate and approved. When cases came to the ears of a Bishop, they met with some pretty severe censure, especially in later days. But it was quite within the power of a Bishop to give leave for the body of a vampire to be exhumed and burned. Just as now, if exceptional circumstances demand it, a Bishop may permit cremation. The Greeks judged that those of the dead who returned and who suffered from incorruptibility must be helped, and the one certain way in which dissolution which secured them rest and repose could most certainly be effected was cremation. Not a measure to be adopted lightly, but nevertheless a measure which, if inevitable, was an act of charity both to the living and to the dead. (pp. 257–58)

16

A Russian Vampire

From W. R. S. Ralston's *Songs of the Russian People* based on Alexander Afansief's *Poeticheskija Vozzryzhenija Slavjan na Prirodu (Poetic Views of the Slavs about Nature)*, 3 vols., Moscow, 1865–69.

A peasant was driving past a grave-yard, after it had grown dark. After him came running a stranger, dressed in a red shirt and a new jacket, who cried,

"Stop! take me as your companion."

"Pray take a seat."

They enter a village, drive up to this and that house. Though the gates are wide open, yet the stranger says, "Shut tight!" for on those gates crosses have been branded. They drive on to the very last house; the gates are barred, and from them hangs a padlock weighing a score of pounds; but there is no cross there, and the gates open of their own accord.

They go into the house; there on the bench lie two sleepers —an old man and a lad. The stranger takes a pail, places it near the youth, and strikes him on the back; immediately the back opens, and forth flows rosy blood. The stranger fills the pail full, and drinks it dry. Then he fills another pail with blood from the old man, slakes his brutal thirst, and says to the peasant:

"It begins to grow light! let us go back to my dwelling."

In a twinkling they found themselves at the grave-yard. The

vampire would have clasped the peasant in its arms, but luckily for him the cocks began to crow, and the corpse disappeared. The next morning, when folks came and looked, the old man and the lad were both dead.

17

Another Russian Vampire

From Elena (Helena) Hahn Petrovna Blavatsky, *Isis Unveiled*,
1877

Madame Blavatsky—born in Russia, 1831; died in America, 1891—is
regarded by some as "traveler, theosophist, editor," and by others as
"one of the most accomplished, ingenious and interesting charlatans of
history." In 1875, she founded the Theosophical Society, which included among its aims the investigation of "the unexplained laws of
nature and the powers latent in man."

Isis Unveiled, in part a history of Eastern occultism and in part a
history of the author's extraordinary adventures, was occasionally dic-
tated to Madame by "mysterious intelligences." The book received
widespread attention both here and abroad.

About the beginning of the present century, there occurred in
Russia, one of the most frightful cases of Vampirism on record.
The governor of the Province Tch——was a man of about sixty
years, of a malicious, tyrannical, cruel, and jealous disposition.
Clothed with despotic authority, he exercised it without stint, as
his brutal instincts prompted. He fell in love with the pretty
daughter of a subordinate official. Although the girl was betrothed
to a young man whom she loved, the tyrant forced her father to
consent to his having her marry him; and the poor victim, despite
her despair, became his wife. His jealous disposition exhibited
itself. He beat her, confined her to her room for weeks together,
and prevented her seeing anyone except in his presence. He finally

Caspar David Friedrich's painting, *Abbey in the Oak Forest*, evokes the haunting mood of the settings of many vampire tales from the early 19th century on. (Verwaltung der Staatlichen Schlösser und Garten, Berlin)

fell sick and died. Finding his end approaching, he made her swear never to marry again; and with fearful oaths threatened that, in case she did, he would return from his grave and kill her. He was buried in the cemetery across the river, and the young widow experienced no further annoyance, until, nature getting the better of her fears, she listened to the importunities of her former lover, and they were again betrothed.

On the night of the customary betrothal-feast, when all had returned, the old mansion was aroused by shrieks proceeding from her room. The doors were burst open and the unhappy woman was found lying on her bed in a swoon. At the same time a carriage was heard rumbling out of the courtyard. Her body was found to be black and blue in places, as from the effect of pinches, and from a slight puncture on her neck drops of blood were oozing. Upon recovering she stated that her deceased husband had suddenly entered her room, appearing exactly as in life, with the exception of a dreadful pallor; that he had upbraided her for her inconstancy, and then beaten and pinched her most cruelly. Her story was disbelieved; but the next morning the guard stationed at the other end of the bridge which spans the river, reported that, just before midnight, a black coach and six had driven furiously past them, towards the town, without answering their challenge.

The new governor, who disbelieved the story of the apparition, took nevertheless the precaution of doubling the guards across the bridge. The same thing happened, however, night after night; the soldiers declaring that the toll-bar at their station near the bridge would rise of itself, and the spectral equipage sweep by them despite their efforts to stop it. At the same time every night the coach would rumble into the courtyard of the house; the watchers, including the widow's family, and the servants, would be thrown into a heavy sleep, and every morning the young victim would be found bruised, bleeding and swooning as before. The town was thrown into consternation. The physicians had no explanation to offer; priests came to pass the night in prayer, but as midnight approached, all would be seized with the terrible lethargy. Finally, the archbishop of the province came, and performed the ceremony of exorcism in person, but the following morning the governor's widow was found worse than ever. She was now brought to death's door.

The governor was now driven to take the severest measures to stop the ever-increasing panic in the town. He stationed fifty Cossacks along the bridge, with orders to stop the spectre-carriage at all hazards. Promptly at the usual hour, it was heard and seen approaching from the direction of the cemetery. The officer of the guard, and a priest bearing a crucifix, planted themselves in front of the toll-bar, and together shouted: "In the name of God and the Czar, who goes there?" Out of the coach window was thrust a well-remembered head, and a familiar voice responded: "The Privy Councillor of State and Governor C——!" At the same moment, the officer, the priest, and the soldiers were flung aside as by an electric shock, and the ghostly equipage passed by them, before they could recover breath.

The archbishop then resolved as a last expedient to resort to the time-honoured plan of exhuming the body, and pinning it to the earth with an oaken stake driven through its heart. This was done with great religious ceremony in the presence of the whole populace. The story is that the body was found gorged with blood, and with red cheeks and lips. At the instant that the first blow was struck upon the stake, a groan issued from the corpse, and a jet of blood spurted high in the air. The archbishop pronounced the usual exorcism, the body was re-interred, and from that time no more was heard of the Vampire.

18

Five Romanian Vampires

The first three accounts below are from the Romanian periodical of peasant art and literature, *Ion Creanga*, which for years was edited by Tudor Pamfile, one of the most competent folklorists Romania has ever had. The stories in *Ion Creanga* were taken down by careful observers, and were published as nearly as possible in the peasants' own words. Based on Summers' translation.

I.   STORY FROM BOTOSANI

Published in Ion Creanga, *Vol. V, p. 11*

A girl and a young man were once in love, but the youth died and became a vampire. The girl knew nothing of this. She happened to be alone in her parents' house, and she put out all the lights and went to bed as usual. Now vampires can enter into empty houses or into unclean houses, but the girl's house was clean and holy, so he could not come in. Instead of coming in he called at the window, speaking in the same tone and using the same words as he did when alive. "Stupid girl, come with me," he said, and took her hand and led her, undressed as she was, to his tomb. "Go in," he said. "No, friend, I'm afraid," she said. He went in first, and called, "Come more quickly." "Wait," she said, "I've lost my beads. They must have fallen hereabouts." And she ran and ran until she saw a house with a light. She went in and found a man called Avram lying dead on a bench. She drew the bolts of the door and lay down in hiding behind the oven. The vampire came after her with true vampire persistency. He knocked at the window, saying "Avram, open the door." Avram was himself a vampire, and was going to obey and open the door. But the hen saw what was happening, and said to the cock, "Crow, so as to save the poor girl." "No, you crow. It is not my turn." So the hen crowed quickly before Avram could get to the door, and the girl escaped, because she was clean and holy, and vampires do not easily get hold of clean souls.

II. STORY FROM SIRET

Published in Ion Creanga, *Vol. VI, p. 17*

An old man with some soldiers was driving in a cart in Transylvania, trying to find where he could get some hay. Night came on during their journey, so they stopped at a lonely house in a plain. The woman of the house received them, put maize porridge (mămăligă) and milk on the table for them, and then went away. The soldiers ate the maize porridge, and after their meal looked for the old woman to thank her, but were unable to find her. Climbing up to the attic to see if she was there, they found seven bodies lying down, one of which was the woman's. They were frightened and fled, and, as they looked back, they saw seven little lights descending on the house. These were the souls of the vampires. Had the soldiers turned the bodies with their faces downwards, the souls would never have been able to enter the bodies again.

III. STORY FROM VAGUILESTI

Recorded by N. I. Dumitrascu; and published in Ion Creanga, *Vol. VII (1914), p. 165*

In Vaguilesti, in Mehedinti, there was a peasant Dimitriu Vaideanu, of Transylvanian origin, who had married a wife in Vaguilesti and settled there. His children died one after the other; seven died within a few months of birth, and some bigger children had died as well. People began to wonder what the cause of all this could be. They took council together, and resolved to take a white horse to the cemetery one night, and see if it would pass over all the graves of the wife's relations. This they did, and the horse jumped over all the graves, until it came to the grave of the mother-in-law, Joana Marta, who had been a witch, renowned far and wide. Then the horse stood still, beating the earth with its feet, neighing, and snorting, unable to step over the grave. Probably there was something unholy there. At night Dimitriu and his son took candles and went to dig up the grave. They were seized with horror at what they saw. There she was, sitting like a Turk, with long hair falling over her face, with all her skin red, and with fingernails frightfully long. They got together brushwood, shavings, and bits of old crosses, they poured wine on her, they put in straw, and set fire to the whole. Then they shovelled the earth back and went home.

IV.

Story from Albata, in the Petesht region, along the Arges River; recorded in 1937, and preserved in the archives of the Institute of Folklore, Bucharest. My translation.

Despite its brevity, this hitherto unpublished tale which I discovered in the archives is interesting on several counts. The events take place near the real Castle Dracula; the report indicates that educated persons as well as peasants believe in vampires; the vampire described herein attacked members of his own family;

and his posture in the grave—leaning on his elbows—is an arrogant one even for a vampire.

The priest Marinescu from the Joitsa Ilfore reported that a colleague in theology believed in the following story: A villager from Albata in Bucharest died and when he was brought back to his village, about three other persons from this same family died. And the people were obliged to dig up the grave of the vampire and they found him leaning on his elbows in the coffin and they plunged a knife into his heart.

V.

Folktale preserved in the archives of the Institute of Folklore, Bucharest

This story, which I turned up in 1969 while doing research in Romania on the historical Prince Dracula, is published here for the first time. It proves beyond doubt that "love conquers all"—even vampirism.

Once there was an emperor who had a daughter. The emperor was obliged to choose the best and most handsome soldiers to guard himself and his country. At the main entrance of his palace was a soldier who was very handsome and very attractive.

The emperor's daughter, who was fourteen or fifteen years old, usually went out through the main entrance. This soldier talked often with her there and the girl fell in love with the soldier.

The soldier brought candy to this little girl and the girl received the candy with pleasure and did not think about the future.

The emperor saw the soldier and he dismissed him from his post and replaced him with another. Next day the emperor's daughter came to see the soldier, but he was not there. She was very sad, became very sick, and finally died. The emperor entombed her in a coffin in a church, and ordered that this dead girl be well guarded.

But what happened? This girl became a vampire, and she ate all the soldiers who came into the church to guard her body. She ate these soldiers at night.

In time she ate almost one hundred soldiers, more exactly ninety-nine. Everyone heard about it, and because of this, no one wanted to enter the church, especially soldiers. The emperor had difficulty finding a soldier to act as watchman.

The emperor remembered the first soldier and decided that it would be better if he were to enter the church to guard her coffin.

When the soldier heard about it, he became dejected because he was afraid. But the emperor gave him clothes, food, money, and arms.

Passing over the bridge, an old beggar saw this soldier as he was going towards the church. She asked the soldier to give her money. The soldier gave some money to her. She said, "I think that you are worried. What happened to you?" The soldier told her the entire story and concluded, "Tomorrow I will be dead."

"Why?" she asked. He told the story to her again and ended, "Now it is my turn. I will be eaten by her." "I can give you a piece of advice," said the beggar. "Before twelve o'clock, five minutes before, you must go to the priest's altar and hide behind the icon. You must remain there for a while. She will look for you. But she will not be able to find you and after that when she cannot find you in the church, she will return to her coffin."

The soldier did all this.

The vampire girl came out and searched vainly for him, right and left. When the cock crowed, she went back into her coffin. The emperor was sure that this soldier was dead. Whereas he had escaped death. The emperor sent five soldiers to bury him. When these soldiers came there, they were very surprised, because they saw him alive. The emperor decided to send this same soldier the next day. The soldier got food, clothes and arms again. He again crossed the bridge and again saw the beggar. The beggar again asked for one cent. He gave it to her. She gave him different advice, "This time fifteen minutes before twelve you must go to the top of the church. The vampire will look for you at the altar and everywhere. When she does not find you in the church or at the altar, she will return to her coffin." So it happened.

The girl cried, "I am the emperor's daughter. I am hungry. I want to eat something." She looked for him in the church but not on the top. The cock crowed and she went back to her coffin.

Next morning the emperor sent five men to bury the soldier. But the soldier was all right.

Next night the emperor sent him again to the church. He gave him more money, clothes and arms. The soldier crossed the bridge and met the beggar. "My dear, why are you so upset?" she asked. He replied, "Tomorrow I will be dead." And she advised him:

"Two minutes before 12 o'clock, you must sleep close to the coffin of the girl and when she comes out she will go out the window and she will look for you outside, everywhere, because she has not eaten for two days and two nights. She is very hungry. You must immediately enter her coffin. And when she returns, she will find you there in the coffin." Here is what happened: She looked for him outside, in all the gardens, but she found nothing to eat. Finally, she returned to her coffin before the cock crowed. She wanted to enter her coffin, but she found the soldier inside. She was very surprised when she saw the soldier in her coffin. She was become a real girl again. She recognized him, of course. He again told her stories. Again the soldiers came to bury him, but they saw both the soldier and the girl alive and happy. They returned to the emperor and told him everything.

19

Vampire in Venice

by Lawrence Durrell

From the novel *Balthazar*, New York, E.P. Dutton & Co.,
Inc., 1958

Anglo-Irish author Lawrence Durrell was born on February 27, 1912, in
India. In 1935 he settled in Corfu, where his writing included extensive
correspondence with Henry Miller, who helped Durrell in getting his
first prose work published. Durrell's most famous work is The Alexandria
Quartet. This series of novels—set in Egypt—consists of *Justine* (1957),
Balthazar (1958), *Mountolive* (1959), and *Clea* (1960).

The narrator of the story below is Pursewarden, a writer and one-
time official in the British Foreign Office. It is carnival time in Alexandria, when the citizens wear masks and "all illicit desires [are] sated,"
and Pursewarden is telling of a similar time in Venice when a friend of
his became intimate with a vampiress whose face he never saw. Le Fanu,
it is interesting to note, also uses a gala time to present the vampiric
Madame la Comtesse, and he obscures her face with a mask.

Pursewarden was telling one of his famous stories in that crisp
uninflected French of his which was just a shade too perfect.

"When I was twenty, I went to Venice for the first time at
the invitation of an Italian poet with whom I had been corresponding, Carlo Negroponte. For a middle-class English youth
this was a great experience, to live virtually by candlelight in this
huge tumbledown palazzo on the Grand Canal with a fleet of

gondolas at my disposal—not to mention a huge wardrobe of cloaks lined with silk. Negroponte was generous and spared no effort to entertain a fellow-poet in the best style. He was then about fifty, frail and rather beautiful, like a rare kind of mosquito. He was a prince and a diabolist, and his poetry happily married the influences of Byron and Baudelaire. He went in for cloaks and shoes with buckles and silver walking-sticks and encouraged me to do the same. I felt I was living in a Gothic novel. Never have I written worse poetry.

"That year we went to the carnival together and got separated though we each wore something to distinguish each other by; you know of course that carnival is the one time of the year when vampires walk freely abroad, and those who are wise carry a pig of garlic in their pockets to drive them off—if by chance one were to be encountered. Next morning I went into my host's room and found him lying pale as death in bed, dressed in the white night-shirt with lace cuffs, with a doctor taking his pulse. When the doctor had gone he said: 'I have met the perfect woman, masked; I went home with her and she proved to be a vampire.' Then drawing up his nightshirt he showed me with exhausted pride that his body was covered with great bites, like the marks of a weasel's teeth. He was utterly exhausted but at the same time excited— and frightening to relate, very much in love. 'Until you have experienced it,' he said, 'you have no idea what it is like. To have one's blood sucked in darkness by someone one adores.' His voice broke. 'De Sade could not begin to describe it. I did not see her face, but I had the impression she was fair, of a northern fairness; we met in the dark and separated in the dark. I have only the impression of white teeth, and a voice—never have I heard any woman say the things she says. She is the very lover for whom I have been waiting all these years. I am meeting her again tonight by the marble griffin at the Footpads' Bridge. O my friend, be happy for me. The real world has become more and more mean-ingless to me. Now at last, with this vampire's love, I feel I can

The image of woman as vampire who beckoned man to his doom was a vivid theme in turn-of-the-century Viennese art and literature. In an 1899 issue of *Ver Sacrum*, the Austrian artist Ernst Stöhr illustrated one of his own poems, in which the man exclaims, "My poor life is the price, You drink my heart's blood." (Thomas B. Hess and Linda Nochlin, eds., *Woman as Sex Object*, New York, Newsweek, 1972)

live again, feel again, write again!' He spent all that day at his papers, and at nightfall set off, cloaked, in his gondola. It was not my business to say anything. The next day once more I found him, pale and deathly tired. He had a high fever, and again these terrible bites. But he could not speak of his experience without weeping—tears of love and exhaustion. And it was now that he had begun his great poem which begins—you all know it—

'Lips not on lips, but on each other's wounds
Must suck the envenomed bodies of the loved
And through the tideless blood draw nourishment
To feed the love that feeds upon their deaths. . . .'

"The following week I left for Ravenna where I had some studies to make for a book I was writing and where I stayed two months. I heard nothing from my host, but I got a letter from his sister to say that he was ill with a wasting disease which the doctors could not diagnose and that the family was much worried because he insisted on going out at night in his gondola on journeys of which he would not speak but from which he returned utterly exhausted. I did not know what to reply to this.

"From Ravenna, I went down to Greece and it was not until the following autumn that I returned. I had sent a card to Negroponte saying I hoped to stay with him, but had no reply. As I came down the Grand Canal a funeral was setting off in choppy water, by twilight, with the terrible plumes and emblems of death. I saw that they were coming from the Negroponte Palazzo. I landed and ran to the gates just as the last gondola in the procession was filling up with mourners and priests. I recognized the doctor and joined him in the boat, and as we rowed stiffly across the canal, dashed with spray and blinking at the stabs of lightning, he told me what he knew. Negroponte had died the day before. When they came to lay out the body, they found the bites:

perhaps of some tropical insect? The doctor was vague. 'The only such bites I have seen,' he said, 'were during the plague of Naples when the rats had been at the bodies. They were so bad we had to dust him down with talcum powder before we could let his sister see the body.' "

Pursewarden took a long sip from his glass and went on wickedly. "The story does not end there; for I should tell you how I tried to avenge him, and went myself at night to the Bridge of the Footpads—where according to the gondolier this woman always waited in the shadow. . . . But it is getting late, and anyway, I haven't made up the rest of the story as yet."

There was a good deal of laughter and Athena gave a well-bred shudder, drawing her shawl across her shoulders. Narouz had been listening open-mouthed, with reeling senses, to this recital: he was spellbound. "But," he stammered, "is all this true?" Fresh laughter greeted his question.

"Of course it's true," said Pursewarden severely, and added: "I have never been in Venice in my life."

Edward Gorey, drawing, 1973. "The Count smiled and
walked on, his cloak fluttering in the breeze, casting a bat-
like shadow on the pathway before him. He could see the
graveyard now, the tilted tombstones rising from the earth
like leprous fingers rotting in the moonlight." From "The
Living Dead."

20

The Living Dead

by Robert Bloch

From *The Midnight People,* edited by Peter Haining, New York, Popular Library, 1968, pp. 184–90

Robert Bloch sold his first story—to the magazine *Weird Tales*—when he was seventeen. Later he contributed many stories to *Unknown Worlds,* to *Fantastic,* and to *Strange Stories.* In 1959, he went to Hollywood. One collection of his short stories was made into a film entitled *Torture Garden;* another group formed the basis of the movie *The House That Dripped Blood.*

In "The Living Dead," Bloch brilliantly transforms a war story into a horrific vampire tale.

All day long he rested, while the guns thundered in the village below. Then, in the slanting shadows of the late afternoon, the rumbling echoes faded into the distance and he knew it was over. The American advance had crossed the river. They were gone at last, and it was safe once more.

Above the village, in the crumbling ruins of the great château atop the wooded hillside, Count Barsac emerged from the crypt.

The Count was tall and thin—cadaverously thin, in a manner most hideously appropriate. His face and hands had a waxen pallor; his hair was dark, but not as dark as his eyes and the hollows beneath them. His cloak was black, and the sole touch of colour about his person was the vivid redness of his lips when they curled in a smile.

He was smiling now, in the twilight, for it was time to play the game.

The name of the game was Death, and the Count had played it many times.

He had played it in Paris on the stage of the Grand Guignol; his name had been plain Eric Karon then, but still he'd won a certain renown for his interpretation of bizarre roles. Then the war had come and, with it, his opportunity.

Long before the Germans took Paris, he'd joined their Underground, working long and well. As an actor he'd been invaluable.

And this, of course, was his ultimate reward—to play the supreme role, not on the stage, but in real life. To play without the artifice of spotlights, in true darkness; this was the actor's dream come true. He had even helped to fashion the plot.

"Simplicity itself," he told his German superiors. "Château Barsac has been deserted since the Revolution. None of the peasants from the village dare to venture near it, even in daylight because of the legend. It is said, you see, that the last Count Barsac was a vampire."

And so it was arranged. The short-wave transmitter had been set up in the large crypt beneath the château, with three skilled operators in attendance, working in shifts. And he, "Count Barsac," in charge of the entire operation, as guardian angel. Rather, as guardian demon.

"There is a graveyard on the hillside below," he informed them. "A humble resting place for poor and ignorant people. It contains a single imposing crypt—the ancestral tomb of the Barsacs. We shall open that crypt, remove the remains of the last Count, and allow the villagers to discover that the coffin is empty. They will never dare come near the spot or the château again, because this will prove that the legend is true—Count Barsac is a vampire, and walks once more."

The question came then. "What if there are sceptics? What if someone does not believe?"

And he had his answer ready. "They will believe. For at night I shall walk—I, Count Barsac."

After they saw him in the make-up, wearing the black cloak, there were no more questions. The role was his.

The role was his, and he'd played it well. The Count nodded to himself as he climbed the stairs and entered the roofless foyer of the château, where only a configuration of cobwebs veiled the radiance of the rising moon.

Now, of course, the curtain must come down. If the American advance had swept past the village below, it was time to make one's bow and exit. And that too had been well arranged.

During the German withdrawal another advantageous use had been made of the tomb in the graveyard. A cache of Air Marshal Goering's art treasures now rested safely and undisturbed within the crypt. A truck had been placed in the château. Even now the three wireless operators would be playing new parts— driving the truck down the hillside to the tomb, placing the *objets d'art* in it.

By the time the Count arrived there, everything would be packed. They would then don the stolen American Army uniforms, carry the forged identifications and permits, drive through the lines across the river, and rejoin the German forces at a predesignated spot. Nothing had been left to chance. Some day, when he wrote his memoirs . . .

But there was not time to consider that now. The Count glanced up through the gaping aperture in the ruined roof. The moon was high. It was time to leave.

In a way he hated to go. Where others saw only dust and cobwebs he saw a stage—the setting of his finest performance. Playing a vampire's role had not addicted him to the taste of blood —but as an actor he enjoyed the taste of triumph. And he had triumphed here.

"Parting is such sweet sorrow." Shakespeare's line. Shakespeare, who had written of ghosts and witches, of bloody apparitions. Because Shakespeare knew that his audiences, the stupid masses, believed in such things—just as they still believed today. A great actor could always make them believe.

The Count moved into the shadowy darkness outside the entrance of the château. He started down the pathway towards the beckoning trees.

It was here, amid the trees, that he had come upon Raymond, one evening weeks ago. Raymond had been his most appreciative audience—a stern, dignified, white-haired elderly man, mayor of the village of Barsac. But there had been nothing dignified about the old fool when he'd caught sight of the Count looming up before him out of the night. He'd screamed like a woman and run.

Probably Raymond had been prowling around, intent on poaching, but all that had been forgotten after his encounter in the woods. The mayor was the one to thank for spreading the rumours that the Count was again abroad. He and Clodez, the oafish miller, had then led an armed band to the graveyard and entered the Barsac tomb. What a fright they got when they discovered the Count's coffin open and empty!

The coffin had contained only dust that had been scattered to the winds, but they could not know that. Nor could they know about what had happened to Suzanne.

The Count was passing the banks of the small stream now. Here, on another evening, he'd found the girl—Raymond's daughter, as luck would have it—in an embrace with young Antoine LeFevre, her lover. Antoine's shattered leg had invalided him out of the army, but he ran like a deer when he glimpsed the cloaked and grinning Count. Suzanne had been left behind and that was unfortunate, because it was necessary to dispose of her. Her body had been buried in the woods, beneath great stones, and there was no question of discovery; still, it was a regrettable incident.

In the end, however, everything was for the best. Now silly superstitious Raymond was doubly convinced that the vampire walked. He had seen the creature himself, had seen the empty tomb and the open coffin; his own daughter had disappeared. At his command none dared venture near the graveyard, the woods, or the château beyond.

Poor Raymond! He was not even a mayor any more—his village had been destroyed in the bombardment. Just an ignorant, broken old man, mumbling his idiotic nonsense about the "living dead."

The Count smiled and walked on, his cloak fluttering in the breeze, casting a bat-like shadow on the pathway before him. He could see the graveyard now, the tilted tombstones rising from the earth like leprous fingers rotting in the moonlight. His smile faded; he did not like such thoughts. Perhaps the greatest tribute to his talent as an actor lay in his actual aversion to death, to darkness and what lurked in the night. He hated the sight of blood, had developed within himself an almost claustrophobic dread of the confinement of the crypt.

Yes, it had been a great role, but he was thankful it was ending. It would be good to play the man once more, and cast off the creature he had created.

As he approached the crypt he saw the truck waiting in the shadows. The entrance to the tomb was open, but no sounds issued from it. That meant his colleagues had completed their task of loading and were ready to go. All that remained now was to change his clothing, remove the make-up and depart.

The Count moved to the darkened truck. And then . . .

Then they were upon him, and he felt the tines of the pitchfork bite into his back, and as the flash of lanterns dazzled his eyes he heard the stern command. "Don't move!"

He didn't move. He could only stare as they surrounded him —Antoine, Clodez, Raymond, and the others, a dozen peasants from the village. A dozen armed peasants, glaring at him in mingled rage and fear, holding him at bay.

But how could they dare?

The American Corporal stepped forward. That was the answer, of course—the American Corporal and another man in uniform, armed with a sniper's rifle. They were responsible. He didn't even have to see the riddled corpses of the three short-wave operators piled in the back of the truck to understand what had happened. They'd stumbled on his men while they worked, shot them down, then summoned the villagers.

Now they were jabbering questions at him, in English, of course. He understood English, but he knew better than to reply. "Who are you? Were these men working under your orders? Where were you going with this truck?"

The Count smiled and shook his head. After a while they stopped, as he knew they would.

The Corporal turned to his companion. "Okay," he said. "Let's go." The other man nodded and climbed into the cab of the truck as the motor coughed into life. The Corporal moved to join him, then turned to Raymond.

"We're taking this across the river," he said. "Hang on to our friend here—they'll be sending a guard detail for him within an hour."

Raymond nodded.

The truck drove off into the darkness.

And as it was dark now—the moon had vanished behind a cloud. The Count's smile vanished, too, as he glanced around at his captors. A rabble of stupid clods, surly and ignorant. But armed. No chance of escaping. And they kept staring at him, and mumbling.

"Take him into the tomb."

It was Raymond who spoke, and they obeyed, prodding their captive forward with pitchforks. That was when the Count recognised the first faint ray of hope. For they prodded him most gingerly, no man coming close, and when he glared at them their eyes dropped.

They were putting him in the crypt because they were afraid of him. Now the Americans were gone, they feared him once more—feared his presence and his power. After all, in their eyes he was a vampire—he might turn into a bat and vanish entirely. So they wanted him in the tomb for safekeeping.

The Count shrugged, smiled his most sinister smile, and bared his teeth. They shrank back as he entered the doorway. He turned and, on impulse, furled his cape. It was an instinctive final gesture, in keeping with his role—and it provoked the appropriate response. They moaned, and old Raymond crossed himself. It was better, in a way, than any applause.

In the darkness of the crypt the Count permitted himself to relax a trifle. He was off stage now. A pity he'd not been able to make his exit the way he'd planned, but such were the fortunes of war. Soon he'd be taken to the American headquarters and interrogated. Undoubtedly there would be some unpleasant moments, but the worst that could befall him was a few months in a prison camp. And even the Americans must bow to him in appreciation when they heard the story of his masterful deception.

It was dark in the crypt, and musty. The Count moved about restlessly. His knee grazed the edge of the empty coffin set on a trestle in the tomb. He shuddered involuntarily, loosening his cape at the throat. It would be good to remove it, good to be out of here, good to shed the role of vampire forever. He'd played it well, but now he was anxious to be gone.

There was a mumbling audible from outside, mingled with another and less identifiable noise—a scraping sound. The Count moved to the closed door of the crypt and listened intently; but now there was only silence.

What were the fools doing out there? He wished the Americans would hurry back. It was too hot in here. And why the sudden silence?

Perhaps they'd gone.

Yes. That was it. The Americans had told them to wait and guard him, but they were afraid. They really believed he was a vampire—old Raymond had convinced them of that. So they'd run off. They'd run off, and he was free, he could escape now . . .

So the Count opened the door.

And he saw them then, saw them standing and waiting, old Raymond staring sternly for a moment before he moved forward. He was holding something in his hand, and the Count recognised it, remembering the scraping sound that he'd heard.

It was a long wooden stake with a sharp point.

Then he opened his mouth to scream, telling them it was only a trick, he was no vampire, they were a pack of superstitious fools . . .

But all the while they bore him back into the crypt, lifting him up and thrusting him into the open coffin, holding him there as the grim-faced Raymond raised the pointed stake above his heart.

It was only when the stake came down that he realised there's such a thing as playing a role too well.

21

The Drifting Snow

by Stephen Grendon

(pseudonym for August William Derleth)

From *The Midnight People*, edited by Peter Haining, New York, Popular Library, 1968, pp. 95–105

Born on February 24, 1909, in Sauk City, Wisconsin, Derleth began writing at age thirteen and was publishing by age fifteen. His output consisted of almost a hundred long and short titles each year. He was made a Guggenheim fellow in 1938, edited some dozen anthologies of supernatural and science-fiction stories, and was regarded as a leading authority on regionalism in American literature.

In the following story, as in Bram Stoker's "Dracula's Guest," it becomes clear that no extreme of weather can keep a vampire from his appointed rounds.

Aunt Mary's advancing footsteps halted suddenly, short of the table, and Clodetta turned to see what was keeping her. She was standing very rigidly, her eyes fixed upon the French windows just opposite the door through which she had entered, her cane held stiffly before her.

Clodetta shot a quick glance across the table towards her husband, whose attention had also been drawn to his aunt; his face vouchsafed her nothing. She turned again to find that the old lady had transferred her gaze to her, regarding her stonily and in silence. Clodetta felt uncomfortable.

"Who withdrew the curtains from the west windows?"

Clodetta flushed, remembering. "I did, Aunt. I'm sorry. I forgot about your not wanting them drawn away."

The old lady made an odd grunting sound, shifting her gaze once again to the French windows. She made a barely perceptible movement, and Lisa ran forward from the shadow of the hall, where she had been regarding the two at table with stern disapproval. The servant went directly to the west windows and drew the curtains.

Aunt Mary came slowly to the table and took her place at its head. She put her cane against the side of her chair, pulled at the chain about her neck so that her lorgnette lay in her lap, and looked from Clodetta to her nephew, Ernest.

Then she fixed her gaze on the empty chair at the foot of the table, and spoke without seeming to see the two beside her.

"I told both of you that none of the curtains over the west windows was to be withdrawn after sundown, and you must have noticed that none of those windows has been for one instant uncovered at night. I took especial care to put you in rooms facing east, and the sitting-room is also in the east."

"I'm sure Clodetta didn't mean to go against your wishes, Aunt Mary," said Ernest abruptly.

"No, of course not, Aunt."

The old lady raised her eyebrows, and went on impassively. "I didn't think it wise to explain why I made such a request. I'm not going to explain. But I do want to say that there is a very definite danger in drawing away the curtains. Ernest has heard that before, but you, Clodetta, have not."

Clodetta shot a startled glance at her husband.

The old lady caught it, and said, "It's all very well to believe that my mind's wandering or that I'm getting eccentric, but I shouldn't advise you to be satisfied with that."

A young man came suddenly into the room and made for the seat at the foot of the table, into which he flung himself with an almost inaudible greeting to the other three.

"Late again, Henry," said the old lady.

Henry mumbled something and began hurriedly to eat. The old lady sighed, and began presently to eat also, whereupon Clodetta and Ernest did likewise. The old servant, who had continued to linger behind Aunt Mary's chair, now withdrew, not without a scornful glance at Henry.

Clodetta looked up after a while and ventured to speak, "You aren't as isolated as I thought you might be up here, Aunt Mary."

"We aren't, my dear, what with telephones and cars and all. But only twenty years ago it was quite a different thing, I can tell you." She smiled reminiscently and looked at Ernest. "Your grandfather was living then, and many's the time he was snowbound with no way to let anybody know."

"Down in Chicago when they speak of 'up north' or the 'Wisconsin woods' it seems very far away," said Clodetta.

"Well, it *is* far away," put in Henry abruptly. "And, Aunt, I hope you've made some provision in case we're locked in here for a day or two. It looks like snow outside, and the radio says a blizzard's coming."

The old lady grunted and looked at him. "Ha, Henry—you're overly concerned, it seems to me. I'm afraid you've been regretting this trip ever since you set foot in my house. If you're worrying about a snowstorm, I can have Sam drive you down to Wausau, and you can be in Chicago tomorrow."

"Of course not."

Silence fell, and presently the old lady called gently, "Lisa," and the servant came into the room to help her from her chair, though, as Clodetta had previously said to her husband, "She didn't need help."

From the doorway, Aunt Mary bade them all goodnight, looking impressively formidable with her cane in one hand and her unopened lorgnette in the other, and vanished into the dusk of the hall, from which her receding footsteps sounded together with those of the servant, who was seldom seen away from her. These two were alone in the house most of the time, and only very brief periods when the old lady had up her nephew Ernest, "Dear John's boy," or Henry, of whose father the old lady never spoke, helped to relieve the pleasant somnolence of their quiet lives. Sam, who usually slept in the garage, did not count.

Clodetta looked nervously at her husband, but it was Henry who said what was uppermost in their thoughts.

"I think she's losing her mind," he declared matter-of-factly. Cutting off Clodetta's protest on her lips, he got up and went into the sitting-room, from which came presently the strains of music from the radio.

Clodetta fingered her spoon idly and finally said, "I do think she is a little queer, Ernest."

Ernest smiled tolerantly. "No, I don't think so. I've an idea why she keeps the west windows covered. My grandfather died out there—he was overcome by the cold one night, and froze on the slope of the hill. I don't rightly know how it happened—I was away at the time. I suppose she doesn't like to be reminded of it."

"But where's the danger she spoke of, then?"

He shrugged. "Perhaps it lies in her—she might be affected and affect us in turn." He paused for an instant, and finally added, "I suppose she *does* seem a little strange to you—but she was like that as long as I can remember; next time you come, you'll be used to it."

Clodetta looked at her husband for a moment before replying. At last she said, "I don't think I like the house, Ernest."

"Oh, nonsense, darling." He started to get up, but Clodetta stopped him.

"Listen, Ernest. I remembered perfectly well Aunt Mary's not wanting those curtains drawn away—but I just felt I had to do it. I didn't want to but—*something made me do it.*" Her voice was unsteady.

"Why, Clodetta," he said, faintly alarmed. "Why didn't you tell me before?"

She shrugged. "Aunt Mary might have thought I'd gone woolgathering."

"Well, it's nothing serious, but you've let it bother you a little and that isn't good for you. Forget it; think of something else. Come and listen to the radio."

They rose and moved towards the sitting-room together. At the door Henry met them. He stepped aside a little, saying, "I might have known we'd be marooned up here," and adding, as Clodetta began to protest, "We're going to be, all right. There's a wind coming up and it's beginning to snow, and I know what that means." He passed them and went into the deserted dining-room, where he stood a moment looking at the too long table. Then he turned aside and went over to the French windows, from which he drew away the curtains and stood there peering out into the darkness. Ernest saw him standing at the window, and protested from the sitting-room.

"Aunt Mary doesn't like those windows uncovered, Henry."

Henry half turned and replied, "Well, *she* may think it's dangerous, but I can risk it."

Clodetta, who had been staring beyond Henry into the night through the French windows, said suddenly, "Why, there's someone out there!"

Henry looked quickly through the glass and replied, "No, that's the snow; it's coming down heavily, and the wind's drifting it this way and that." He dropped the curtains and came away from the windows.

Clodetta said uncertainly, "Why, I could have sworn I saw someone out there, walking past the window."

"I suppose it does look that way from here," offered Henry,

who had come back into the sitting-room. "But personally, I think you've let Aunt Mary's eccentricities impress you too much."

Ernest made an impatient gesture at this, and Clodetta did not answer. Henry sat down before the radio and began to move the dial slowly. Ernest had found himself a book, and was becoming interested, but Clodetta continued to sit with her eyes fixed upon the still slowly moving curtains cutting off the French windows. Presently she got up and left the room, going down the long hall into the east wing, where she tapped gently upon Aunt Mary's door.

"Come in," called the old lady.

Clodetta opened the door and stepped into the room where Aunt Mary sat in her dressing-robe, her dignity, in the shape of her lorgnette and cane, resting respectively on her bureau and in the corner. She looked surprisingly benign, as Clodetta at once confessed.

"Ha, thought I was an ogre in disguise, did you?" said the old lady, smiling in spite of herself. "I'm really not, you see, but I have a sort of bogy about the west windows, as you have seen."

"I wanted to tell you something about those windows, Aunt Mary," said Clodetta. She stopped suddenly. The expression on the old lady's face had given way to a curiously dismaying one. It was not anger, not distaste—it was a lurking suspense. Why, the old lady was afraid!

"What?" she asked Clodetta shortly.

"I was looking out—just for a moment or so—and I thought I saw someone out there."

"Of course, you didn't, Clodetta. Your imagination, perhaps, or the drifting snow."

"My imagination? Maybe. But there was no wind to drift the snow, though one has come up since."

"I've often been fooled that way, my dear. Sometimes I've gone out in the morning to look for footprints—there weren't any, ever. We're pretty far away from civilisation in a snowstorm, despite our telephones and radios. Our nearest neighbour is at the foot of the long, sloping rise—over three miles away—and all wooded land between. There's no highway nearer than that."

"It was so clear. I could have sworn to it."

"Do you want to go out in the morning and look?" asked the old lady shortly.

"Of course not."

"Then you didn't see anything?"

It was half question, half demand. Clodetta said, "Oh, Aunt Mary, you're making an issue of it now."

"Did you or didn't you in your own mind see anything, Clodetta?"

"I guess I didn't, Aunt Mary."

"Very well. And now do you think we might talk about something more pleasant?"

"Why, I'm sure—I'm sorry, Aunt. I didn't know that Ernest's grandfather had died out there."

"Ha, he's told you that, has he? Well?"

"Yes, he said that was why you didn't like the slope after sunset—that you didn't like to be reminded of his death."

The old lady looked at Clodetta impassively. "Perhaps he'll never know how near right he was."

"What do you mean, Aunt Mary?"

"Nothing for you to know, my dear." She smiled again, her sternness dropping from her. "And now I think you'd better go, Clodetta; I'm tired."

Clodetta rose obediently and made for the door, where the old lady stopped her. "How's the weather?"

"It's snowing—hard, Henry says—and blowing."

The old lady's face showed her distaste at the news. "I don't like to hear that, not at all. Suppose someone should look down that slope tonight?" She was speaking to herself, having forgotten Clodetta at the door. Seeing her again abruptly, she said, "But you don't know, Clodetta. Goodnight."

Germaine Richier, *The Bat Man*, sculpture, 1956. (The Wadsworth Atheneum. E. Irving Blomstrann, photographer)

Clodetta stood with her back against the closed door, wondering what the old lady could have meant. *But you don't know, Clodetta.* That was curious. For a moment or two the old lady had completely forgotten her.

She moved away from the door, and came upon Ernest just turning into the east wing.

"Oh, there you are," he said. "I wondered where you had gone."

"I was talking a bit with Aunt Mary."

"Henry's been at the west windows again—and now *he* thinks there's someone out there."

Clodetta stopped short. "Does he really think so?"

Ernest nodded gravely. "But the snow's drifting frightfully, and I can imagine how that suggestion of yours worked on his mind."

Clodetta turned and went back along the hall. "I'm going to tell Aunt Mary."

He started to protest, but to no avail, for she was already tapping on the old lady's door, was indeed opening the door and entering the room before he could frame an adequate protest.

"Aunt Mary," she said, "I didn't want to disturb you again, but Henry's been at the French windows in the dining-room, and he says he's seen someone out there."

The effect on the old lady was magical. "He's seen them!" she exclaimed. Then she was on her feet, coming rapidly over to Clodetta. "How long ago?" she demanded, seizing her almost roughly by the arms. "Tell me, quickly. How long ago did he see them?"

Clodetta's amazement kept her silent for a moment, but at last she spoke, feeling the old lady's keen eyes staring at her. "It was some time ago, Aunt Mary, after supper."

The old lady's hands relaxed, and with it her tension. "Oh," she said, and turned and went back slowly to her chair, taking her cane from the corner where she had put it for the night.

"Then there *is* someone out there?" challenged Clodetta, when the old lady had reached her chair.

For a long time, it seemed to Clodetta, there was no answer. Then presently the old lady began to nod gently, and a barely audible "Yes" escaped her lips.

"Then we had better take them in, Aunt Mary."

The old lady looked at Clodetta earnestly for a moment; then she replied, her voice firm and low, her eyes fixed upon the wall beyond. "We can't take them in, Clodetta—because they're not alive."

At once Henry's words came flashing into Clodetta's memory —"She's losing her mind"—and her involuntary start betrayed her thought.

"I'm afraid I'm not mad, my dear—I hoped at first I might be, but I wasn't. I'm not, now. There was only one of them out there at first—the girl; Father is the other. Quite long ago, when I was young, my father did something which he regretted all his days. He had a too strong temper, and it maddened him. One night he found out that one of my brothers—Henry's father— had been very familiar with one of the servants, a very pretty girl, older than I was. He thought she was to blame, though she wasn't, and he didn't find out until too late. He drove her from the house, then and there. Winter had not yet set in, but it was quite cold, and she had some five miles to go to her home. We begged Father not to send her away—though we didn't know what was wrong then—but he paid no attention to us. The girl had to go.

"Not long after she had gone, a biting wind came up, and close upon it a fierce storm. Father had already repented his hasty action, and sent some of the men to look for the girl. They didn't find her, but in the morning she was found frozen to death on the long slope of the hill to the west."

The old lady sighed, paused a moment, and went on. "Years later—she came back. She came in a snowstorm, as she went; but she had become vampiric. We all saw her. We were at supper table, and Father saw her first. The boys had already gone up-stairs, and Father and the two of us girls, my sister and I, did not recognise her. She was just a dim shape floundering about in the snow beyond the French windows. Father ran out to her, calling to us to send the boys after him. We never saw him alive again. In the morning we found him in the same spot where years before the girl had been found. He, too, had died of exposure.

"Then, a few years after—she returned with the snow, and she brought him along; he, too, had become vampiric. They stayed until the last snow, always trying to lure someone out there. After that, I knew, and had the windows covered during the winter nights, from sunset to dawn, because they never went beyond the west slope.

"Now you know, Clodetta."

Whatever Clodetta was going to say was cut short by running footsteps in the hall, a hasty rap, and Ernest's head appearing suddenly in the open doorway.

"Come on, you two," he said, almost gaily, "There *are* people out on the west slope—a girl and an old man—and Henry's gone out to fetch them in!"

Then, triumphant, he was off. Clodetta came to her feet, but the old lady was before her, passing her and almost running down the hall, calling loudly for Lisa, who presently appeared in night-cap and gown from her room.

"Call Sam, Lisa," said the old lady, "and send him to me in the dining-room."

She ran on into the dining-room, Clodetta close on her heels. The French windows were open, and Ernest stood on the snow-covered terrace beyond, calling his cousin. The old lady went directly over to him, even striding into the snow to his side, though the wind drove the snow against her with great force. The wooded western slope was lost in a snowfog; the nearest trees were barely discernible.

"Where could they have gone?" Ernest said, turning to the

old lady, whom he had thought to be Clodetta. Then, seeing that it was the old lady, he said, "Why, Aunt Mary—and so little on, too! You'll catch your death of cold."

"Never mind, Ernest," said the old lady. "I'm all right. I've had Sam get up to help you look for Henry—but I'm afraid you won't find him."

"He can't be far; he just went out."

"He went before you saw where; he's far enough gone."

Sam came running into the blowing snow from the dining-room, muffled in a greatcoat. He was considerably older than Ernest, almost the old lady's age. He shot a questioning glance at her and asked, "Have they come again?"

Aunt Mary nodded. "You'll have to look for Henry. Ernest will help you. And remember, don't separate. And don't go far from the house."

Clodetta came with Ernest's overcoat, and together the two women stood there, watching them until they were swallowed up in the wall of driven snow. Then they turned slowly and went back into the house.

The old lady sank into a chair facing the windows. She was pale and drawn, and looked, as Clodetta said afterwards, "as if she'd fallen together." For a long time she said nothing. Then, with a gentle little sigh, she turned to Clodetta and spoke.

"Now there'll be three of them out there."

Then, so suddenly that no one knew how it happened, Ernest and Sam appeared beyond the windows, and between them they dragged Henry. The old lady flew to open the windows, and the three of them, cloaked in snow, came into the room.

"We found him—but the cold's hit him pretty hard, I'm afraid," said Ernest.

The old lady sent Lisa for cold water, and Ernest ran to get himself other clothes. Clodetta went with him, and in their rooms told him what the old lady had related to her.

Ernest laughed. "I think you believed that, didn't you, Clodetta? Sam and Lisa do, I know, because Sam told me the story long ago. I think the shock of Grandfather's death was too much for all three of them."

"But the story of the girl, and then——"

"That part's true, I'm afraid. A nasty story, but it did happen."

"But those people Henry and I saw!" protested Clodetta weakly.

Ernest stood without movement. "That's so," he said, "I saw them, too. Then they're out there yet, and we'll have to find them!" He took up his overcoat again, and went from the room, Clodetta protesting in a shrill unnatural voice. The old lady met him at the door of the dining-room, having overheard Clodetta pleading with him. "No, Ernest—you can't go out there again," she said. "There's no one out there."

He pushed gently into the room and called to Sam, "Coming, Sam? There are still two of them out there—we almost forgot them."

Sam looked at him strangely. "What do you mean?" he demanded roughly. He looked challengingly at the old lady, who shook her head.

"The girl and the old man, Sam. We've got to get them, too."

"Oh, *them*," said Sam. "They're dead!"

"Then I'll go out alone," said Ernest.

Henry came to his feet suddenly, looking dazed. He walked forward a few steps, his eyes travelling from one to the other of them yet apparently not seeing them. He began to speak abruptly, in an unnatural child-like voice.

"The snow," he murmured, *"the snow—the beautiful hands, so little, so lovely—her beautiful hands—and the snow, the beautiful lovely snow, drifting and falling about her. . . ."*

He turned slowly and looked towards the French windows,

the others following his gaze. Beyond was a wall of white, where the snow was drifting against the house. For a moment Henry stood quietly watching; then suddenly a white figure came forward from the snow—a young girl, cloaked in long snow-whips, her glistening eyes strangely fascinating.

The old lady flung herself forward, her arms outstretched to cling to Henry, but she was too late. Henry had run towards the windows, had opened them, and even as Clodetta cried out, had vanished into the wall of snow beyond.

Then Ernest ran forward, but the old lady threw her arms around him and held him tightly, murmuring, "You shall not go! Henry is gone beyond our help!"

Clodetta came to help her, and Sam stood menacingly at the French windows, now closed against the wind and the sinister snow. So they held him, and would not let him go.

"And tomorrow," said the old lady in a harsh whisper, "we must go to their graves and stake them down. We should have gone before."

In the morning they found Henry's body crouched against the bole of an ancient oak, where two others had been found years before. There were almost obliterated marks of where something had dragged him, a long, uneven swath in the snow, and yet no footprints, only strange, hollowed places along the way as if the wind had whirled the snow away, and only the wind.

But on his skin were signs of the snow vampire—the delicate small prints of a young girl's hands.

22

Drink My Red Blood

by Richard Matheson

From *The Midnight People*, edited by Peter Haining, New York, Popular Library, 1968, pp. 132–39

Richard Matheson is most famous for his novel *I Am Legend*, which was twice made into a movie. One film version, solidly based on the story, was entitled *The Last Man on Earth;* it appeared in 1964 with Vincent Price in the leading role. A second version, loosely contrived from the novel, was released under the title *The Omega Man;* Charlton Heston played the lead. Traditionally, the vampire is a rare, legendary being in the world of humans, but in *I Am Legend* Matheson turns the tables—for a single human being is portrayed in a world of vampires and mutants; as the last man on earth, he becomes legend after he dies and the other creatures inherit the earth.

In *Drink My Red Blood*, which predates *I Am Legend*, Matheson rings an interesting change on the usual age of the fictional vampire, and does unexpected things to the reader's sympathies.

The people on the block decided definitely that Jules was crazy when they heard about his composition.

There had been suspicions for a long time.

He made people shiver with his blank stare. His coarse guttural tongue sounded unnatural in his frail body. The paleness of his skin upset many children. It seemed to hang loose around his flesh. He hated sunlight.

And his ideas were a little out of place for the people who lived on the block.

Jules wanted to be a vampire.

People declared it common knowledge that he was born on a night when winds uprooted trees. They said he was born with three teeth. They said he'd used them to fasten himself on his mother's breast drawing blood with the milk.

They said he used to cackle and bark in his crib after dark. They said he walked at two months and sat staring at the moon whenever it shone.

Those were things that people said.

His parents were always worried about him. An only child, they noticed his flaws quickly.

They thought he was blind until the doctor told them it was just a vacuous stare. He told them that Jules, with his large head might be a genius or an idiot. It turned out he was an idiot.

He never spoke a word until he was five. Then one night coming up to supper, he sat down at the table and said, "Death."

His parents were torn between delight and disgust. They finally settled for a place in between the two feelings. They decided that Jules couldn't have realised what the word meant.

But Jules did.

From that night on, he built up such a large vocabulary that everyone who knew him was astonished. He not only acquired every word spoken to him, words from signs, magazines, books; he made up his own words.

Like nighttouch. Or killove. They were really several words that melted into each other. They said things Jules felt but couldn't explain with other words.

He used to sit on the porch while the other children played hop-scotch, stickball and other games. He sat there and stared at the sidewalk and made up words.

Until he was twelve Jules kept pretty much out of trouble. Of course there was the time they found him undressing Olive Jones in an alley. And another time he was discovered dissecting a kitten on his bed.

But there were many years in between. Those scandals were forgotten.

In general he went through childhood merely disgusting people.

He went to school but never studied. He spent about two or three terms in each grade. The teachers all knew him by his first name. In some subjects like reading and writing he was almost brilliant.

In others he was hopeless.

One Saturday when he was twelve, Jules went to the movies. He saw *Dracula*.

When the show was over he walked, a throbbing nerve mass, through the little girl and boy ranks.

He went home and locked himself in the bathroom for two hours.

His parents pounded on the door and threatened but he wouldn't come out.

Finally he unlocked the door and sat down at the supper table. He had a bandage on his thumb and a satisfied look on his face.

The morning after he went to the library. It was Sunday. He sat on the steps all day waiting for it to open. Finally he went home.

The next morning he came back instead of going to school.

He found *Dracula* on the shelves. He couldn't borrow it because he wasn't a member and to be a member he had to bring in one of his parents.

So he stuck the book down his pants and left the library and never brought it back.

He went to the park and sat down and read the book through. It was late evening before he finished.

He started at the beginning again, reading as he ran from

street light to street light, all the way home.

He didn't hear a word of the scolding he got for missing lunch and supper. He ate, went in his room and read the book to the finish. They asked him where he got the book. He said he found it.

As the days passed Jules read the story over and over. He never went to school.

Late at night, when he had fallen into an exhausted slumber, his mother used to take the book into the living-room and show it to her husband.

One night they noticed that Jules had underlined certain sentences with dark shaky pencil lines.

Like: "The lips were crimson with fresh blood and the stream had trickled over her chin and stained the purity of her lawn death robe."

Or: "When the blood began to spurt out, he took my hands in one of his, holding them tight and, with the other seized my neck and pressed my mouth to the wound. . . ."

When his mother saw this, she threw the book down the garbage chute.

The next morning when Jules found the book missing he screamed and twisted his mother's arm until she told him where the book was.

Then he ran down to the cellar and dug in the piles of garbage until he found the book.

Coffee grounds and egg yolk on his hands and wrists, he went to the park and read it again.

For a month he read the book avidly. Then he knew it so well he threw it away and just thought about it.

Absence notes were coming from school. His mother yelled. Jules decided to go back for a while.

He wanted to write a composition.

One day he wrote it in class. When everyone was finished

writing, the teacher asked if anyone wanted to read their compositions to the class.

Jules raised his hand.

The teacher was surprised. But she felt charity. She wanted to encourage him. She drew in her tiny jab of a chin and smiled.

"All right," she said, "pay attention, children. Jules is going to read us his composition."

Jules stood up. He was excited. The paper shook in his hands.

"My Ambition by . . ."

"Come to the front of the class, Jules, dear."

Jules went to the front of the class. The teacher smiled lovingly. Jules started again.

"My Ambition by Jules Dracula."

The smile sagged.

"When I grow up I want to be a vampire."

The teacher's smiling lips jerked down and out. Her eyes popped wide.

"I want to live forever and get even with everybody and make all the girls vampires. I want to smell of death."

"Jules!"

"I want to have a foul breath that stinks of dead earth and crypts and sweet coffins."

The teacher shuddered. Her hands twitched on her green blotter. She couldn't believe her ears. She looked at the children. They were gaping. Some of them were giggling. But not the girls.

"I want to be all cold and have rotten flesh with stolen blood in the veins."

"That will . . . hrrumph!"

The teacher cleared her throat mightily.

"That will be all, Jules," she said.

Jules talked louder and desperately.

"I want to sink my terrible white teeth in my victims' necks. I want them to . . ."

"Jules! Go to your seat this instant!"

"I want them to slide like razors in the flesh and into the veins," read Jules ferociously.

The teacher jolted to her feet. Children were shivering. None of them were giggling.

"Then I want to draw my teeth out and let the blood flow easy in my mouth and run hot in my throat and . . ."

The teacher grabbed his arm. Jules tore away and ran to a corner. Barricaded behind a stool he yelled:

"And drip off my tongue and run out of my lips down my victim's throats! I want to drink girls' blood!"

The teacher lunged for him. She dragged him out of the corner. He clawed at her and screamed all the way to the door and the principal's office.

"That is my ambition! That is my ambition! That is my ambition!"

It was grim.

Jules was locked in his room. The teacher and the principal sat with Jules' parents. They were talking in sepulchral voices.

They were recounting the scene.

All along the block parents were discussing it. Most of them didn't believe it at first. They thought their children made it up.

Then they thought what horrible children they'd raised if the children could make up such things.

So they believed it.

After that everyone watched Jules like a hawk. People avoided his touch and look. Parents pulled their children off the street when he approached. Everyone whispered tales of him.

There were more absence notes.

Jules told his mother he wasn't going to school any more. Nothing would change his mind. He never went again.

When a truant officer came to the apartment Jules would run over the roofs until he was far away from there.

A year wasted by.

Jules wandered the streets searching for something; he didn't know what. He looked in alleys. He looked in garbage cans. He looked in lots. He looked on the east side and the west side and in the middle.

He couldn't find what he wanted.

He rarely slept. He never spoke. He stared down all the time. He forgot his special words.

Then.

One day in the park, Jules strolled through the zoo.

An electric shock passed through him when he saw the vampire bat.

His eyes grew wide and his discoloured teeth shone dully in a wide smile.

From that day on, Jules went daily to the zoo and looked at the bat. He spoke to it and called it the Count. He felt in his heart it was really a man who had changed.

A rebirth of culture struck him.

He stole another book from the library. It told all about wild life.

He found the page on the vampire bat. He tore it out and threw the book away.

He learned the section by heart.

He knew how the bat made its wound. How it lapped up the blood like a kitten drinking cream. How it walked on folded wing stalks and hind legs like a black furry spider. Why it took no nourishment but blood.

Month after month Jules stared at the bat and talked to it. It became the one comfort in his life. The one symbol of dreams come true.

One day Jules noticed that the bottom of the wire covering the cage had come loose.

He looked around, his black eyes shifting. He didn't see anyone looking. It was a cloudy day. Not many people were there.

Jules tugged at the wire.

It moved a little.

Then he saw a man come out of the monkey house. So he pulled back his hand and strolled away whistling a song he had just made up.

Late at night, when he was supposed to be asleep he would walk barefoot past his parents' room. He would hear his father and mother snoring. He would hurry out, put on his shoes and run to the zoo.

Every time the watchman was not around, Jules would tug at the wiring.

He kept on pulling it loose.

When he had finished and had to run home, he pushed the wire in again. Then no one could tell.

All day Jules would stand in front of the cage and look at the Count and chuckle and tell him he'd soon be free again.

He told the Count all the things he knew. He told the Count he was going to practise climbing down walls head first.

He told the Count not to worry. He'd soon be out. Then, together, they could go all around and drink girls' blood.

One night Jules pulled the wire out and crawled under it into the cage.

It was very dark.

He crept on his knees to the little wooden house. He listened to see if he could hear the Count squeaking.

He stuck his arm in the black doorway. He kept whispering.

He jumped when he felt a needle jab in his finger.

With a look of great pleasure on his thin face, Jules drew the fluttering hairy bat to him.

He climbed down from the cage with it and ran out of the zoo; out of the park. He ran down the silent streets.

It was getting late in the morning. Light touched the dark skies with grey. He couldn't go home. He had to have a place.

He went down an alley and climbed over a fence. He held

A vampire bat. (J. R. Eyerman, Time-LIFE Picture Agency)

tight to the bat. It lapped at the dribble of blood from his finger.

He went across a yard and into a little deserted shack.

It was dark inside and damp. It was full of rubble and tin cans and soggy cardboard and excrement.

Jules made sure there was no way the bat could escape.

Then he pulled the door tight and put a stick through the metal loop.

He felt his heart beating hard and his limbs trembling.

He let go of the bat. It flew to a dark corner and hung on the wood.

Jules feverishly tore off his shirt. His lips shook. He smiled a crazy smile.

He reached down into his pants pocket and took out a little penknife he had stolen from his mother.

He opened it and ran a finger over the blade. It sliced through the flesh.

With shaking fingers he jabbed at his throat. He hacked. The blood ran through his fingers.

"Count! Count!" he cried in frenzied joy. "Drink my red blood! Drink me! Drink me!"

He stumbled over the tin cans and slipped and felt for the bat. It sprang from the wood and soared across the shack and fastened itself on the other side.

Tears ran down Jules' cheeks.

He gritted his teeth. The blood ran across his shoulders and across his thin hairless chest.

His body shook in fever. He staggered back towards the other side. He tripped and felt his side torn open on the sharp edge of a tin can.

His hands went out. They clutched the bat. He placed it against his throat. He sank on his back on the cool wet earth. He sighed.

He started to moan and clutch at his chest. His stomach heaved. The black bat on his neck silently lapped his blood.

Jules felt his life seeping away.

He thought of all the years past. The waiting. His parents. School. Dracula. Dreams. For this. This sudden glory.

Jules's eyes flickered open.

The side of the reeking shack swam about him.

It was hard to breathe. He opened his mouth to gasp in the air. He sucked it in. It was foul. It made him cough. His skinny body lurched on the cold ground.

Mists crept away in his brain.

One by one like drawn veils.

Suddenly his mind was filled with terrible clarity.

He knew he was lying half-naked on garbage and letting a flying bat drink his blood.

With a strangled cry, he reached up and tore away the furry throbbing bat. He flung it away from him. It came back fanning his face with its vibrating wings.

Jules staggered to his feet.

He felt for the door. He could hardly see. He tried to stop his throat from bleeding so.

He managed to get the door open.

Then, lurching into the dark yard, he fell on his face in the long grass blades.

He tried to call out for help.

But no sounds save a bubbling mockery of words came from his lips.

He heard the fluttering wings.

Then, suddenly they were gone.

Strong fingers lifted him gently. Through dying eyes Jules saw the tall dark man whose eyes shone like rubies.

"My son," the man said.

Uan deme quaden thyrãne Dracole wyda·

"Concerning a Great Tyrant, Dracula the Voevod." Woodcut from a late-15th-century German pamphlet, now in Budapest. (Szechenyi Collection, Budapest)

23

Dracula's Guest

by Bram Stoker

First published in the collection *Dracula's Guest and Other Weird Stories*, Routledge, London, 1914

At twilight on an April evening in 1912, Bram Stoker, author of *Dracula*—the greatest of all vampire tales—was busy working on a collection of his short stories. Now sixty-four years old and in poor health, he had spread out some of his early stories on his sickbed. Among this unpublished material was "Dracula's Guest," which, he had decided, was to head the collection. Stoker died that spring evening, leaving his task unfinished.

"Dracula's Guest" had originally been conceived as the first chapter of *Dracula* but was not included when the book came out in 1897. Since Stoker's editors had considered the manuscript to be too long to make a commercially viable book, Stoker had deleted the opening.

The story contains a detail of particular interest to devotees of vampire fiction. On his way to Transylvania, Jonathan Harker stops off at the hotel Vierjahreszeiten in Munich. (This hotel, by the way, still exists. I stayed there in 1970.) From there he goes to a deserted village, where he finds a bier with the inscription "Countess Dolingen of Gratz in Styria. Sought and found. Death 1801." Joseph Sheridan Le Fanu, in *his* vampire story *Carmilla* (1872), invented a countess whose activities did indeed take place in Styria, southeastern Austria, and who had been laid out in just such a tomb as Stoker's hero encountered. Thus, in *Dracula's Guest*, Stoker acknowledged the inspiration afforded by Le Fanu, and in a special way paid up an intellectual debt.

When we started for our drive the sun was shining brightly on Munich, and the air was full of the joyousness of early summer. Just as we were about to depart, Herr Delbrück (the maître d'hôtel of the Quatre Saisons, where I was staying) came down, bareheaded, to the carriage and, after wishing me a pleasant drive, said to the coachman, still holding his hand on the handle of the carriage door:

"Remember you are back by nightfall. The sky looks bright but there is a shiver in the north wind that says there may be a sudden storm. But I am sure you will not be late." Here he smiled, and added, "for you know what night it is."

Johann answered with an emphatic, "ja, mein Herr," and, touching his hat, drove off quickly. When we had cleared the town, I said, after signalling to him to stop:

"Tell me, Johann, what is to-night?"

He crossed himself, as he answered laconically:

"Walpurgis Nacht." Then he took out his watch, a great, old-fashioned German silver thing as big as a turnip, and looked at it, with his eyebrows gathered together and a little impatient shrug of his shoulders. I realised that this was his way of respectfully protesting against the unnecessary delay, and sank back in the carriage, merely motioning him to proceed. He started off rapidly, as if to make up for lost time. Every now and then the horses seemed to throw up their heads and sniff the air suspiciously. On such occasions I often looked round in alarm. The road was pretty bleak, for we were traversing a sort of high, wind-swept plateau. As we drove, I saw a road that looked but little used, and which seemed to dip through a little, winding valley. It looked so inviting that, even at the risk of offending him, I called Johann to stop—and when he had pulled up, I told him I would like to drive down that road. He made all sorts of excuses, and frequently crossed himself as he spoke. This somewhat piqued my curiosity, so I asked him various questions. He answered fencingly, and repeatedly looked at his watch in protest. Finally I said:

"Well, Johann, I want to go down this road. I shall not ask you to come unless you like; but tell me why you do not like to go, that is all I ask." For answer he seemed to throw himself off the box, so quickly did he reach the ground. Then he stretched out his hands appealingly to me, and implored me not to go. There was just enough of English mixed with the German for me to understand the drift of his talk. He seemed always just about to tell me something—the very idea of which evidently frightened him—but each time he pulled himself up, saying, as he crossed himself:

"Walpurgis Nacht!"

I tried to argue with him, but it was difficult to argue with a man when I did not know his language. The advantage certainly rested with him, for although he began to speak in English, of a very crude and broken kind, he always got excited and broke into his native tongue—and every time he did so, he looked at his watch. Then the horses became restless and sniffed the air. At this he grew very pale, and, looking around in a frightened way, he suddenly jumped forward, took them by the bridles and led them on some twenty feet. I followed, and asked why he had done this. For answer he crossed himself, pointed to the spot we had left and drew his carriage in the direction of the other road, indicating a cross, and said, first in German, then in English: "Buried him—him what killed themselves."

I remembered the old custom of burying suicides at crossroads: "Ah! I see, a suicide. How interesting!" But for the life of me I could not make out why the horses were frightened.

Whilst we were talking, we heard a sort of sound between a yelp and a bark. It was far away; but the horses got very restless, and it took Johann all his time to quiet them. He was pale, and said; "It sounds like a wolf—but yet there are no wolves here now."

"No?" I said, questioning him; "isn't it long since the wolves were so near the city?"

"Long, long," he answered, "in the spring and summer; but with the snow the wolves have been here not so long."

Whilst he was petting the horses and trying to quiet them, dark clouds drifted rapidly across the sky. The sunshine passed away, and a breath of cold wind seemed to drift past us. It was only a breath, however, and more in the nature of a warning than a fact, for the sun came out brightly again. Johann looked under his lifted hand at the horizon and said:

"The storm of snow, he comes before long time."

Then he looked at his watch again, and, straightway holding his reins firmly—for the horses were still pawing the ground restlessly and shaking their heads—he climbed to his box as though the time had come for proceeding on our journey.

I felt a little obstinate and did not at once get into the carriage.

"Tell me," I said, "about this place where the road leads," and I pointed down.

Again he crossed himself and mumbled a prayer, before he answered: "It is unholy."

"What is unholy?" I enquired.

"The village."

"Then there is a village?"

"No, no. No one lives there hundreds of years."

My curiosity was piqued: "But you said there was a village."

"There was."

"Where is it now?"

Whereupon he burst out into a long story in German and English, so mixed up that I could not quite understand exactly what he said, but roughly I gathered that long ago, hundreds of years, men had died there and been buried in their graves; and sounds were heard under the clay, and when the graves were opened, men and women were found rosy with life, and their mouths red with blood. And so, in haste to save their lives (aye, and their souls!—and here he crossed himself) those who were left fled away to other places, where the living lived, and the dead were dead and not—not something. He was evidently afraid to speak the last words. As he proceeded with his narration, he grew more and more excited. It seemed as if his imagination had got hold of him, and he ended in a perfect paroxysm of fear—white-faced, perspiring, trembling and looking round him, as if expecting that some dreadful presence would manifest itself there in the bright sunshine on the open plain. Finally, in an agony of desperation, he cried:

"Walpurgis Nacht!" and pointed to the carriage for me to get in. All my English blood rose at this, and, standing back, I said:

"You are afraid, Johann—you are afraid. Go home; I shall return alone; the walk will do me good." The carriage door was open. I took from the seat my oak walking-stick—which I always carry on my holiday excursions—and closed the door, pointing back to Munich, and said, "Go home, Johann—Walpurgis Nacht doesn't concern Englishmen."

The horses were now more restive than ever, and Johann was trying to hold them in, while excitedly imploring me not to do anything so foolish. I pitied the poor fellow, he was so deeply in earnest; but all the same I could not help laughing. His English was quite gone now. In his anxiety he had forgotten that his only means of making me understand was to talk my language, so he jabbered away in his native German. It began to be a little tedious. After giving the direction, "Home!" I turned to go down the cross-road into the valley.

With a despairing gesture, Johann turned his horses towards Munich. I leaned on my stick and looked after him. He went slowly along the road for a while: then there came over the crest of the hill a man tall and thin. I could see so much in the distance.

When he drew near the horses, they began to jump and kick about, then to scream with terror. Johann could not hold them in; they bolted down the road, running away madly. I watched them out of sight, then looked for the stranger, but I found that he, too, was gone.

With a light heart I turned down the side road through the deepening valley to which Johann had objected. There was not the slightest reason, that I could see, for his objection; and I daresay I tramped for a couple of hours without thinking of time or distance, and certainly without seeing a person or a house. So far as the place was concerned, it was desolation itself. But I did not notice this particularly till, on turning a bend in the road, I came upon a scattered fringe of wood; then I recognised that I had been impressed unconsciously by the desolation of the region through which I had passed.

I sat down to rest myself, and began to look around. It struck me that it was considerably colder than it had been at the commencement of my walk—a sort of sighing sound seemed to be around me, with, now and then, high overhead, a sort of muffled roar. Looking upwards I noticed that great thick clouds were drifting rapidly across the sky from North to South at a great height. There were signs of coming storm in some lofty stratum of the air. I was a little chilly, and, thinking that it was the sitting still after the exercise of walking, I resumed my journey.

The ground I passed over was now much more picturesque. There were no striking objects that the eye might single out; but in all there was a charm of beauty. I took little heed of time and it was only when the deepening twilight forced itself upon me that I began to think of how I should find my way home. The brightness of the day had gone. The air was cold, and the drifting of clouds high overhead was more marked. They were accompanied by a sort of far-away rushing sound, through which seemed to come at intervals that mysterious cry which the driver had said came from a wolf. For a while I hesitated. I had said I would see the deserted village, so on I went, and presently came on a wide stretch of open country, shut in by hills all around. Their sides were covered with trees which spread down to the plain, dotting, in clumps, the gentler slopes and hollows which showed here and there. I followed with my eye the winding of the road, and saw that it curved close to one of the densest of these clumps and was lost behind it.

As I looked there came a cold shiver in the air, and the snow began to fall. I thought of the miles and miles of bleak country I had passed, and then hurried on to seek the shelter of the wood in front. Darker and darker grew the sky, and faster and heavier fell the snow, till the earth before and around me was a glistening white carpet the further edge of which was lost in misty vagueness. The road was here but crude, and when on the level its boundaries were not so marked as when it passed through the cuttings, and in a little while I found that I must have strayed from it, for I missed underfoot the hard surface, and my feet sank deeper in the grass and moss. Then the wind grew stronger and blew with ever increasing force, till I was fain to run before it. The air became icy cold, and in spite of my exercise I began to suffer. The snow was now falling so thickly and whirling around me in such rapid eddies that I could hardly keep my eyes open. Every now and then the heavens were torn asunder by vivid lightning, and in the flashes I could see ahead of me a great mass of trees, chiefly yew and cypress and heavily coated with snow.

I was soon amongst the shelter of the trees, and there, in comparative silence, I could hear the rush of the wind high overhead. Presently the blackness of the storm had become merged in the darkness of the night. By-and-by the storm seemed to be passing away: it now only came in fierce puffs or blasts. At such moments the weird sound of the wolf appeared to be echoed by many similar sounds around me.

Now and again, through the black mass of drifting cloud, came a straggling ray of moonlight, which lit up the expanse, and showed me that I was at the edge of a dense mass of cypress and yew trees. As the snow had ceased to fall, I walked out from the shelter and began to investigate more closely. It appeared to me that, amongst so many old foundations as I had passed, there might be still standing a house in which, though in ruins, I could find some sort of shelter for a while. As I skirted the edge of the copse, I found that a low wall encircled it and following this I presently found an opening. Here the cypresses formed an alley leading up to a square mass of some kind of building. Just as I caught sight of this, however, the drifting clouds obscured the moon, and I passed up the path in darkness. The wind must have grown colder, for I felt myself shiver as I walked; but there was hope of shelter, and I groped my way blindly on.

I stopped, for there was a sudden stillness. The storm had passed; and in sympathy with nature's silence, my heart seemed to cease to beat. But this was only momentarily; for suddenly the moonlight broke through the clouds, showing me that I was in a graveyard, and that the square object before me was a great massive tomb of marble, as white as the snow that lay on and all around it. With the moonlight there came a fierce sigh of the storm, which appeared to resume its course with a long, low howl, as of many dogs or wolves. I was awed and shocked, and felt the cold perceptibly grow upon me till it seemed to grip me by the heart. Then while the flood of moonlight still fell on the marble tomb, the storm gave further evidence of renewing, as though it was returning on its track. Impelled by some sort of fascination, I approached the sepulchre to see what it was, and why such a thing stood alone in such a place. I walked around it, and read, over the Doric door, in German—

COUNTESS DOLINGEN OF GRATZ

IN STYRIA

SOUGHT AND FOUND DEATH

1801

Atkinson Grimshaw, *Whitby Harbor by Moonlight*, painting, 1867. Bram Stoker based his description of Count Dracula's arrival in England upon accounts of an actual shipwreck off Whitby—that of the Russian schooner *Demeter*, which was loaded with sand from the Danube delta. Although *Dracula* was not published until after Grimshaw's death, there are many analogies between the novel and the artist's inventive, misty paintings. (Ferrers Gallery, London)

On the top of the tomb, seemingly driven through the solid marble—for the structure was composed of a few vast blocks of stone—was a great iron spike or stake. On going to the back I saw, graven in great Russian letters:

"The dead travel fast."

There was something so weird and uncanny about the whole thing that it gave me a turn and made me feel quite faint. I began to wish, for the first time, that I had taken Johann's advice. Here a thought struck me, which came under almost mysterious circumstances and with a terrible shock. This was Walpurgis Night!

Walpurgis Night, when, according to the belief of millions of people, the devil was abroad—when the graves were opened and the dead came forth and walked. When all evil things of earth and air and water held revel. This very place the driver had specially shunned. This was the depopulated village of centuries ago. This was where the suicide lay; and this was the place where I was alone—unmanned, shivering with cold in a shroud of snow with a wild storm gathering again upon me! It took all my philosophy, all the religion I had been taught, all my courage, not to collapse in a paroxysm of fright.

And now a perfect tornado burst upon me. The ground shook as though thousands of horses thundered across it; and this time the storm bore on its icy wings, not snow, but great hailstones which drove with such violence that they might have come from the thongs of Balearic slingers—hailstones that beat down leaf and branch and made the shelter of the cypresses of no more avail than though their stems were standing corn. At the first I had rushed to the nearest tree; but I was soon fain to leave it and seek the only spot that seemed to afford refuge, the deep Doric doorway of the marble tomb. There, crouching against the massive bronze door, I gained a certain amount of protection from the beating of the hailstones, for now they only drove against me as they ricocheted from the ground and the side of the marble.

As I leaned against the door, it moved slightly and opened inwards. The shelter of even a tomb was welcome in that pitiless tempest, and I was about to enter it when there came a flash of forked lightning that lit up the whole expanse of the heavens. In the instant, as I am a living man, I saw, as my eyes were turned into the darkness of the tomb, a beautiful woman, with rounded cheeks and red lips, seemingly sleeping on a bier. As the thunder broke overhead, I was grasped as by the hand of a giant and hurled out into the storm. The whole thing was so sudden that, before I could realise the shock, moral as well as physical, I found the hailstones beating me down. At the same time I had a strange dominating feeling that I was not alone. I looked towards the tomb. Just then there came another blinding flash which seemed to strike the iron stake that surmounted the tomb and to pour through to the earth, blasting and crumbling the marble, as in a burst of flame. The dead woman rose for a moment of agony, while she was lapped in the flame, and her bitter scream of pain was drowned in the thundercrash. The last thing I heard was this mingling of dreadful sound, as again I was seized in the giant-grasp and dragged away, while the hailstones beat on me, and the air around seemed reverberant with the howling of wolves. The last sight that I remembered was a vague, white, moving mass, as if all the graves around me had sent out the phantoms of their sheeted dead, and that they were closing in on me through the white cloudiness of the driving hail.

Gradually there came a sort of vague beginning of consciousness; then a sense of weariness that was dreadful. For a time I remembered nothing; but slowly my senses returned. My feet seemed positively racked with pain, yet I could not move them. They seemed to be numbed. There was an icy feeling at the back of my neck and all down my spine, and my ears, like my feet, were dead, yet in torment; but there was in my breast a sense of warmth which was, by comparison, delicious. It was as a nightmare—a physical nightmare, if one may use such an expression; for some heavy weight on my chest made it difficult for me to breathe.

This period of semi-lethargy seemed to remain a long time, and as it faded away I must have slept or swooned. Then came a sort of loathing, like the first stage of sea-sickness, and a wild desire to be free from something—I knew not what. A vast stillness enveloped me, as though all the world were asleep or dead —only broken by the low panting as of some animal close to me. I felt a warm rasping at my throat, then came a consciousness of the awful truth, which chilled me to the heart and sent the blood surging up through my brain. Some great animal was lying on me and now licking my throat. I feared to stir, for some instinct of prudence bade me lie still; but the brute seemed to realize that there was now some change in me, for it raised its head. Through my eyelashes I saw above me the two great flaming eyes of a gigantic wolf. Its sharp white teeth gleamed in the gaping red mouth, and I could feel its hot breath fierce and acrid upon me.

For another spell of time I remembered no more. Then I became conscious of a low growl, followed by a yelp, renewed again and again. Then seemingly very far away, I heard a "Holloa! holloa!" as of many voices calling in unison. Cautiously I raised my head and looked in the direction whence the sound came; but the cemetery blocked my view. The wolf still continued to yelp in a strange way, and a red glare began to move round the grove of cypresses, as though following the sound. As the voices drew closer, the wolf yelped faster and louder. I feared to make either sound or motion. Nearer came the red glow, over the white pall which stretched into the darkness around me. Then all at once from beyond the trees there came at a trot a troop of horsemen bearing torches. The wolf rose from my breast and made for the cemetery. I saw one of the horsemen (soldiers by their caps and their long military cloaks) raise his carbine and take aim. A companion knocked up his arm, and I heard the ball whizz over my head. He had evidently taken my body for that of the wolf.

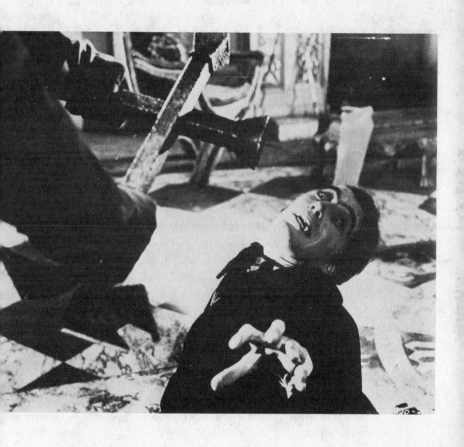

In the final scene of Hammer Films' *The Horror of Dracula*
(1958), Dracula (Christopher Lee) disintegrates in the sunlight before a cross fashioned from two candelabra by Van
Helsing (Peter Cushing). (Universal Pictures. Photo The
Bettmann Archive)

Another sighted the animal as it slunk away, and a shot followed. Then, at a gallop, the troop rode forward—some towards me, others following the wolf as it disappeared amongst the snow-clad cypresses.

As they drew nearer I tried to move, but was powerless, although I could see and hear all that went on around me. Two or three of the soldiers jumped from their horses and knelt beside me. One of them raised my head, and placed his hand over my heart.

"Good news, comrades!" he cried. "His heart still beats!"

Then some brandy was poured down my throat; it put vigour into me, and I was able to open my eyes fully and look around. Lights and shadows were moving among the trees, and I heard men call to one another. They drew together, uttering frightened exclamations; and the lights flashed as the others came pouring out of the cemetery pell-mell, like men possessed. When the further ones came close to us, those who were around me asked them eagerly:

"Well, have you found him?"

The reply rang out hurriedly:

"No! no! Come away quick—quick! This is no place to stay, and on this of all nights!"

"What was it?" was the question, asked in all manner of keys. The answer came variously and all indefinitely as though the men were moved by some common impulse to speak, yet were restrained by some common fear from giving their thoughts.

"It-it-indeed!" gibbered one, whose wits had plainly given out for the moment.

"A wolf—and yet not a wolf!" another put in shudderingly.

"No use trying for him without the sacred bullet," a third remarked in a more ordinary manner.

"Serve us right for coming out on this night! Truly we have earned our thousand marks!" were the ejaculations of a fourth.

"There was blood on the broken marble," another said after

a pause—"the lightning never brought that there. And for him —is he safe? Look at his throat! See, comrades, the wolf has been lying on him and keeping his blood warm."

The officer looked at my throat and replied:

"He is all right; the skin is not pierced. What does it all mean? We should never have found him but for the yelping of the wolf."

"What became of it?" asked the man who was holding up my head, and who seemed the least panic-stricken of the party, for his hands were steady and without tremor. On his sleeve was the chevron of a petty officer.

"It went to its home," answered the man, whose long face was pallid, and who actually shook with terror as he glanced around him fearfully. "There are graves enough there in which it may lie. Come, comrades—come quickly! Let us leave this cursed spot."

The officer raised me to a sitting posture, as he uttered a word of command; then several men placed me upon a horse. He sprang to the saddle behind me, took me in his arms, gave the word to advance; and, turning our faces away from the cypresses, we rode away in swift, military order.

As yet my tongue refused its office, and I was perforce silent. I must have fallen asleep; for the next thing I remembered was finding myself standing up, supported by a soldier on each side of me. It was almost broad daylight, and to the north a red streak of sunlight was reflected, like a path of blood, over the waste of snow. The officer was telling the men to say nothing of what they had seen, except that they found an English stranger, guarded by a large dog.

"Dog! that was no dog," cut in the man who had exhibited such fear. "I think I know a wolf when I seen one."

The young officer answered calmly: "I said a dog."

"Dog!" reiterated the other ironically. It was evident that his courage was rising with the sun; and, pointing to me, he said, "Look at his throat. Is that the work of a dog, master?"

Instinctively I raised my hand to my throat, and as I touched it I cried out in pain. The men crowded round to look, some stooping down from their saddles; and again there came the calm voice of the young officer:

"A dog, as I said. If aught else were said we should only be laughed at."

I was then mounted behind a trooper, and we rode on into the suburbs of Munich. Here we came across a stray carriage, into which I was lifted, and it was driven off to the Quatre Saisons— the young officer accompanying me, whilst a trooper followed with his horse, and the others rode off to their barracks.

When we arrived, Herr Delbrück rushed so quickly down the steps to meet me, that it was apparent he had been watching within. Taking me by both hands he solicitously led me in. The officer saluted me and was turning to withdraw, when I recognized his purpose, and insisted that he should come to my rooms. Over a glass of wine I warmly thanked him and his brave comrades for saving me. He replied simply that he was more than glad, and that Herr Delbrück had at the first taken steps to make all the searching party pleased; at which ambiguous utterance the maître d'hôtel smiled, while the officer pleaded duty and withdrew.

"But Herr Delbrück," I enquired, "how and why was it that the soldiers searched for me?"

He shrugged his shoulders, as if in depreciation of his own deed, as he replied:

"I was so fortunate as to obtain leave from the commander of the regiment in which I served, to ask for volunteers."

"But how did you know I was lost?" I asked.

"The driver came hither with the remains of his carriage, which had been upset when the horses ran away."

"But surely you would not send a search-party of soldiers merely on this account?"

"Oh, no!" he answered; "but even before the coachman arrived, I had this telegram from the Boyar whose guest you are," and he took from his pocket a telegram which he handed to me, and I read:

BISTRITZ.

"Be careful of my guest—his safety is most precious to me. Should aught happen to him, or if he be missed, spare nothing to find him and ensure his safety. He is English and therefore adventurous. There are often dangers from snow and wolves at night. Lose not a moment if you suspect harm to him. I answer your zeal with my fortune.—Dracula."

As I held the telegram in my hand, the room seemed to whirl around me; and, if the attentive maître d'hôtel had not caught me, I think I should have fallen. There was something so strange in all this, something so weird and impossible to imagine, that there grew on me a sense of my being in some way the sport of opposite forces—the mere vague idea of which seemed in a way to paralyse me. I was certainly under some form of mysterious protection. From a distant country had come, in the very nick of time, a message that took me out of the danger of the snow-sleep and the jaws of the wolf.

In MGM's *London After Midnight* (1927), Lon Chaney played a double role of vampire and detective. He was one of the first to popularize the image of the vampire in human form with top hat and bat-like cape. (© 1927 Metro-Goldwyn-Mayer Distributing Corporation. Renewed 1955 Loew's Incorporated.)

24

Are Vampires Less Frequent Today?

From Montague Summers, *The Vampire in Europe*, London, Routledge and Kegan Paul, 1928; reprint Hyde Park, N.Y., University Books, Inc., 1968; pp. xviii–xix

Cases of vampirism may be said to be in our time a rare occult phenomenon. Yet whether we are justified in supposing that they are less frequent to-day than in past centuries I am far from certain. One thing is plain:—not that they do not occur but that they are carefully hushed up and stifled. More than one such instance has come to my own notice. . . .

Mrs. Hayes informs me of a vampiric existence which befell her only some ten years ago, but happily in this case no actual harm was done, perhaps because the evil force (although none the less dangerous in intent) was something old and waning and had not at the time collected a sufficient reserve of that new strength for which it was so eagerly athirst in order that it might manifest itself more potently and with intensely active malice.

In June, 1918, it chanced that Mrs. Hayes took a small house at Penlee, South Devon, not far from Dartmouth. She writes: "I had a friend staying with me, but otherwise we were quite alone in the place. One morning we came down to find in the middle of the parquet floor of the sitting-room the mark of a single cloven hoof in mud. The house and windows were very small, so it was quite impossible for an animal to have got in, nor indeed were such the case could it have managed so as to leave one single footprint. We hunted everywhere for a second trace but without success. For several nights I had most unpleasant and frightening experiences with an invisible but perfectly tangible being. I had no peace until I had hung the place with garlic, which acted like a charm. I tried it as a last resource."

In a recent book, *Oddities*, Commander Gould has spoken of the Devil's Footsteps that have from time to time appeared in South Devon, and it might very well be thought that the haunting at Penlee was the evocation of demonism whose energies persist, that formerly Satanists dwelt or assembled on the spot and diabolic rites were celebrated, but the purgation of the house by garlic unmistakably betrays that the horror was due to a definite vampiric origin. I have no doubt that there are many localities similarly infested, and that from time to time the vampire manifests in a greater or less degree, but the exact nature of these molestations is unrecognized and the happenings unrecorded.

Author Raymond T. McNally frequently lectures on vampire and other folklore at campuses around the country and is a well-known figure on TV. In 1967, Dr. McNally was one of a party of men who discovered the authentic Castle Dracula. His journey to this ruined site in Transylvania began in Cleveland, Ohio, where he spent his childhood leisure looking at vampire and monster movies. It continued via Fordham University in New York; the Free University in Berlin, which awarded him a Ph.D. in Russian history; the USSR, which admitted him as an American Exchange Scholar; and Boston College, where one of his colleagues was the Romanian scholar Dr. Radu Florescu. The penultimate stop was Bucharest; here, over a glass of plum brandy, McNally and Florescu pledged to seek the long-lost castle of the 15th-century prince named Dracula. The story of the castle and its notorious owner, plus a detailed account of vampire lore, was published in *In Search of Dracula* (New York Graphic Society, 1972).

Dr. McNally teaches history at Boston College, and resides in Brookline, Mass.

A Contemporary Romanian Vampire

An episode that I witnessed in an area familiar to both Bram Stoker's fictional Count Dracula and Romania's historical Prince Dracula.

In 1969 I was passing through the village of Rodna, which is located near the Borgo Pass. Noticing a burial taking place in the village graveyard, I stopped to watch. As I talked with some of the bystanders, they told me that the deceased was a girl from the village who had recently died by suicide. The villagers were afraid that she would become a vampire after death. So they did what had to be done—and what I had read about for so many years. They plunged a stake through the heart of the corpse.